AND

BROOMSTICKS

BEWITCHED BY CHOCOLATE
MYSTERIES

BOOK FIVE

H.Y. HANNA

CONTENTS

CHAPTER ONE

"Caitlyn? Did you hear me? Come over here and stir the cauldron."

Caitlyn Le Fey started guiltily and blinked as she came out of her thoughts. She looked across the dimly lit kitchen, to where an old woman with flashing dark eyes, a hooked nose, and wild grey hair stood by a large black cauldron hanging in the fireplace. It looked like a scene straight out of a children's fairy-tale: the sinister old witch hunched over her bubbling cauldron, conjuring potions and spells... except that this old woman was her grandmother and the cauldron held nothing more sinister than simmering caramel sauce.

Not that her grandmother was any ordinary old woman, of course. The Widow Mags was regarded with fear and suspicion by the village residents, not just because of her intimidating looks and cantankerous manner, but also because of her reputation as the "local witch". Oh yes, they whispered. That had to be the explanation. How else could the chocolates in her shop taste so amazing? They *had* to have been bewitched by dark magic.

The irony was, there *was* no magic involved in the making of the chocolates. Those delicious truffles, chocolate bars, and bonbons were simply the result of the best cocoa beans, the freshest cream, and purest ingredients, all expertly combined with the Widow Mags's chocolatier skills—no artificial charms, potions, or spells included.

Well, okay... maybe a bit of magic is used sometimes to save time and effort, thought Caitlyn with a smile, glancing at the mixing bowl on the table next to her, in which a spatula was moving around and around completely by itself, bewitched to stir the melted chocolate within. *But it's really no different to the modern appliances used in many kitchens...*

"Are you deaf, child?"

"Oh! Sorry..." Caitlyn sprang up and hurried over to her grandmother. She gripped the ladle and began stirring the bubbling caramel.

"Good, good..." said the Widow Mags, watching her. "Not too quickly... Slow and steady..."

Caitlyn inhaled deeply as a sweet, buttery aroma

rose from the cauldron. "Ohhh... this smells amazing! What's in it?"

"Pure refined sugar, fresh butter, vanilla extract, double cream, and some flakes of sea salt... which should all combine to turn into soft, chewy salted caramel when cooled. That's if it hasn't burnt in the pan, waiting for you to come over."

Caitlyn ducked her head. "Sorry, Grandma—my mind wandered for a moment."

"Humph..." The Widow Mags gave her a disgruntled look. "Your mind seems to be completely lost in the woods, if you ask me! You've been mooning about, in a world of your own, ever since you got back from Huntingdon Manor last week."

Caitlyn winced inwardly at the mention of that day. The memories she was constantly fighting to suppress rose up to swamp her, and in a second, she was standing on the steps of Huntingdon Manor again... and there, smiling down at her in a way that made her heart race, was its handsome owner, Lord James Fitzroy...

"I'll be back as soon as I can," he'd said, as he followed the butler into the house to take an urgent phone call.

And she had stood dreamily on the front steps, thinking of that look in his warm grey eyes, until a movement overhead had caught her eye...

Caitlyn had frowned, squinting at it... It looked

like—yes, a pair of flying glasses! The Widow Mags's runaway spectacles, in fact. She uttered the counter-spell, breaking the enchantment, and laughed with elation as the flying spectacles transformed back into an ordinary pair of reading glasses again. She'd done it! She'd finally been able to make magic do her bidding...

Then she turned around and saw James standing there, staring at her...

"Who are you? What... what was that?" he asked, his eyes filled with shock and horror.

"I..." Caitlyn's voice seemed to have died in her throat. What had he seen? How much could she tell him? Did she dare tell him the truth about herself? She wanted to—oh, how she wanted to!—but she was terrified. She had only just begun to hope that James might have feelings for her... would those feelings be destroyed if he learned that she was a witch?

He came swiftly towards her and grabbed her hand, turning it over so that he could see the glasses. He stared down at the worn plastic frames, lying lifeless in her palm. Caitlyn saw bewilderment cloud his face and doubt fill his eyes.

"I... I could have sworn..." he muttered. Then he dropped her hand and gave her a sheepish look. "I think I must be hallucinating... I thought... I thought I saw these spectacles flying through the air and you—" he gave an uncertain laugh, "—but of course, I can't have. Spectacles don't fly!" He passed a hand

4

over his face. "I must be more tired than I realise. My mind is playing tricks on me."

He started to turn away but Caitlyn caught his arm impulsively.

"No, wait—!" She swallowed. "What if... what if you're not wrong?"

"What do you mean?"

Her heart was pounding. She couldn't believe she was doing this. James had given her an easy way out, a ready-made explanation that he would readily accept... so why didn't she just embrace it gratefully and let everything be swept under the carpet?

But it was as if a mad impulse had awakened inside her—like a child who had been warned that a hot flame could burn, but who couldn't resist reaching out to touch it anyway. She licked her lips and said:

"What if you did see the spectacles flying?"

James gave a rueful smile. "You're going to be teasing me about that forever now, aren't you?"

"No, I'm serious," Caitlyn insisted. "What if what you saw was... was real?"

"Real?" James chuckled. "You mean, there really was a pair of flying spectacles? And what were you doing? Conjuring up a spell to capture them?"

Caitlyn took a deep breath. "Yes."

James stared at her.

"It was actually a reverse Levitation spell... because the spectacles were just normal reading glasses to begin with, and they were bewitched to

5

fly… so I performed a counter-spell…"

"A counter-spell," James repeated blankly.

"Yes." Caitlyn gave him a hesitant smile. "James… I… I've been wanting to tell you for so long… I… you see, I'm a witch."

There was silence. James looked at her. Then he looked away. Then he looked at her again. Caitlyn recoiled from the disappointment she saw in his eyes. Her heart sank.

"James—" she started to say.

"No, don't," he said sharply. "Don't keep talking such nonsense."

"What…? What do you mean?" Caitlyn faltered. "It's not nonsense. I'm telling you the truth."

James's grey eyes had gone cold. "I thought you were different, Caitlyn. I never thought you'd turn out to be one of those silly girls who believed in all this paranormal rubbish… messing around with Ouija boards and crystals and voodoo mumbo jumbo… jumping on the trendy witchcraft bandwagon and pretending you're a witch—"

"But… but I'm not pretending!" Caitlyn cried. "I really am a witch!"

James gave an impatient sigh. "There are no such things as witches. They're simply the product of folktales and superstitions, made up by simple folk who didn't have the benefit of a scientific education."

"But—"

"Look, an old woman who is experienced with herbs and spices might use some to cure an illness or

save a crop from pests—and in the olden days, people would call her a witch, because it looked like she'd performed magic. But nowadays, we know it's the chemical compounds in the herbs that healed the sick or protected the crops and livestock."

"But it's more than that!" Caitlyn burst out. "I mean, yes, I know a lot of so-called 'witches' were simply old women who lived alone and their skills as herbalists were misunderstood... but there is real magic as well. Magic that can transform things, bring things to life, make things fly. You saw it just now: you saw me—"

"Stop." He held a hand up. "Please, stop. I can't bear to hear such ridiculous nonsense coming from your lips." He made an involuntary movement, an expression of dismay on his face. "My God, you sound exactly like her..."

"No, wait—you have to listen to me," Caitlyn cried, catching hold of his arm. "I never believed in witchcraft and magic before either! But when I arrived in Tillyhenge, I learned the truth: that the reason I'd always felt different and struggled to fit in wasn't just because I was adopted... or because I was really English, despite my American upbringing... it was because I was descended from a long line of witches—witches who have a special affinity for working with chocolate! And the Widow Mags... and Bertha... and Evie... they are my family." Caitlyn gave him a hesitant smile. "I never dreamt that when I came to England to search for answers about my past, I would stumble into a new world and discover my real identity... but it's true. Magic is real. It exists. Look... look, I'll show you..."

She glanced around, then picked up a leaf from the ground. Holding it up in front of James's face, she said, "I'll change this into chocolate... watch!"

She took a deep breath and focused on the leaf in her hands, summoning her will and trying to imagine the waxy green surface transforming into smooth milk chocolate. It was difficult, though, with James standing there watching her; her mind felt fuzzy and unfocused, and she found it hard to concentrate. The leaf quivered in her hand but remained unchanged.

James sighed. "Caitlyn—"

"No! No, just wait... let me try again..." Caitlyn said desperately. She bit her lip and stared at the leaf harder, almost trembling with the effort.

Nothing happened.

She wanted to scream with frustration. How many times had she done it—tapped something carelessly and transformed it into chocolate? It was the one form of magic that she seemed to have mastered. And yet here... now... it was failing her.

"It... it should work," she stammered "I don't know why... maybe it's just... I'm not focusing properly... I'm... I'm a bit nervous with an audience... but I promise, I've done it so many times..."

She trailed off as she saw the expression on James's face. He'd said nothing, just stood there silently, looking at her. But the expression in his eyes made her flinch. It wasn't disappointment—it was even worse than that. It was pity.

"I... I'm not making it up..." she said weakly. "I really... there is magic..."

She broke off as the butler appeared at the front door again, with another telephone call for the master of Huntingdon Manor. The look of relief on James's face stabbed her like a knife. He cleared his throat, muttered an excuse, then disappeared into the house, leaving her standing alone on the steps...

Now, Caitlyn could still feel the sense of hurt and loss that had washed over her, almost as if she was still standing there on those steps, with the sky empty and grey above her and the wind rustling inconsolably through the nearby trees, and the acrid smell of burning in the air—

Wait... what acrid smell of burning?

"CAITLYN!"

CHAPTER TWO

Caitlyn looked down and gasped in horror. The beautifully bubbling caramel was now a charred sludge, with blackened crusts around the edge of the cauldron and smoke rising from the molten centre.

"Oh! I'm so sorry!" Caitlyn cried, grabbing the forgotten ladle and frantically trying to stir the sticky blackened mess.

The Widow Mags hurried over and snatched the cauldron off the fire, then turned to glower at her.

"That batch of caramel is ruined now! What on earth were you doing, child? You simply had to stir it."

"I'm sorry," said Caitlyn miserably. "I... I guess my mind wandered for a moment..."

The Widow Mags gave her a sharp look but didn't

say anything. Instead, she heaved the cauldron over to the large kitchen sink and turned on the tap. Steam rose in a hissing cloud as the cauldron filled with cool water.

"I can make up a new batch," Caitlyn offered.

The old witch sighed. "Never mind. We can do without the caramel today. I'll make more tomorrow."

She returned to the large wooden table in the centre of the kitchen and picked up her piping bag once more. But as she bent over the freshly baked chocolate ganache cake and began squeezing out the melted chocolate in intricate swirls, the piping bag slipped from her fingers. It fell to the floor and split open, splattering melted chocolate everywhere. The Widow Mags made a sound of frustration and bent down painfully.

"Oh, let me..." Caitlyn crouched down quickly next to her grandmother.

She picked up the broken bag and wiped the floor, then watched as the Widow Mags fashioned a new piping bag from a section of waxed baking paper. The old witch seemed to struggle as she tried to fold the paper into a cone shape, flexing her gnarled fingers and grimacing.

"Is it your arthritis?" asked Caitlyn tentatively. "Shall I—"

"I'm fine!" the Widow Mags growled.

She finally tucked the paper into shape, then turned towards the bowl of melted chocolate on the table and poured a large spoonful into the paper cone. Twisting the top to seal the cone, she snipped the tip off the pointed end and bent over the cake once more. But Caitlyn could see that her grandmother's fingers were stiff and awkward, struggling to squeeze the piping bag with the control needed to create the delicate chocolate art.

She opened her mouth to volunteer to help, then shut it again. She didn't think she had enough skill to create those intricate chocolate swirls and decorations. She also wasn't sure if her grandmother would appreciate her offer. Proudly independent, the Widow Mags hated showing weakness in front of others and, despite being a witch, she was just like many senior citizens who struggled with the fact that they could no longer do many things with ease.

"Why don't you just use magic?" Caitlyn asked, puzzled. "Then you wouldn't have to use your hands. You could just direct the piping bag to—"

"No. The arthritis in my hands... it affects that too," said the Widow Mags gruffly, flexing her fingers again.

"Oh." Caitlyn was taken aback. "I... I thought—"

"That magic is a cure-all?" said the Widow Mags dryly. "That is what people always think. But working magic is a skill, no different to learning to play an instrument or mastering fine carpentry or delicate needlework—it still requires a certain dexterity and strength, in your body as well as your mind." She gave a defeated shrug. "Anyway, I have learned to live with the arthritis. It comes and goes... and the herbal tonics that Bertha prepares for me are a great help."

As if on cue, the back door of the cottage swung open and a pleasant-faced, middle-aged woman in a voluminous purple kaftan came bustling in, followed by a girl of about eighteen. It was Bertha, the Widow Mags's oldest daughter (and Caitlyn's aunt), and *her* daughter, Evie.

Caitlyn felt a rush of affection as she saw them. One of the nicest things about coming to England was discovering her new family and getting to know them. Well, her grandmother had turned out to be more prickly than she'd expected, but her aunt had been exactly the sort of gentle, maternal presence that Caitlyn had yearned for all her life. And as for her cousin, Evie... Caitlyn smiled as she looked at the gangly girl, with her frizzy red hair and teenage acne. Evie was like the little sister she'd never had, and although only four years separated them, somehow she felt immeasurably older and wiser.

"Caitlyn—guess who we saw in the village green just now!" Evie exclaimed, rushing forwards. "James! I mean, Lord Fitzroy."

"Oh." Caitlyn swallowed, hoping that her colour hadn't risen. "Um... how nice."

She saw the Widow Mags glance at her, but the old witch made no comment as Evie babbled on:

"He's invited us all to the Manor for dinner

tonight! He said he has some friends staying with him, so he thought it would be nice to have a dinner party to introduce everyone—oh, and Sir Henry and his wife are coming too."

"I'm afraid Mother and I won't be able to go," said Bertha. "We have an appointment with the GP in town—he has a late night clinic this evening."

"I don't see why I need to go and see him," the Widow Mags grumbled. "Nothing wrong with me."

"Mother, you know it's important that you see the doctor at least once a year to have a general check-up, especially at your age," said Bertha patiently. "My herbal tonics are good but they're no substitute for checking your heart and your cholesterol and blood pressure... and besides, your arthritis seems to be flaring up more frequently lately. The doctor might have some helpful ideas for treatment and management." She turned back to Caitlyn and Evie, and smiled. "But you two girls can go to the dinner party—and it'll be lovely for you to catch up with Pomona."

"Pomona?" Caitlyn sat upright. "Pomona is back from London?"

Bertha looked at her in surprise. "I thought you knew. Hasn't she called you?"

"Oh... er... perhaps I missed her call," said Caitlyn, although she knew it was unlikely. She had been watching her phone like a hawk—she was sure she couldn't have missed a call from her American cousin. She felt the familiar worry and confusion fill her again. She hadn't seen Pomona since they had parted in Harrods Department Store in London, over a week ago, and since then, there had only been a few brief texts and one phone call, in which Pomona had sounded vague and distracted.

Of course, it wasn't as if her cousin had to report to her daily. Even before they had come to England, they had led very different lives. As the daughter of a top Hollywood actress, Pomona was the original "celebrity princess", spending most of her time at parties, premieres, and publicity events. In a way, Caitlyn had grown up in the same world; after all, her adoptive mother, Barbara Le Fey—sister to Pomona's mother—had been a famous singer in her own right. But where Pomona had revelled in the limelight and flaunted her glamorous looks with easy confidence, Caitlyn had been shy and bookish, staying away from social events and downplaying her luminous hazel eyes and vivid red hair.

But despite the differences in their personality and lifestyle, the two girls had been close from childhood, more sisters than cousins. And even when they had been apart, they had always stayed in touch, with long chatty phone calls, emails, and texts. Caitlyn had never known a time when Pomona had seemed so distant.

Then a memory stirred in her mind: a tall, dark man with saturnine good looks standing by her cousin, looking down at Pomona with an unreadable expression in his piercing blue eyes. *Thane Blackmort.* the "Black Tycoon". An enigmatic billionaire who was as notorious for his sex appeal as for his immense wealth and power. Caitlyn had never felt so uneasy as that day when she'd had to walk away, leaving Pomona in Blackmort's company.

But there had been nothing she could do. Pomona was an adult, and besides, her cousin had always been more than capable of taking care of herself in her various flings and romances. If anything, it was usually the poor man that Caitlyn worried for. Still, Blackmort was nothing like Pomona's usual "bad boys" ...

Caitlyn shook her anxious thoughts away as she realised that Evie was talking again:

"...and James said he was just thinking about giving a dinner party when Pomona rang and asked if she could stay at the Manor when she came back to Tillyhenge. So it was perfect timing. He thought it would be a nice 'welcome back' dinner for her as well."

"Pomona rang him?" said Caitlyn in surprise.

Evie turned innocent eyes towards Caitlyn. "Didn't he tell you, Caitlyn? He always seems to tell you everything."

This time, Caitlyn couldn't stop the hot colour coming to her cheeks, and she looked down as she mumbled, "Um... I haven't... er... seen much of James lately... We just... um... happen to miss each other every time he's in the village or I'm up at the Manor."

She didn't add that she had a feeling that James was avoiding her. They hadn't been alone together since that fateful day last week and the few brief words they had exchanged since then had always been stilted greetings in the company of other people. The thought that James could be so repulsed by her that he didn't even want to see her made her squirm with hurt and misery.

"Well, I'm sure you can all have a good catch-up at dinner tonight," said Bertha with a smile.

Her comforting tone soothed Caitlyn's feelings and she cheered up slightly. Yes, there had to be a good reason why Pomona hadn't contacted her. She would see her cousin tonight and it would all be explained. And as for James... She sighed. Well, at least with so many people around, there wouldn't be any awkward silences...

"I've brought a nice dress," said Evie, giving Caitlyn a half-bashful, half-excited smile. "It's my first proper dinner party—I'm even going to wear heels! Is it okay if I change in your room? Mum says we can go together. Dinner's at eight-thirty."

Caitlyn brightened. "I'd love to help you get ready, Evie. Oh, but you'd better put your heels in a bag and change into them once we get there. That's what I'm going to do because I think the walk over the hill will ruin them—"

"You're not planning to walk to the Manor, are

you?" asked Bertha in alarm.

Caitlyn looked at her in surprise. "Yes, why? The sun doesn't set till after eight still, so there will be plenty of light. We can go out the back door here, straight up over the hill and down the other side into the Manor grounds—it only takes about twenty minutes. I love the long summer days in England," she added with a grin. "It makes you feel like you get an extra half day."

"It'll already be twilight by the time you set off," said Bertha, frowning. "It's not safe—not with the stories that have been going around the village lately."

"What stories?" asked Caitlyn.

Evie turned round eyes on her. "Haven't you heard? Everyone's been talking about it. There was a man found dead last weekend, in one of the country lanes. They say when they found him, his eyes were wide and staring, and he had a look of terror on his face. The police couldn't work out how he died... but everyone in the village knows." Evie leaned forwards, dropping her voice to a whisper. "He'd been killed by the Black Shuck!"

CHAPTER THREE

"The what?" said Caitlyn. "What's the Black Shuck?"

Evie shuddered. "It's a huge black dog that's supposed to haunt lonely country lanes at night. It comes on a carpet of mist and its footfalls make no sound. Oh, it's terrible luck if you meet it when out walking! They say it's an omen of death and it means you're going to die within a year." Evie frowned. "Or was it someone in your family will die within a year? There are different stories—"

"Oh, it's a legend," said Caitlyn. "You mean it's just a creature from folklore."

"Witches are creatures from folklore too," the Widow Mags spoke up.

Caitlyn turned to look at her. "You mean... you believe the Black Shuck is real?"

"There *is* something haunting the woods and countryside around Tillyhenge," insisted Evie, before the old witch could answer. "Mrs Parsons at the post office shop said her niece saw it with her own eyes. She was walking home last weekend from her babysitting job—the niece, I mean, not Mrs Parsons—and it was late and she decided to take the shortcut through the fields... and then suddenly, the Black Shuck was there, walking next to her. She screamed and ran all the way until she got home."

"Maybe it was just the farmer's dog?"

Evie shook her head vehemently. "No, she said it was huge—as big as a calf."

"Well, maybe it *was* a calf then," suggested Caitlyn.

Evie shook her head again. "No, no, she said it was definitely a dog—a big black dog, with red eyes and huge fangs and shaggy black fur! She heard it howling as she ran away—it made her blood run cold."

"Whether the Black Shuck is real or not, I agree that there *is* something out in the country lanes around Tillyhenge," said Bertha briskly. "It could be a man—or a gang of criminals—or a ghostly demon hound—but whatever it is, it isn't safe for you girls to walk alone to the Manor tonight. I want you to go in Caitlyn's car."

"Yes, Aunt Bertha."

"Yes, Mum."

***

It was a full moon that night and despite the sun having only just set, the pale glowing orb was already high in the sky. Caitlyn drove carefully as she navigated out of Tillyhenge and joined the motorway. It was actually easier and more straightforward walking to the Manor than driving—the geography of the Cotswolds countryside and the way Tillyhenge lay nestled in a small "valley" meant that although the village was situated just on the other side of the hill at the edge of the Fitzroy estate, there was no direct road access between them. You had to take the route through the woods out of Tillyhenge and join the main motorway which circled around the valley, almost doubling back on yourself, before you could reach the official road that led in through the main gates of the Huntingdon Manor parklands.

Still, there was little traffic tonight and they soon found themselves rolling up the sweeping driveway in front of the majestic eighteenth-century Georgian manor house. There were a few strange cars parked next to James's green Range Rover on one side of the driveway and Caitlyn slid her rented Volkswagon Beetle in next to them. She killed the engine, picked up her bag, then paused to look in the rearview mirror.

"You look gorgeous," said Evie, watching her.

Caitlyn plucked at the fabric of her dress. "Do you think this is too clingy? I'm worried my bum is going to look enormous."

"Don't worry, Mum says most women in England are pear-shaped," said Evie ingenuously. "You're not really fat—you just have big hips."

"Er... thanks," said Caitlyn dryly. "That makes me feel better... I think." She fidgeted with the strap of her dress. She wasn't used to dressing up; unlike Pomona who ate, drank, and breathed fashion, Caitlyn spent most of her days in faded T-shirts and jeans, chosen more for their comfort than their design flair. Until she had come to Tillyhenge and met James Fitzroy, she had never really cared about how she looked. In fact, if anything, she had always tried to fade into the background. But in the past few months, she'd discovered that there was something thrilling about having a handsome man look at you with admiration...

Evie touched her own hair self-consciously and asked shyly, "What about me? Do... do I look okay?"

Caitlyn smiled at the other girl. "You look fantastic. That colour really suits you."

Evie flushed with pleasure. She *was* looking very pretty tonight, with her usually frizzy red hair tamed with copious amounts of mousse, and her gangly limbs concealed in the soft folds of a periwinkle-blue cotton dress. Her cheeks were pink with excitement and her eyes, carefully highlighted with make-up, sparkled with anticipation.

"I... I suppose none of the daytime staff will be here anymore," she said in a carefully casual voice.

Caitlyn looked at her in puzzlement, then grinned as it dawned on her. "You mean Chris Bottom?"

Evie flushed even more and looked down, plucking a fold of her dress. "It's just... he's never seen me dressed up... maybe he would notice me if he saw me like this..."

"I'm sure Chris notices you," Caitlyn said gently, thinking that she wasn't really lying. She just wasn't sure if Chris noticed Evie in the way that the latter hoped. With his "surfer" good looks and easy smile, Chris Bottom was usually inundated with female attention. And although his reputation as the local teen heartthrob hadn't gone to his head— in fact, he was an incredibly nice and down-to-earth young man—he was still unlikely to notice Evie's shy interest amongst all the bolder overtures from the more confident girls at their high school.

"Anyway, Chris probably won't be here," said Evie with a sigh. "He's only working for James part-time so he's probably gone home already."

"You never know. He's got a summer job as a sort of handyman and general dogsbody around the estate, hasn't he? Maybe he'll still be fixing a light bulb in the house somewhere," Caitlyn teased. Then she opened the car door and added with a laugh, "Come on, we'd better go in, otherwise everyone will have finished dinner while we're still here checking our appearance!"

Evie wobbled unsteadily as they walked from the car. It was the first time she had worn high heels and she was tottering around like someone on stilts.

"You have to stand up straight and put your heel down first," said Caitlyn, trying to help. "Don't hunch over—throw your weight backwards."

"I'm... I'm trying!" said Evie, tripping and staggering sideways. She gave Caitlyn a despairing look. "I should have worn flats! These heels are so hard to walk in... I always wanted a pair of stilettos and Mum bought me these as a special treat... but now I just know I'm going to trip and fall on my face in front of everyone!"

"No, you won't," Caitlyn assured her. "Just keep your head up, look straight ahead, and walk confidently."

"Easy for you to say," muttered Evie, taking another tottering step forwards. Then she paused and brightened. "Wait—I know! I can cast a spell on my shoes so that they'll walk by themselves!"

Caitlyn looked at her uneasily. "Evie, are you sure that's a good idea—"

"Yes, yes, it'll be brilliant!" said the other girl. She screwed up her eyes, pointed to her shoes and chanted:

Stilettos with grace,
Now gather apace,

With my feet inside,
Enable me to glide!

Caitlyn took an involuntary step back, eyeing the shoes warily. Evie might have been born knowing that she was a witch and grown up surrounded by spells and potions, but her own talents in the magic department seemed to be sadly lacking. In fact, the only thing that was reliable about Evie's spells was that they usually went spectacularly wrong.

Now, the shoes glowed like hot coals for a moment, making Caitlyn worry that Evie might burn her feet, then the glow faded to a faint shimmer. Caitlyn blinked, then stared at the shoes again. They still looked like the same pair of high-heeled stilettos, but there was something subtly different. They seemed strangely... *animate.*

The next moment, her eyes widened in surprise as Evie took a deep breath and started walking towards the front door of the Manor again. Her cousin literally *glided.* It was amazing. She walked like a supermodel sashaying down the catwalk.

"Wow," said Caitlyn, impressed. "Evie, that's incredible!"

The younger girl beamed. "Told ya!"

Caitlyn chuckled and was about to follow Evie when she froze.

"Listen!" she said. "Did you hear that?

Evie turned around, halfway up the Manor's front steps. "Hear what?"

"That... that sound..." Caitlyn turned and scanned the dark woods beyond the manor house. "It sounded like... some kind of animal..."

Evie listened but there was nothing now except the rustling of leaves as the wind moved through the trees. Twilight was almost over and the sky had darkened to an inky blue, with just a hint of pink on the western horizon. High above them, the full moon glowed, casting a silvery light over the landscape.

"I don't hear anything," said Evie. "Maybe you imagined it?"

"No, I heard it," Caitlyn insisted. "It was... a mournful cry... like... like..."

"A fox bark? They do sound very odd—not like a dog barking, more like a strange bird screaming—"

"No, it wasn't a fox," said Caitlyn. "I know what a fox bark sounds like. This was more like... like howling—"

"Howling? We don't have wolves in England. Maybe it was a dog then." Evie's eyes widened. "Oooh, do you think it was the Black Shuck?"

Caitlyn gave a sheepish laugh. "No, it was probably just a farmer's dog. It just sounded so eerie for a moment..." She shook her head, as if to clear it. "You're right, my imagination is running away with me. Come on, let's go in."

They were met at the front door by Giles Mosley, the Manor's new butler—a man so stiffly "correct" and proper that he was almost a caricature.

Although he normally favoured a conservative dark suit, tonight, in honour of the dinner party, he was dressed in full butler regalia, in a black jacket with tails, grey waistcoat, white wing collar shirt, and a black tie. He even had white gloves on. Clearing his throat importantly, he greeted them with grave ceremony, calling them "madam" and making Evie giggle, then escorted them to the Ante-Chamber where the guests had gathered for pre-dinner drinks.

Caitlyn hesitated as she entered, bracing herself to meet James. She saw him almost immediately, his tall figure dominating the room as he stood talking to a couple by the fireplace. It was easy to see why he had been voted "Most Eligible Bachelor in Britain" several years running: with his aristocratic features, dark curling hair, and lithe, muscular physique—not to mention his title and wealth—James Fitzroy was a modern Mr Darcy come to life.

He glanced up as they came in and Caitlyn saw something flicker in his dark grey eyes, then a polite mask came down over his face as he came towards them. She was seized by a sudden panic. How was she to greet him? She'd never been comfortable with the European custom of casual hugs and kisses, and now with the strained atmosphere between them, it was even more inconceivable to greet James with a peck on the cheek. And yet shaking hands seemed ridiculously unnatural and formal as well. Thankfully, Mosley the butler came to the rescue, arriving at the same time as James and bearing a silver tray with an assortment of drinks.

"Hello Evie. Caitlyn..." James gave them a perfunctory smile, then seized on the convenient distraction provided by the butler and waved a hand towards the tray. "What will you have?"

"Ooh, can I have a champagne?" asked Evie, wide-eyed.

"Of course," said James, reaching for one of the crystal flutes filled with fizzy gold liquid.

Mosley cleared his throat pointedly, his expression appalled. "Sir! Allow me..." With great flourish, he flicked a white-gloved hand, lifted a champagne flute from the tray, and presented it to Evie.

It was all done with such comical self-importance that Caitlyn felt a smile tugging at her lips and, when she glanced up, she caught a twinkle of amusement in James's dark grey eyes too. Their gazes met. Caitlyn caught her breath—for a moment, it was almost as if last week had never happened and they were just sharing a moment of amusement, like they'd often done. Then James stiffened, the warmth fading from his eyes, and he looked away. Caitlyn felt like someone out in the cold who had seen a doorway open into a warm room... and then suddenly had it slam in her face.

She was grateful when the butler—completely oblivious to the undercurrents—turned towards her and enquired:

"And what would madam like to drink?"

"Oh... er... just something non-alcoholic. I'm driving."

Mosley gestured to various glasses on the tray. "Orange juice? Tonic water? Perrier?"

"Er... orange juice is fine."

Caitlyn accepted her glass and sipped it, grateful to have something to do with her hands. An awkward silence descended on them. Evie was looking around, over-awed with the surroundings, and it was obvious she wasn't going to help with the conversation. Finally, James cleared his throat and said to Evie:

"I'm glad you came tonight. I believe this is the first time you've been here—at least, since I inherited the title?"

Evie nodded shyly. "I came with Mum once when she dropped off some herbal salve for the head gardener, but I stayed in the car."

"I must give you a little tour after dinner," said James with a smile. Then his gaze shifted beyond them and he said, "Ah, Chris... did you want to speak to me?"

They turned to see a teenage boy standing in the doorway of the Ante-Chamber. Evie gave a muffled squeak. It was Chris Bottom. He pushed his shock of sun-bleached blond hair off his forehead as he leaned against the doorjamb and addressed James:

"I've fixed the modem in your office. It's working

fine now. I thought I'd push off... unless there was something else you wanted me to do?"

"No, no, that's super. Thanks very much. But why don't you join us for a drink or even stay for dinner?" invited James. He gestured towards Evie. "Look, Evie's here—you go to the same school, don't you? You could sit together."

"Thanks but I—*Evie?*" Chris did a double take.

Evie went bright red as he stared at her. "H-h-hi Chris," she stammered.

"Chris, would you like some champagne? Or a glass of wine, perhaps?" asked James, beckoning for Mosley with the tray.

"Uh... no, no thanks... I have to get back... Dad and Aunt Vera will be expecting me for dinner. It's roast tonight and Aunt Vera gets really annoyed if we're not sitting at the table when the lamb comes out of the oven," Chris said, talking to James but still staring at Evie.

"Oh, well... perhaps next time then," said James.

Chris nodded absently and turned to go, although his eyes remained riveted on Evie.

James held up a hand. "Actually, Chris, I was just telling Evie that I'd give her a little tour of the Manor, since this is her first visit... but I won't be able to do it until after dinner. If you've got a moment, perhaps you could show her around?"

"Uh... sure." Chris held a hand out to Evie. "Come on, I'll show you the Library and the other rooms on the visitors' tour."

Evie stood rooted to the spot, looking like she was going to faint. Caitlyn gave her a surreptitious nudge. *Thank goodness for the bewitched high heels*, she thought as Evie's feet seemed to suddenly move of their own accord and she walked gracefully over to join Chris at the door.

CHAPTER FOUR

.

It was only after Evie and Chris had left that Caitlyn realised she was now in exactly the situation she'd been dreading: she was alone with James. Even though Evie hadn't said much, her cousin had still acted as a sort of buffer. Desperately, Caitlyn looked around, searching for a distraction. Then she frowned slightly as she realised something she should have noticed as soon as she'd arrived, if she hadn't been so pre-occupied.

"Where's Pomona?" she blurted. "I thought she was back from London tonight."

"Yes, she is—she arrived a short while before you did, actually, and I did try to persuade her to join us for drinks, but she insisted on going up to her room first. She said she had to 'freshen up and change for dinner'." James's forehead knit in puzzlement "To be honest, I didn't understand why she had to change. Her dress was lovely and more than appropriate for a dinner party, but Pomona seemed horrified when I suggested that she just come as she was."

Cailtyn smiled to herself. Maybe she had been worrying for nothing. It didn't sound like Pomona had changed at all. Her cousin's standards of fashion and glamour were so high that she wouldn't be seen dead in outfits most other women would have thought perfectly fine. Besides, Pomona never passed up any excuse to change into a new ensemble.

James glanced at his watch. "Hmm... I would have thought that she'd be down here by now."

Caitlyn laughed. "Oh, Pomona's probably decided to wash her hair or do a revitalising facial and total body scrub or something. She'll make a grand entrance in a moment, looking so fabulous that you'll agree all her extra primping was worth it."

"*You* look fine without it," James said. "More than fine, actually."

Caitlyn blushed, torn between delight that James had noticed her appearance and embarrassment over how to reply. She was immensely relieved when a scrap of black fur seemed to materialise out of nowhere and scampered up to her.

"Nibs!" She bent down to scoop the little kitten into her arms. "I didn't realise that you were in here."

"He shouldn't be in here," said James dryly. "I was worried about him getting under guests' feet so I left him in my study, together with Bran, but the little monkey must have got out somehow."

"Has he been giving you trouble?" asked Caitlyn, cuddling the kitten close to her chest.

James's face softened. "No—well, no more than usual," he said with a chuckle. "Of course, most of the staff simply can't resist his cheeky little face, so they let him get away with murder."

The arrival of the kitten seemed to have eased the tension between them and James's manner warmed perceptibly as he talked about Nibs. Caitlyn was glad that at least they still had this between them. They had rescued the kitten together from a disused quarry in the woods and although he was originally meant to live at the Manor, Nibs had had his own ideas. After stowing away with Caitlyn and hitching a ride back to the chocolate shop, the little kitten had wormed his way into the Widow Mags's heart. Like a typical cat, Nibs had soon managed to have things arranged exactly how he wanted: now he lived part of the time at the Manor and the rest of the time at the chocolate shop, and was ridiculously spoilt in both his homes.

"He can come and live at the chocolate shop full-time if he's too much hassle at the Manor," Caitlyn offered.

"Good God, no," said James, laughing. "I think I'd have a mutiny on my hands! The staff are all besotted with Nibs—they'd be bereft if he wasn't here. Even Old Palmer, the head gardener, seems to be softening. I actually caught him patting Nibs on the head the other day, when he thought nobody was looking. And Bran would be desolate. They eat together, sleep together, do everything together..." James shook his head, chuckling. "I think they're almost becoming as much of a tourist attraction as the Manor itself; people love seeing a huge English mastiff being led around by a tiny kitten." He glanced across the room at the couple he had been talking to earlier and added, "But I'd better put him back in my study now. Sir Henry's wife, Sherry, said she's allergic to cats and I wouldn't want Nibs to trigger a bad reaction."

He reached for the kitten and Caitlyn reluctantly passed Nibs over. As James turned to go, Evie re-entered the Ante-Chamber. The girl's face was flushed and she was walking as if she was in a dream. She barely acknowledged James as she passed him heading out; instead she drifted slowly across the room to where Caitlyn was standing.

"How was the tour?" asked Caitlyn with a grin.

Evie's cheeks were pink. "We only saw half of the rooms, then Chris had to go. But he... he said that he'd show me around the rest of the place the next time I come up to the Manor." She leaned closer and whispered, "My feet are killing me! I didn't realise I'd be walking around so much..." She took the weight off one foot and wriggled it, grimacing.

"Do you think it's okay if I slip my shoes off for a moment?"

Caitlyn glanced around, then pointed to a chair tucked against the wall behind them. "Why don't you go and sit there for a moment? Then it won't be so obvious if you take your shoes off."

As Evie hurried to comply, breathing an audible sigh of relief as she eased her toes out of the pointed stilettos, Caitlyn turned and eyed the other guests curiously. There was a young man of about James's age, fashionably dressed in a trendy top and dark jeans, who was talking earnestly to an older man with the most enormous sideburns Caitlyn had ever seen. Beside them, a stout middle-aged woman was talking to the couple that James had been with earlier. Caitlyn recognised the woman as Mrs Gibbs, a Tillyhenge resident—one of the bossy ladies who presided over the village committee and spent most of her time complaining about the tourists—and she realised that the couple must be Sir Henry Pritchard and his wife.

While she had never met Sir Henry, Caitlyn had heard his name mentioned several times in the village. A wealthy, self-made businessman who owned the lands adjoining the Fitzroy estate, Sir Henry was known for his blunt, down-to-earth manner and his love of a good drink. He was a regular at the village pub and was proud of his humble beginnings as a farmer's son, despite having been given a knighthood by the Queen. With his balding head, red, jowly face, and faded tweed waistcoat stretched over his bulging belly, he looked exactly like the stereotype of the "English country squire".

He was a startling contrast to his well-groomed wife, who looked at least twenty years younger and had the sort of slim, taut figure that was achieved from hours at the gym and iron-control over one's diet. She was sipping her glass of wine now with small, tight movements, as she stood beside her husband and watched him talking loudly.

Sir Henry's booming voice carried easily across the room: "...so I told him, he could sod off and take his fancy machines back where he came from!"

"Quite right, Sir Henry, quite right," said Mrs Gibbs, nodding her head approvingly. "I'm glad we have someone like you to stand up to those smug big-city executives—"

"Big city? Pah! Bunch of nancy-boys—wouldn't last one day on a farm, I tell you! Oh no, here in the country, we need a *real* man... eh, poochykins?" Sir Henry leered suddenly at his wife.

She simpered. "Ooh yes, honeybun—a real man like you."

Sir Henry guffawed and gave his wife an affectionate smack on the bum, for all the world as if she was a favourite mare. She jumped slightly, but her smile didn't slip and Caitlyn blinked in disbelief. The woman must have had the forbearance of a saint!

At that moment, James returned to the Ante-Chamber and the butler hurried up to him.

"Sir... Mrs Pruett is wondering if you will be sitting down soon? She is worried some of the dishes will spoil if kept warm for much longer and she is keen to start serving."

"We're just waiting for one more guest, Mosley."

"Would that be Miss Pomona Sinclair, sir?"

"Yes." James glanced at his watch and frowned. "I'm hoping she'll be down any minute..."

"Very good, sir. Would you like a fresh drink?"

"Oh, don't worry, Mosley. I'll sort myself out—I know where the bar is," said James, indicating the antique bar cabinet in the corner of the room.

"Sir! You must allow me—"

James grinned at the butler's distress. "Honestly, Mosley, I can manage. I know it's probably not what you're used to but I'm more than happy to look after myself. I was doing it for years, you know, before I inherited the title. Oh, it's no reflection on your service—you're an exemplary butler," he added hastily. "I'm just used to being more independent."

"Of course, sir," said Mosley stiffly. "As the new master of Huntingdon Manor, it is understandable that you'd want to break with tradition."

"I certainly don't intend to turn my back on tradition and etiquette," said James with a laugh. "But maybe we can just respect them in a slightly more relaxed way, eh?"

The butler watched James wander off to the bar

cabinet with such a pained expression on his face that Caitlyn wanted to laugh. Then she saw Mosley turn towards the connecting door that led to the Dining Room and a look of bewilderment crossed his face. Caitlyn followed the direction of his gaze and nearly gasped out loud in horror.

A pair of stiletto heels was walking by itself across the room.

Caitlyn swung her gaze around to where Evie was still sitting on the chair by the wall. Her young cousin was staring dreamily into space, swinging her bare feet against the chair, but on the floor in front of her was now an empty space. Her high heels, freed of her feet, had obviously decided to go walking by themselves.

"Evie!" Caitlyn hissed.

"Huh?" Evie started, then came out of her reverie, blinking. She looked around in confusion. "Yes?"

Caitlyn pointed frantically. "Evie, your shoes!"

Evie turned to look, then her eyes bulged and she made a strangled sound in her throat. She sprang up from her chair and rushed over to where Caitlyn was standing.

"What do I do?" she asked.

"You need to go and catch your shoes!"

"No, wait—I can reverse the spell from here," said Evie confidently, pointing a finger at the stilettos and chanting something under her breath.

There was a loud crackling, like the sound of

static, and the stilettos glowed like hot coals again. Caitlyn watched hopefully but instead of subsiding back into a normal pair of high heels, the stilettos sprang into the air and began dancing a jig.

"Evie...!" Caitlyn groaned. "What are you doing?"

"I... I thought I was un-bewitching them!" cried Evie. "Maybe... maybe they're too far away. I need to get closer."

"We need to catch them before someone sees them!"

The stilettos were now mincing along the edge of the Persian carpet, stopping every so often to do a twirl as they danced to some imaginary music. Thankfully, the other guests were too engrossed in conversation to notice, but Mosley was staring at them, his mouth slightly open. He rubbed his eyes and was just about to take another look when Caitlyn rushed in front of him, blocking his view, and gabbled:

"Er... Mosley, I hate to be a bother but I was wondering if you could make up a mocktail for me? I'm feeling a bit left out drinking boring old orange juice while everybody else is enjoying champagne."

"Certainly... madam... Er... What would you like?" asked Mosley in a distracted voice as he leaned to one side, trying to peer behind Caitlyn's shoulder.

She shifted around so that she kept blocking his view. "I'd like a blend of fresh orange juice and apple juice... and um... cranberry juice... with lemonade and some... er... passionfruit puree... and... and mint leaves... and... er..." She racked her brains for something that would really complicate the order and keep him busy. "Er... and a raw egg."

That got his attention at last. He stared at her. "A... a raw egg, madam?"

"Yes," said Caitlyn stoically. "Mixed in thoroughly. Oh, and it must be free range."

The butler gave her a funny look but, to her relief, his training had obviously disciplined him to take guests' peculiarities in his stride. He departed to the kitchen to hunt for the free-range raw egg to mix into her drink. As soon as he had gone, Caitlyn turned around to see Evie skulking on the other side of the room. Her cousin was creeping up behind the pair of stilettos, which was hovering next to the other guests' feet, as if it wanted to go up and say hello to the other shoes.

Evie made a sudden dive but the stilettos darted sideways at the last moment, neatly evading her hands. They skipped away from her, pausing only to raise one pointy heel at her in a rude gesture.

Caitlyn groaned and buried her face in her hands. She couldn't believe this was happening. Evie rushed after the shoes... and collided straight into James, who was returning from the bar cabinet with his drink.

"Evie!" he said in surprise as he caught her arm and steadied her.

"Oh! J-James... I mean, Lord Fitzroy—"

"Come on, you're not seriously going to call me by my title," he said with a chuckle. "What's the matter, Evie? Where are you going in such a rush?"

"Oh... um... er..."

Caitlyn saw Evie glance over James's shoulder, then turn to shoot her an agonised look. She followed Evie's gaze and saw the reason for the anguish. The pair of stiletto heels were skipping towards the Ante-Chamber door. In fact, even as she watched, they pirouetted through the open doorway and disappeared.

Yikes. They couldn't have a pair of bewitched high heels running loose in the Manor!

Hurrying past a bewildered Mosley, who had returned carrying the mocktail, Caitlyn rushed out of the room and set off in pursuit.

CHAPTER FIVE

The stilettos were just disappearing around the corner at the end of the hallway when Caitlyn stepped out of the Ante-Chamber. She chased after them. They were surprisingly fast—she tried several times to put on a burst of speed to catch them, but somehow they always managed to dart around a corner or skip up a flight of stairs before she could reach them.

Soon she found herself in the rear of the Manor, hurrying up a flight of back stairs—the old servants' staircase—to the upper floor. A long, empty hallway stretched before her. Caitlyn had stayed in the Manor before so she was familiar with the upper storey, but this wasn't the wing where the guest bedrooms were located—this seemed to be a wing she hadn't seen before. From the dim lighting and the stale air, this was obviously a section of the Manor that wasn't used very much. In front of her, the stilettos slowed, as if they felt unsure in this quiet, disused wing.

Caitlyn quickly took advantage of the opportunity. She pounced, grabbing the stilettos by their heels and sweeping them off the floor. But as she straightened, her attention was caught by something at the other end of the corridor. She frowned, straining her eyes to see. Was there a figure down there?

The stilettos wriggled in her grasp but Caitlyn barely noticed as she began walking farther down the corridor. As her eyes grew accustomed to the dim light, she realised that this section of the corridor looked familiar. Yes, she *had* been here before—she had come up the zigzag staircase at the other end. It was the time Nibs had climbed up a tree and got himself stuck on a window ledge. She had come in through a concealed door from the gardens and rushed up the staircase to rescue him.

She could see the same door now and, yes, there was someone hovering in front of it. They were so engrossed in examining the door that they hadn't even noticed her. Caitlyn heard a female voice muttering and her eyes widened as she recognised the American accent.

"Pomona?"

The figure jumped, then spun around.

"Holy guacamole, Caitlyn, you scared the jeepers

outta me!"

Pomona was a classic Californian beauty, all tanned brown limbs, blue eyes, and big blonde hair, with generous curves that she liked to flaunt in glamorous, revealing outfits. She came forwards now, looking like someone dressed to go to an Oscars awards party, in a sequinned gown that hugged every line of her body.

"Pomie, what are you doing here?"

"Oh, I got, like, a bit lost as I was heading downstairs... man, these big English country houses with all their corridors... anyway, I sorta found myself here and then I saw that door." Pomona gestured to the thick oak door covered in metal studs, like a relic from a medieval dungeon. "It looked so weird... I guess I was being nosy." She grinned. "I thought it might be like Bluebeard's room!"

"It's not—I've been in there. It's just the Fitzroy Portrait Gallery."

"Oh, so *that's* the Portrait Gallery."

"Yes, I told you about it, remember? I came up here when I was rescuing Nibs and the window ledge he was on was in that room. Also, that night when I came up here with Antoine de Villiers... It's got oil paintings of all the Fitzroy ancestors on one wall."

"Isn't it also where James said his dad kept his occult collection?" said Pomona excitedly.

"Yes... but I didn't see anything special when I

went in, just lots of furniture covered with white sheets."

"Didn't you lift up the sheets to have a look?" demanded Pomona. "Jeez, I would have been so curious! I can't believe you didn't even have a peek!"

"I... I just wanted to get out of there quickly," said Caitlyn. She didn't know how to explain the oppressive atmosphere in the room and she was embarrassed to admit that the place had creeped her out. She took Pomona's arm. "Anyway, I think we'd better get back downstairs. They're all waiting for you—you're holding up dinner."

"Oh, sheesh... I didn't think of that," said Pomona, sounding genuinely contrite. She fell into step beside Caitlyn as they began making their way back to the Ante-Chamber. "Why are you holding a pair of stilettos, by the way?"

"Huh? Oh, these." Caitlyn looked down. She'd almost forgotten about Evie's shoes. The stilettos seemed to have given up the fight now and hung limply in her grasp. "They're Evie's. They were sort of... um... moving independently, you could say, and I came out to catch them."

Pomona laughed. "Man, I'd forgotten what it's like here in Tillyhenge—all the cool magical stuff that happens all the time. I'm so glad I'm back!"

"You never rang me to tell me that you were coming," said Caitlyn, unable to keep the note of accusation out of her voice.

"Hey, I thought it would be nice to surprise you,"

said Pomona, grinning.

"Oh." Caitlyn was taken aback by the easy explanation. Could it really have been that simple? "I thought... maybe... well, you seemed a bit... "

"A bit what?"

"You just... well, you didn't seem to text or call much when you were in London..."

"Oh, honey..." Pomona gave her a swift hug. "Sorry! I guess I just got too caught up in all the stuff that was going on. It was like one wild, non-stop party! I mean, I've been to some pretty awesome Hollywood events but this was, like, on a totally different level, you know? And when you're with Thane, it's just like—I don't know—time stops or something, you know? I mean, I don't think the guy even sleeps. Once, we were talking during one of his parties and he asked me if I'd ever seen the northern lights and when I said no but I always wanted to, he just, like, called up his private jet—you know, the one that's in all the press 'cos it's all painted black—and man, you should see the inside, black marble and ebony leather and everything—and he flew me and a bunch of other guests to the Arctic! I couldn't believe it. One minute I was sitting in London, the next I was in this igloo hotel up in Iceland somewhere... and all these local people kept telling Thane that it was too early in the season to see the Aurora but he just waved them away... and then it got dark and he went outside, like, with no coat or anything, and we could all see him through the glass walls of the igloo... and he raised his hand up and... holy guacamole, the whole sky just lit up! It was like he summoned the northern lights or something..." She gave a lusty sigh. "Thane Blackmort's got it all: he's rich, he's hot, he sure knows how to live it up... and he's so freaking mysterious..."

Caitlyn watched her speak with troubled eyes. "So you were with him the whole time?"

"Yeah, it was, like, the best time of my life!" Pomona's cheeks were flushed, her eyes unnaturally bright. Then she seemed to collect herself and gave Caitlyn a slightly guilty look. "Well, except when I'm with you, of course. We have the best fun together."

"Um... so where's Blackmort now?" asked Caitlyn.

"Oh, he had to go on some business trip."

Caitlyn felt a stab of hurt. So Pomona had only bothered to return when Thane Blackmort wasn't around anymore. There was silence between them as they descended the back stairs and rejoined the hallway leading to the main part of the house. Then Caitlyn spoke up hesitantly:

"Pomie... You're not... um... getting too involved with Blackmort, are you?"

Her cousin raised her chin. "What do you mean?"

"Well, nobody really knows anything about him... and there are all those stories going around—"

48

Pomona's eyes flashed. "I would have thought you, of all people, would know better than to believe in random gossip and rumours. Or do you also think that the Widow Mags is, like, an evil witch plotting to hex the whole village with her chocolates?"

"That's different," Caitlyn protested. "Besides, we know the Widow Mags, whereas you don't really know Blackmort."

"What do you mean? I do know him," said Pomona.

Caitlyn started to retort, then sighed and let it go. She didn't want to fight with Pomona on the first night her cousin was back. Pomona must have sensed something too, because just before they reached the doorway to the Ante-Chamber, she paused and reached out to squeeze Caitlyn's hand.

"Look, I'm a big girl now and I can take care of myself. So quit worrying, okay? Anyway..." She gave Caitlyn a familiar teasing smile. "We should be talking about *your* love life. So, tell me—have you and James kissed yet?"

"Pomie!" Caitlyn gasped, glancing quickly around to make sure that no one had heard, even though they were alone in the hallway. "I keep telling you—it's... it's not like that between James and me."

Pomona rolled her eyes. "Oh, pul-lease! There were sparks coming off you two from the day you met! I don't think I've ever seen a couple who are so obviously *meant* for each other."

"I think you're reading too much into things. And anyway, even if James had felt something for me, he... he's changed his mind," Caitlyn said in a small voice.

Pomona frowned at her. "What do you mean, he's changed his mind?"

"I told him."

"Told him? Told him what?"

"The truth about me... That... that I'm a witch."

Pomona goggled at her. "And?"

"And he wouldn't believe me!" Caitlyn burst out. "Can you believe that? I finally work up the courage to tell him the truth and he thinks I'm lying! That I'm just a fraud."

"A fraud? You mean, he thinks you're *pretending* to be a witch?"

Caitlyn threw her hands up. "Yeah, isn't it ridiculous? And he was so upset about it too; he looked at me with such... such *disappointment* in his eyes! Like he had thought better of me and I'd let him down. He actually said that he never thought I'd be 'one of those silly girls who believed in all this paranormal rubbish... messing around with Ouija boards and crystals and voodoo mumbo jumbo'—that's what he said."

"Hey, I take offence at that! I'm one of those 'silly girls' who believes in paranormal rubbish and I love Ouija boards!" said Pomona jokingly. Then she sobered and said, "You know what, Caitlyn? I kinda get where he's coming from."

Caitlyn looked at her incredulously.

"No, listen... remember I told you about that ex-girlfriend of his? The one he was with at college? I didn't tell you all the details. See, they were together for a couple of years—it sounded pretty serious—and then she got interested in the occult and became, like, totally obsessed with druids and magic and witchcraft and stuff. She joined some weird coven group and started believing that she was a witch." Pomona rolled her eyes. "Seriously, the girl sounded totally nuts. Like, once, she dragged James down to Stonehenge and made him wait up till sunrise with her and then watch her while she stripped naked and danced around, chanting stuff... and once she served him a cup of potion she made up, which had live lizards and frogs in it... and then he walked into her room at college one day and found blood everywhere. She'd been trying to do some kind of 'blood magic' and she'd cut herself really badly. James had to rush her to the hospital—she would probably have been a goner if he hadn't saved her."

Caitlyn stared at her cousin. "You... you told me that James broke up with a girlfriend in college because she became obsessed with magic and witchcraft. I thought that sounded a bit extreme at the time... but I didn't realise it was like this."

Pomona nodded. "Oh yeah, she was the one who was 'extreme', not him! I think a lotta guys would have bailed long before that. James was a saint to stick around as long as he did. Maybe he felt some kinda stupid loyalty... you know how he's always so noble and nice, like the way he's always giving his staff second chances. But that trip to the hospital was the final straw. He just couldn't take the crazy anymore. He said it was like his girlfriend had become a totally different person. After she recovered, he broke it off with her... and I think since then, he's been, like, really paranoid about any girl who shows too much interest in the occult." She shrugged. "You can't really blame him."

"But he seems fine with you," Caitlyn pointed out. "And you're completely obsessed with the paranormal."

Pomona chuckled. "Yeah, but he's not interested in me romantically. He just sees me as, like, a kooky friend that you humour but you don't take seriously. You know, it's like when you watch people do crazy stuff in a TV show and you laugh and enjoy it, 'cos they're not anybody you really care about. They're just entertainment."

"That's not true. James cares about you."

"Oh sure, he'd save me if I was, like, drowning or whatever. But I'm not really important to his life— I'm not the woman he loves."

Caitlyn flushed and turned away. "Who says *I* am? Anyway," she continued hurriedly as Pomona growled with irritation, "I still don't understand why James is so against the idea of magic. I mean... fine, his ex-girlfriend might have been crazy, but that doesn't mean magic itself doesn't exist. You know, he even saw the Widow Mags's flying spectacles but he convinced himself that it was just a hallucination! He wouldn't even believe what he saw with his own eyes—he had to turn it into some kind of rational, scientific phenomenon, instead of just accepting that maybe magic could be real."

Pomona eyed her sideways. "Well, you never used to believe in magic either. You used to laugh at me whenever I talked about witchcraft and divination."

Caitlyn hung her head. "Okay, I was wrong—I admit it. But see? I *have* opened my mind; I'm not just rejecting it outright."

"Well, then... maybe it's more than his ex-girlfriend," Pomona said thoughtfully. "Maybe it's to do with his dad as well."

Caitlyn looked at her in surprise. "What does James's father have to do with this?"

"Well, his dad was obsessed with the occult too, right? I know James doesn't talk about him much, but from the bit I've heard, the old Lord Fitzroy used to have this weird obsession with witchcraft and magic as well. That's why he's got an occult collection."

"So? I still don't see—"

"So maybe James resented his father's obsession when he was growing up... or... or maybe it's even simpler than that! Maybe he just doesn't wanna become like his dad!"

Caitlyn looked at her blankly.

Pomona made an impatient gesture. "Look how James is into changing things up and modernising the estate. Ever since he inherited the title, he's been, like, breaking with tradition and showing that there's going to be a new approach now. So maybe rejecting magic is also his way of showing that he's not like his dad. You know—we all wanna rebel against becoming our parents, right?"

"Since when did you become so 'deep'?" asked Caitlyn sarcastically.

Pomona laughed and flicked her hair in an exaggerated fashion. "Hey, I'm not a blonde bimbo *all* the time. Only on Tuesdays and Saturdays."

Caitlyn looked at her cousin. When Pomona was standing next to her like this, joking and laughing, it was as if nothing had changed and it was hard to believe that she might ever have been vague and distant. *It's only when she's with Blackmort,* thought Caitlyn. And she hoped fervently that her cousin would stay away from London and Blackmort's influence.

CHAPTER SIX

One way the new Lord Fitzroy *was* very different from his father was his casual attitude to meals. James had been adamant that he didn't want to follow his father's custom of a three-course dinner in the formal Dining Room every evening, opting instead for simple meals of sandwiches or soup and bread, on a tray in his study. He had been bewildered when Mrs Pruett, the Manor's cook—far from appreciating the lighter workload—had been hurt and upset at being deprived of the chance to create the elaborate menus she had been used to.

Tonight, however, she had obviously seized the rare chance of a proper dinner party to flex her culinary muscles, and they were met by a smorgasbord of gourmet delights when they finally entered the Dining Room. There was roasted

Devonshire chicken with *foie gras* stuffing, Cornish cod fillet in garlic butter, braised beef ribs with creamed parsnips, a classic shepherd's pie, grilled calf liver with sautéed onions, griddled baby leeks and buttered green beans, and even a plate of fresh oysters with tangy citrus dressing.

The delicious aromas rising from the table made Caitlyn's stomach growl and she would have been quite content to just eat and enjoy her meal in silence. But the other guests were in a talkative mood. Sir Henry, in particular, seemed keen to share his opinion on everything from politics to pyjamas, and since Caitlyn was sitting near him, she found it almost impossible to ignore him as he drowned out all other conversation. She also couldn't help hearing the cringe-worthy nicknames he and his wife called each other. They were so awful that she didn't know whether to laugh or gag.

"Pass the hollandaise sauce, would you, flopsymop?"

"Here you go, diddykins!"

Caitlyn turned to catch Pomona's eye, wanting to share her amusement, but her cousin was busily talking to the man with the enormous sideburns—Professor Kynan Thrope. From the brief introductions just before they sat down, Caitlyn had gathered that Thrope was a Cambridge professor and she was surprised to see Pomona speaking to him in such an animated manner. Stuffy academics didn't usually capture her cousin's interest, not unless they were young and good-looking, but Pomona was hanging on to his every word. Curious, she tried to tune out Sir Henry's booming voice and leaned closer to hear their conversation.

"...yes, it was certainly an interesting field trip. I'm hoping to return to Puerto Rico next year and spend more time exploring the legend of the *chupacabras,* perhaps interview the residents of the more remote villages, where there have been several sightings."

"Man, I always thought academics studied really boring stuff but this is so cool!" said Pomona.

Professor Thrope smiled. "Well, I suppose my field trips are quite different from those of my colleagues. You see, I'm a cryptozoologist."

"Ooh!" Pomona opened her eyes wide. "That's a monster hunter, isn't it?"

The professor laughed. "Yes, you could call me that. I have been called worse."

"What do you mean?"

He gave a rueful smile. "Ah, well... the academic community does not take kindly to a man who decides to devote his life to the study of mythical creatures. My biologist colleagues have the glory of discovering important new species of fish or insect, whereas I simply court contempt and ridicule for spending my time searching for beasts from folklore which, according to modern science, simply cannot exist."

"But they do exist!" said Pomona. "I believe in

unicorns and mermaids and kelpies and sea serpents! I know they're still out there—we just haven't been able to find them."

The professor beamed at her. "Thank you, my dear. I am glad to know that there are people who still have the imagination to believe in the incredible."

"So have you seen them?" asked Pomona breathlessly. "Have you seen any monsters?"

Professor Thrope gave her an apologetic look. "Ah, well, the study of cryptids is not an exact science. We have to rely on anecdotal accounts and reported sightings, more than anything else. It is rare that we get to witness the creatures for ourselves. Usually, however, those who spend many years in the field are eventually rewarded. I myself, for example, was extremely lucky to catch a glimpse of Nessie one winter morning—"

"You saw the Loch Ness Monster?" Pomona squealed in delight. "Omigod! What did it look like?"

"It was quite far away and it was a very foggy morning, but as far as I could see, it had a long, serpentine neck ending in a small head, and it seemed to have a large, streamlined body—it moved very smoothly through the water."

"Wow..." Pomona breathed.

The young man sitting on their other side, obviously overhearing their conversation, turned towards them and said: "I thought most of the Nessie sightings were clever hoaxes."

The professor inclined his head in acknowledgement. "Yes, many of them were shown to be faked photographs created by pranksters, but there are some stories which haven't been discredited."

"I wish there was some monster here in the Cotswolds," said Pomona with a wistful sigh. "I'd love to see a real-life beastie from folklore!"

The young man chuckled. "You might get your wish sooner than you think. Have you asked Professor Thrope why he's here in Tillyhenge? He was telling me about it over drinks earlier—he's here hunting the Black Shuck! Oh, forgive me..." He held a hand out to Pomona. "I don't believe we've been properly introduced. I'm Nathan Lewis. I'm an investigative journalist. I'm freelance now but I used to be with the BBC... an old mate of James's. We used to work together, before the jammy sod decided to give it all up to become 'lord of the manor'," he said, laughing and raising his voice so that James would hear.

James looked up from the other end of the table, where he was politely listening to Sir Henry complain about the current British Prime Minister, and grinned at his friend's teasing. "Don't believe anything Nathan tells you," he called. "He's known to have the fastest tongue at the BBC."

"Hey, I'm not the one telling tall tales here," said Nathan, raising his hands in a defensive gesture. Then he turned back to the cryptozoologist and gave him an apologetic smile. "Sorry, Professor, hope you didn't take offence."

"Not at all," said Professor Thrope with a twinkle in his eye. "I'm used to the teasing. It goes with the territory."

"But seriously, Professor, why are you looking for the Black Shuck here in the Cotswolds? I thought it haunts the coastline and countryside around East Anglia."

The professor nodded. "Yes, you're right, the Black Shuck is a creature from the folklore of Norfolk, Suffolk, and the Cambridgeshire fens. In fact, one of the legends originates in Littleport, in Cambridgeshire, where I was born. However, I believe that the Black Shuck is simply one variation of the same creature that has been seen all over the British Isles. If you look back through history, there are many recorded sightings of ghostly black dogs across the different counties in England. There's the Barghest of Yorkshire, Padfoot of Leeds, the Yeth Hound of Devon, the Gurt Dog of Somerset, Hairy Jack of Lincolnshire—"

"Don't forget the hellhounds of Dartmoor, which supposedly inspired *The Hound of the Baskervilles*," said Nathan with a grin.

"Yes, the black phantom hound comes in many incarnations and I personally believe that they are all sightings of one creature, which travels around the British Isles. You see, all the stories share common details, such as the description of the dog being a huge ghostly hound with shaggy black fur and flaming red eyes, which haunts graveyards, dark forests, and crossroads—"

"And it's an omen of death!" said Nathan excitedly. "Once you see it, you're going to die—isn't that right?"

"Oh no!" said Professor Thrope, looking distressed. "That is the common belief, yes, but I feel that it's a misconception, borne out of the fear of the unknown. After all, if the creature really wanted to harm, wouldn't there have been more deaths by now? No, I believe that it is more likely to be a guardian, guiding travellers at night onto the right path or guarding them from danger. There have been numerous reports of ghostly black dogs accompanying people who are out walking in the countryside alone, late at night. Especially women—"

"Yes, yes!" Evie spoke up from across the table. "Mrs Parsons down at the village post office—she said her niece saw the Black Shuck when she was walking home last weekend. It appeared beside her as she was taking a shortcut through the fields."

"Indeed?" Professor Thrope sat up with interest. "I'd like to interview this young lady. Would you be able to help me contact her?"

"What's this then?" said Sir Henry, distracted from his political diatribe at last. He turned from the other end of the table where he had been monopolising James, Mrs Gibbs, and his wife.

"What are you all talking about? The Black Shuck? Load of superstitious twaddle!"

His wife caught his arm, her face anxious. "Oh, but squidypooh, there have been sightings all around Tillyhenge recently. I've been hearing the staff talk about it all week. It's not just superstition—there really is something out there!"

"Nonsense!" her husband roared. "The Black Shuck is just a stupid story made up to scare children."

"What about that tramp who was found dead last weekend?" Mrs Gibbs spoke up. She shuddered. "They say he died with a look of terror on his face, and his clothes were all torn... and the police have no idea how he died."

"Actually, they do," said James quietly. "I just spoke to Inspector Walsh this morning. They're still waiting for the results of the post-mortem, but they think the man could have simply had a heart attack while he was walking. There was a large blackberry bush near where he was found—he may have crashed into that while he was staggering around and got tangled in its thorny branches, which would explain the torn clothes and bloody scratches on his skin."

"That death was no heart attack," Mrs Gibbs said darkly. "And those were not normal scratches on his skin. They were claw marks."

Evie gasped and Lady Pritchard gave a squeal of fear, whilst Pomona's eyes sparkled with excitement. Caitlyn felt her own pulse quicken.

Professor Thrope leaned forwards, his face intent. "Really? Are you certain?"

"Well, I haven't seen them myself," Mrs Gibbs admitted. "But I have it on good authority. The farmer who found the body... he's been telling everyone in the village what he saw. I spoke to his wife yesterday, in fact, and she was terrified. She thought one of her family might be next, because the Black Shuck is supposed to be an omen of death, but I told her that she should be safe enough since she didn't see the creature with her own eyes, nor did her husband or son." She held up a bony finger and wagged it. "But it doesn't matter what the police say—everyone knows that it was the Black Shuck."

"Mrs Gibbs..." James looked at her in surprise. "I wouldn't have thought that you'd be the type to believe in superstitions and rumours."

The woman drew herself up with dignity. "Lord Fitzroy, I believe that there are things out there that science cannot explain—things which make no sense, which should not be possible and yet which people have seen with their own eyes. They are real, even if you cannot find a logical explanation for them."

Caitlyn saw James's eyes flicker towards her for a moment and she felt her cheeks warming. There was an uncomfortable silence around the table. Then Nathan said with a grin:

"Well, personally, if I'm ever out late at night and see the Black Shuck coming towards me, I'm just going to yell a very firm 'SIT'!"

CHAPTER SEVEN

The rest of the meal passed relatively peacefully and by the time the plates were cleared away and dessert was served, everyone was in a more congenial mood. In addition to a freshly baked Victoria sponge cake and a beautiful multi-layered fruit trifle, Mrs Pruett had also arranged a selection of chocolate truffles, bonbons, and fudge pieces on a silver platter, to be passed around with tea and coffee. Caitlyn felt a warm glow as she watched the guests savouring the rich, velvety chocolates. It was always wonderful seeing people taste the Widow Mags's mouth-watering creations for the first time.

"Marvellous chocolates!" said Sir Henry with his mouth full. "Best I've tasted in years! Where did you say they came from, James?"

James smiled and nodded at Caitlyn. "Caitlyn

brought them tonight—courtesy of the Widow Mags. You know her shop, perhaps, Sir Henry? It's the chocolate shop in the village called *Bewitched by Chocolate.*"

"Oh!" Mrs Gibbs, who had just picked up a truffle from the platter, hastily put it back. "I didn't realise these chocolates are from *there.*"

Caitlyn bit her lip and she saw Pomona bristle across the table, whilst Evie shrank down in her chair.

"Why, what's the matter with chocolates from *there*?" asked Nathan, pausing with a piece of caramel fudge halfway to his mouth.

Sir Henry roared with laughter. "Mrs Gibbs, you're not getting your knickers in a twist about *those* stories now, are you?"

"What stories?" asked Professor Thrope, his eyes gleaming with interest. "Is this another local legend?"

"This is no legend—it's the truth," Mrs Gibbs hissed. "The Widow Mags is a witch and her chocolates are tainted with black magic! God only knows what she puts in them to make them taste so good—"

"She doesn't put anything in them except the finest cacao beans and the freshest ingredients!" cried Caitlyn angrily. "You have no right to insinuate—"

Mrs Gibbs rounded on her. "Young lady, I know what I've seen with my own eyes. I was there at the

Fitzroy Garden Party—I saw the Widow Mags conjure up butterflies from that chocolate cake! And what about the attack of chocolate warts on the poor ladies of Tillyhenge? And that... that strange blue fire in the stone circle on the hill? I keep an eye out for what's happening in the village and I know there are unnatural forces at work." She wagged a finger in Caitlyn's face. "Can you look me in the eye and tell me that the Widow Mags isn't a witch?"

"I... I..." Caitlyn stammered, very conscious of James's gaze on her. She didn't know how to answer. How could she say "yes" and expose the Widow Mags in front of all these people? But how could she say "no" when only a few days ago, she had been pleading with James to believe in magic and witchcraft?

Then James's voice cut in, cool and polite: "Mrs Gibbs, while I respect your right to your own opinion, I really cannot allow you to malign a fellow village resident in this fashion. The Widow Mags is a skilled chocolatier who makes the most delicious handmade chocolates I have ever had the fortune to taste. I have no qualms about serving—or eating—her chocolates and I must ask you to please refrain from speaking further on this subject."

Mrs Gibbs flushed bright red. She looked around the table, trying to find support, then sat back stiffly, her mouth set in a tight line. The rest of the table shifted uncomfortably—all except for Sir Henry, who as usual seemed completely oblivious to any undercurrents. He chewed a chocolate truffle noisily, smacking his lips with delight, and said:

"Mmm… bloody good chocolates… if this woman's a witch, I want her in my kitchen! Here, smoochypie, have some more—" He grabbed a large handful from the platter and shoved it onto his wife's plate. She made a face and pushed the plate back towards him.

"Oh, I can't have anymore, cuddleplum. In fact, I don't think I should have had any… I'd forgotten that chocolates always give me a migraine." She massaged her head, grimacing. "I think I might be getting one of my terrible migraines now…"

"You'd better go and lie down in a dark room, dear," said Mrs Gibbs, looking at her in concern. "My sister gets migraines and if she doesn't nip it in the bud quick, she could be out for days."

"I'll ask one of the maids to show you to a guest room," said James, springing up.

"Oh, I don't want to be a bother—"

"It's no bother at all. In fact, why don't you stay at the Manor tonight? Then you don't have to worry about getting up again—you can just relax and go to sleep," James urged.

With a few more protests, Lady Pritchard finally got up. Sir Henry patted his wife's hand absent-mindedly as she leaned across to give him a peck on the cheek. Then she bade the other guests goodnight and followed a maid out of the room.

"Don't know what's wrong with the woman—

always getting these migraines," grumbled Sir Henry after she had gone.

"Perhaps she ought to get it checked out by a doctor?"

"She has! Bloody doctor always coming round... If it's not this thing, then it's that... Friend of mine thinks she's one o' those hypomaniacs."

James's lips twitched. "I think you mean hypochondriac."

Sir Henry waved a hand. "Aye. That." He picked up a chocolate bonbon from his plate and stuffed it in his mouth. "Anyway, good of you to have her to stay."

"It's my pleasure—and you're very welcome to join her, of course."

"No, no, like to sleep in my own bed," said Sir Henry. "Besides, have to get back—early meeting tomorrow morning. That blasted sales agent from Blackmort Developments is coming to see me again. Wants a final answer on their offer."

Pomona's ears perked up. "Blackmort?"

"Is Thane Blackmort trying to buy part of your land too?" asked Mrs Gibbs with a frown.

Sir Henry glowered. "Yes, the section next to the Fitzroy estate—that strip of forest around the hill with the stone circle. Don't know why—nothing there of commercial value."

"It gives access to the hill," said James suddenly. "If you can't get to the hill through Tillyhenge or through the Fitzroy estate, the only other way is through your land."

"Eh?"

"Blackmort has been very keen to purchase that area of land from me. He has been offering all sorts of inducements, from tripling his asking price to giving me a share in his other property portfolios. I've told him several times already that I'm not interested in selling, but he doesn't seem willing to take no for an answer. Now it seems he's trying to get access to the hill through your property— although I don't know what good that will do him if he doesn't own the land that the hill is actually on."

"Wants to build a modern development on that hill, that's what he wants," said Sir Henry. "Clever sod's done it all up and down the countryside. Big apartment and townhouse complex, with tennis courts and swimming pools and cafés and shops and whatnot."

"It's disgusting," said Mrs Gibbs, shaking her head.

"What's disgusting about that?" asked Pomona indignantly. "Sounds pretty awesome to me; he's giving people the chance to live in a beautiful place, with cool facilities and stuff. I'll bet it's great for the local economy."

"Yes, but at what cost, dear?" said Mrs Gibbs sharply. "The British countryside is already under threat. We have to protect what little we have left! The Cotswolds, in particular, is known as an area of 'outstanding natural beauty'—we have a duty to preserve it, not let it be destroyed by a greedy businessman—"

"Thane isn't a greedy businessman! He's just got, like, great vision and ambition..." Pomona flushed and trailed off as she saw everyone around the table staring at her.

"Humph! If Thane Blackmort isn't an example of a greedy businessman, then I don't know what is!" said Sir Henry. "And who is he, eh? No one knows a thing about him! Pops up one day, proud as you please, calling himself the 'Black Tycoon', and starts buying up property left, right, and centre. Could be Russian mafia or some bloody arms dealer, for all you know!"

"You're probably just going to laugh at me again for listening to gossip, but there's been a lot of talk about him too," said Mrs Gibbs primly. "They say bad things have happened to those who oppose him: business rivals, government officials, anyone who tries to make things difficult for Thane Blackmort has mysteriously become ill or disappeared."

James laughed. "Mrs Gibbs, I really think that is salacious gossip now. Surely you're not suggesting that Blackmort could be resorting to assassination or poisoning to remove them? I'm sure it's all just coincidence. I agree that I don't like Blackmort's methods or his ruthless reputation but—"

"Sometimes you have to be ruthless to get things done," protested Pomona. "All the greatest leaders in history were pretty ruthless men. You don't get anywhere by being weak."

"That excuse has been used many times in history to enable men to do terrible things," Nathan spoke up, his voice uncharacteristically serious. Caitlyn was surprised to see the sombre expression on his face. After his joking, irreverent manner all evening, it was a reminder that there was a serious investigative journalist beneath that humorous exterior. He glanced at James, then added, "It's possible to be a strong leader without resorting to ruthless methods and dodgy ethics."

Pomona looked as if she was going to argue, then she bit her lip and sat back in her chair. Suddenly, Caitlyn was desperate for the dinner to be over. She felt exhausted by the constant tensions and undercurrents that kept arising in the middle of seemingly innocent conversation. And it seemed that the other guests shared her thoughts because everyone began draining their teas and coffees and making noises of departure. As Mrs Gibbs rose from the table, however, she looked at Sir Henry and said:

"You're not going to sell, Sir Henry, are you?"

"Certainly not! They've been trying to force my hand by getting to my brother. He was on the phone to me last weekend, pestering me to agree to sell the land." Sir Henry scowled. "I have no doubt that Blackmort contacted him and told him that they're doubling their offer. My brother's always been a weak one for money—he'll roll over and beg if you offer him enough cash! But I'm not budging." He stood up and drained his cup. "I've already told that greasy little weasel of a sales agent once and I'll tell him again tomorrow: the only way they're getting that land is over my dead body!"

CHAPTER EIGHT

Since Nathan and Professor Thrope were staying at the Manor, the two men bade everyone goodnight and retired to their rooms. Pomona gave Caitlyn and Evie each a hug, then followed their example, leaving James to see the rest of the guests out.

"I've called Mrs Gibbs a taxi, sir," said Mosley, as they gathered in the foyer.

"Thank you, Mosley. Can you call one for Sir Henry as well?"

"Eh? Nonsense, I don't need a taxi," the older man blustered, staggering slightly as he turned towards the front door. Mosley hurried to steady him but Sir Henry brushed the butler's hand off with an impatient noise. "Don't fuss, man! I'm fine, I'm fine... just need to find the keys to my car..." he mumbled as he fished in his pockets.

James frowned at him. "You're not thinking of driving, are you, Sir Henry? You've had far too much to drink."

"No, no, I'll leave the car here... going to walk back to my place."

"*Walk?*" The others looked at him in astonishment.

"Sir Henry! Surely you can't be planning to walk all the way back along the motorway on foot?" cried Mrs Gibbs.

"Of course not," Sir Henry growled. "What d'you take me for? There's a shortcut between the Fitzroy estate and mine: footpath running through the woods and down to the village. Passes by the driveway here and then passes by my house. Won't take more than fifteen minutes, I reckon."

"You're not talking about Dead Man's Walk, are you?" asked Mrs Gibbs, horrified. "You can't walk there!"

"Why not?" Sir Henry demanded. "Marvellous summer weather we're having. Do me good to get some fresh air."

"But, Sir Henry... Dead Man's Walk is haunted!" cried Mrs Gibbs.

"Rubbish!" Sir Henry scoffed. "I've walked that path dozens of times, Mrs Gibbs, and never had any trouble. Would have come that way tonight, actually, if the wife hadn't made such a fuss about her shoes."

"It's not just silly superstition," Mrs Gibbs

insisted. "That tramp who was murdered last weekend—his body was found at the village end of Dead Man's Walk."

"The police haven't concluded that it's murder; he may have died of natural causes," James reminded her. Then he turned to Sir Henry. "But nevertheless, I have to agree with Mrs Gibbs, sir— not that I believe that the path is haunted—but it may not be wise for you to attempt the walk so late at night, and in your... er... condition..." he added, eyeing Sir Henry's flushed face. The older man was looking very drunk, with a slightly nauseated expression and a visible tremor in his hands.

"Oh, stop fussing, boy—you're as bad as my wife," said Sir Henry irritably. He wagged a finger at James. "Young chaps nowadays haven't got any stuffing. *You* might be sloshed after a few glasses but *I* have no problem holding my drink. If your father was still alive, he could tell you some stories—spent many a night drinking up half the cellar, we did!" He gave a bark of laughter, then sobered and clapped a hand on James's shoulder. "Never got the chance to tell you this at the funeral, but he was a good man, your father. A great man. The things he did for his country... someday, you'll realise..." Sir Henry trailed off, seeming lost in thought for a moment, then took a breath and said briskly, "Anyway, it's a fine job you're doing with the estate, James. Your father would have been proud of you."

There was an awkward moment of silence and Caitlyn felt slightly embarrassed to be standing there listening. It felt almost as if she was intruding on a private moment.

James cleared his throat, looking surprised and touched. "Er... thank you, Sir Henry... I really appreciate the sentiment. But... won't you consider staying the night here?"

"No, I'm walking home," said the older man obstinately. "And don't keep going on about it—you're giving me a bloody headache! Give me a light and I'll be fine. In fact, I'll give you odds that I get home before you do!"

Taking a torch from Mosley, Sir Henry nodded to them all, then—swaying slightly—he walked out the front door. The door had barely shut behind him when Mrs Gibbs turned towards James and said:

"Lord Fitzroy, you have to stop him!"

James sighed. "Mrs Gibbs, I think that would involve physically restraining him and I don't think Sir Henry would take kindly to that—"

"Better that than having him killed by the Black Shuck!"

James gave her a tired smile. "I don't think there is any danger of that, Mrs Gibbs. You really mustn't let yourself be frightened by the village gossip and rumours. There is no evidence that the death last weekend was due to a supernatural cause or even the result of foul play. I am sure Sir Henry will be quite safe walking that path home. It really is quite a short distance and will only take ten or fifteen minutes—" The sound of a horn outside interrupted him. "Ah, that must be your taxi now."

Still looking distressed, Mrs Gibbs gathered her things and left. Caitlyn and Evie followed her out the door and headed to their car, with James escorting them. He held open the car doors and waited courteously for them to get in.

Settling into her seat, Caitlyn lowered the window and looked up at him. "Thank you for dinner. It was a—" She stumbled over the word "lovely" to describe the tense evening and instead amended it to "—a very interesting experience."

He gave her a wry smile, obviously reading her mind, and started to say something. Then his eyes flicked to Evie sitting in the passenger seat and he took a step back from the car instead.

"Good night. Drive safely." Giving them a wave, he walked back to the Manor and disappeared through the front door.

Caitlyn started the engine, frowning as the car gave a hoarse cough before spluttering into life. It was the third time she had heard that sound in the past few days and she wondered if she should take the vehicle somewhere to be serviced. She sighed. Really, if she was going to remain in England, she knew she should just buy a car of her own, instead of continuing to use a rental vehicle. Even though she was fortunate that her inheritance from her adoptive mother meant that she had no need to worry about funds, it was still an unnecessary waste of money to continue paying hire car rates.

As she drove along the driveway, joining the private road that ran through the Manor parklands and out onto the main road, Caitlyn pondered what make of car to buy. *A Volkswagen Beetle, like this one? Or maybe something with more space in the trunk? I mean, in the boot,* she thought with a wry smile. If she was going to live in England, she'd better start talking like the Brits and calling things by their British names! Her mind busy, she drove absently along the darkened road until she was jolted out of her reverie by the car dipping sharply to one side. The front right wheel sank into a pothole and the entire vehicle thumped and rattled as it bounced out of the hole again, making both girls smack their heads on the ceiling.

"Ow!"

"Sorry, sorry!" Caitlyn gasped. "My fault—I wasn't paying attention..."

She gripped the steering wheel tighter, trying to drive more carefully, but as the car rolled shakily forwards, she heard that hoarse coughing sound coming from the engine again. And then, as she listened in dismay, the engine wheezed, spluttered... and died.

They rolled to a stop and the headlights went dead.

"Oh rats," Caitlyn muttered. She pumped the accelerator and turned the ignition a few times but the car remained silent.

"What happened?" asked Evie.

"I don't know. The engine just died. Maybe it's something to do with the battery... I thought it sounded a bit funny when it started—and it's been sounding like that the last few days..." Caitlyn sighed and peered out of the window at the dark woods around them. "I think we're going to have to follow Sir Henry's example and walk."

"*Walk?* We're not going to walk all the way back to Tillyhenge?" Evie's voice was shrill with dismay.

"No, no, just back to the Manor. We'll have to get a breakdown service to come and look at the car, but I suppose they won't come until tomorrow morning now. I guess we'll have to impose on James's hospitality and ask to stay the night... I hope he hasn't gone to bed yet..."

The two girls got out of the car and Caitlyn looked hopefully at her cousin. "I don't suppose you have a flashlight—I mean, a torch?"

Evie shook her head.

"Never mind, it's a full moon," said Caitlyn, glancing at the sky. "We should have enough light to see our way and we just need to follow this road back until we join up with the driveway."

They started walking, although it wasn't quite as well-lit as Caitlyn had anticipated. The full moon was still high in the sky but there was now a bank of clouds which drifted in front of the moon every so often, obscuring the pale glow so that the landscape was cast into shadows. It gave a surreal effect—almost like someone switching the lights on and off—as things came into sharp focus for a moment under the brilliant moonlight, only to fade into darkness again a moment later.

It was slow going, especially as both of them were wearing high heels, and even the spell on Evie's stilettos seemed to have worn off. Caitlyn could see that the younger girl was hobbling; her own feet were beginning to get painful blisters.

"Do you think we could walk barefoot?" asked Evie. Without waiting for a reply, she slipped off her stilettos, then made a few mincing steps on the road as the rough tarmac hurt her tender soles. "Ow... ow..." She did a little sideways jump, off the tarmac and onto the softer ground beneath the trees at the side of the road. "Ohhh... this is better! Caitlyn, take off your shoes and walk here, with me. It's so much nicer."

Caitlyn hesitated, then complied. She had to admit that Evie was right—the ground of the forest floor was soft and cool to walk on, and it made the going much easier.

"This is great!" said Evie, trotting ahead.

"Evie, wait up..." said Caitlyn, hitching her skirts higher and hurrying after the other girl.

She soon realised that although the ground was softer, it was a lot darker here under the trees. Even when the moon was not obscured by clouds, it was still dim, and when it went behind the clouds, they were plunged into almost total darkness. She faltered to a stop every time that happened, putting her hands out like a blind woman and groping in front of her as she slowly inched forwards. But Evie didn't seem so cautious. Caitlyn could hear her young cousin blundering through the undergrowth ahead, muttering "Ow!" every so often as she crashed into a tree or a prickly bush. Finally, after a particularly long spell of darkness, the moon came out again and Caitlyn straightened, breathing a sigh of relief. Ahead of her, she heard Evie give a small cheer and she smiled to herself.

Then her smile faded as she looked around her. She was surrounded by a wall of tree trunks, leaves, and branches in every direction, with no sign of the road.

"Evie...?" she called. "Evie, where are you?"

A voice sounded at her elbow, making her jump. "I'm here. What's the matter?"

"Evie, where's the road?"

The other girl turned and pointed. "I thought it was ther—" She broke off as she peered at the trees around them in confusion. "Oh."

They must have wandered away from the road and into the forest during the last spell of darkness. Now, they were hopelessly lost, with no idea of which direction they'd come from and which direction they should go in. Caitlyn felt a flare of panic, which she quickly dampened down. She took a deep breath. It wasn't as if they were lost in the wilderness, she reminded herself. They were on Fitzroy land and, large as the estate was, it was still a contained area. If they kept walking, they would either hit the boundary or—hopefully—find themselves in the manicured grounds closer to the house, from which they could easily reach the Manor.

"Let's just keep walking," said Caitlyn, giving her cousin a nudge. "I think the house is that way," she added with false confidence. "If we just keep heading in that direction, we should come out somewhere near the rose garden, I think."

Evie nodded and fell into step beside her, although she could see that the younger girl's former high spirits had evaporated. Now, her cousin peered nervously into the undergrowth around them, starting at every sound and clutching Caitlyn's arm in alarm. Finally, the trees around them thinned and they came out into a sort of clearing, where the track they were following ended in a T-junction with a wider path. The latter cut straight across in front of them, from left to right, and they turned their heads from one side to the other in uncertainty.

"Which way should we go? Left... or right?" asked Evie.

Caitlyn was about to answer when something caught her eye. It was a crude wooden sign that someone had pinned to a tree by the side of the wider path. She stepped closer and her heart gave an uncomfortable jolt as the moonlight fell on the roughly etched letters:

<— DEAD MAN'S WALK —>

She heard Evie's sharp intake of breath next to her as her cousin also saw the words on the sign.

"Oh my Goddess—this is Dead Man's Walk! We can't take this, we can't!" Evie whimpered.

"Well, we can't stand here all night," said Caitlyn. She glanced over her shoulder. "And I'm not going back the way we came—there's no guarantee that we'll find the road again and we could walk around in circles all night. Come on, remember what Sir Henry said? He takes this shortcut all the time."

"What about what Mrs Gibbs said?" Evie retorted.

"You're just letting silly village gossip get to you—"

"It's not silly gossip!" cried Evie. "The Black Shuck is real and this is where he's been seen..." She stared wildly at the woods around them, as if expecting a demon hound to jump out at them any moment.

Caitlyn felt a twinge of unease but resolutely pushed it away. Keeping her voice light and joking, she said: "Well, the longer we stand here, the more likely we are to meet him—so we'd better get going." She looked thoughtfully again from left to right. "If this is Dead Man's Walk, then that means one side ends at the Manor and the other ends at Sir Henry's estate. Either one will do. So we just need to stay on it and walk to the end. Come on... let's go... left," she decided.

She set off at a brisk pace and heard Evie scurry to keep up with her. If it wasn't for the route's spooky reputation, it would almost have been a nice walk. The path was wide and well-worn, and whether by nature's design or man-made intervention, the trees on either side had few overhanging branches, so that the way was clearly lit by moonlight. But somehow, Caitlyn couldn't stop herself glancing uneasily at the trees closing in on either side or shake off the insidious thought that while the moonlight showed the path clearly, it also showed *their* movements clearly to anyone—or any*thing*—that was watching them...

Evie reached out suddenly and grabbed Caitlyn's arm so hard that the latter winced.

"Evie... do you mind not holding on so tightly?" Caitlyn asked.

"Oh, sorry..." the younger girl mumbled. "I just... I thought I saw..." She trailed off and looked over her shoulder.

Caitlyn turned to follow her gaze. "What?"

Evie stared for a moment longer, then sighed and shook her head. "Nothing."

Caitlyn was about to start walking again when Evie gripped her arm again, this time squeezing even harder.

"There! Between those trees! *Oh my Goddess—*" Her voice went shrill with fear. *"Can you see those red eyes?"*

Caitlyn whirled around to look, peering frantically into the undergrowth around them. She was just about to open her mouth and say that she couldn't see anything, when she froze.

A pair of red eyes glowed from the shadows between two trees.

Her heart stuttered in her chest. Beside her, she could hear Evie's breathing, fast and scared... then she realised that the sound was actually her *own* breathing.

Caitlyn took a stumbling step backwards, groping for her cousin's hand. The younger girl made a whimpering sound. Caitlyn gave her a shove.

"Evie—RUN!"

CHAPTER NINE

Caitlyn burst into a run, pumping her legs hard, fighting the urge to look back. She ran without thinking until she was gasping for breath and her lungs were screaming in protest. Next to her, Evie was also gasping and panting, and both girls looked fearfully over their shoulders as they stumbled to a stop.

There was nothing behind them. The path lay empty, a pale winding ribbon disappearing into the woods beyond. Above the dark treeline, the moon glowed serenely in the night sky. Everything looked calm and peaceful. It almost made a mockery of their panicked flight. For a moment, Caitlyn felt a flicker of doubt. Could she have imagined it?

"Is it... is it gone?" asked Evie in a quavering voice.

"I think so... I mean... There *was* something chasing us, wasn't there? What if we just panicked over nothing?" said Caitlyn sheepishly.

"What do you mean? I saw it! You did too! Those red eyes—it was the Black Shuck!"

"Yes, I saw the red eyes but... it could have been any forest animal, like a... a deer or a wild boar... Maybe all the talk tonight just over-stimulated our imaginations and we saw what we wanted to see. After all, there *are* deer on Fitzroy land and—"

"No, I know what I saw!" cried Evie, tears of frustration coming to her eyes. "And you saw it too! Why won't you believe it? It's the Black Shuck! And—listen!" She broke off. "What's that?"

"Aww, come on, Evie, not again—"

"No, listen!" Evie insisted, clutching Caitlyn's arm.

Caitlyn paused, then felt herself stiffen as she heard the sound. A loud rustling. Somewhere in the undergrowth around them... although she couldn't tell which direction it was coming from. She swung around, peering frantically in all directions.

Then a weight like a hand—or a paw—landed on her shoulder. Caitlyn shrieked.

"Ouch!" came a crotchety voice. "Must you scream so loudly? I'm sure my eardrums have been shattered."

Caitlyn whirled to find herself facing a stooped old man who was wincing and holding his hands over his ears. He was wearing a black suit which looked like it belonged to the last century, and his few strands of grey hair were combed carefully over his balding head.

"Viktor!" she cried in mingled relief and exasperation. "Don't sneak up on me like that!"

"I was not sneaking! Vampires never sneak. We glide through the darkness—"

"Did you see anything while you were gliding?" asked Caitlyn. "Like... like a pair of red eyes?"

"Eh? Red eyes? No... but I did see some marvellous red currants!" Viktor smacked his gummy lips. "Big, juicy berries... and no nasty thorns either, like those gooseberry bushes—though I must say, currants can be quite tart even when ripe. Gooseberries, on the other hand, have a wonderful flavour which changes when they turn soft..."

Caitlyn resisted the urge to roll her eyes. Once Viktor started on the subject of his favourite fruits, the conversation was a lost cause. Still, she couldn't help smiling inwardly as she watched him, with his rheumy eyes bright and his gnarled old hands gesticulating excitedly. If someone had told her, when she came to England to search for her real family, that she would find a vampire uncle too, she would have laughed in their face. And yet now she couldn't imagine life without Viktor: grumbling about his lost fangs, proudly telling everyone that he was a "fruitarian", crashing into trees in his adorable fruit bat form...

"We were being chased by the Black Shuck!" Evie piped up.

"Eh?" Viktor broke off and peered at her. "The Black Shuck?"

Evie nodded eagerly. "The ghostly black hound—did you see it? It was right there, in the trees! It was coming after us!"

"Well, we didn't actually see it chasing us," Caitlyn reminded her. "We just saw red eyes—at least, we think we did, but maybe we were wrong—"

Evie opened her mouth to argue but they were interrupted by a screech from the forest behind them. Caitlyn shrank down, peering wildly around.

"What's that?" asked Evie in a terrified whisper, huddling close to Caitlyn.

Viktor cocked his head. "That? Oh, that's a barn owl."

Caitlyn relaxed and straightened up again. "Come on... this is getting silly. We can't stand here all night being scared by the night noises of the forest. Let's get back to the Manor." She turned to the elderly vampire. "Viktor, we got a bit lost and we weren't sure we were walking in the right direction. Do you know if—"

"Never fear!" said Viktor, puffing his bony chest out. "With my vampire-sensory perception, I can always find my way, even in the darkest night, the thickest fog, the murkiest sea! I shall lead you right to the Manor's front door. Follow me!" He hunched over, and before Caitlyn could blink, he had transformed into a fuzzy brown fruit bat. Squeaking importantly, the little creature opened its leathery wings and took to the air... then crashed into the tree next to them.

"Viktor! Are you all right?" Caitlyn cried, rushing over to the tree.

The fruit bat was lying on its back, slightly stunned but otherwise unhurt. Caitlyn bent to pick it up but it squeaked indignantly so she let it roll over by itself. A minute later, a scrawny old man sat at the base of the tree, rubbing his balding head and scowling at her.

"A slight miscalculation, that was all," said Viktor huffily. "Perhaps I need to launch myself from a higher tree—"

"Er... never mind, Viktor," said Caitlyn hastily. "I think we'll just keep following the path. I'm sure it will lead to the Manor. You go back to your red currant bush."

Fifteen minutes later, she breathed a sigh of relief as they stepped out of the woods and onto the manicured lawns surrounding the manor house. And she was even more relieved to find that Mosley was still up. The butler looked startled to find the two girls standing on the doorstep but, true to his training, asked no questions and escorted them to a guestroom with smooth aplomb—for all the world as if midnight visitors asking to stay the night were a perfectly normal daily occurrence.

As soon as he'd left them, Evie undressed and

sank wearily into one of the twin beds. She was obviously exhausted by her eventful evening and was fast asleep within seconds. Caitlyn tried to follow suit but found herself too restless to lie still. Finally, she threw back the covers and padded barefoot to the window. Pulling the curtains back, she peered out into the night. This side of the Manor looked onto part of the formal gardens and, beyond them, she could see the dark silhouettes of the tree tops—part of the woods that they had just walked through—outlined by the silvery light of the moon.

Then she stiffened. A howl... faint and eerie... sounded in the distance. It was brief, lasting barely more than a few seconds, and she wondered if she had imagined it. She pressed her nose against the windowpane, her breath misting the cold glass as she strained her ears to hear it again.

Nothing.

Caitlyn stood for several more minutes at the window, listening and waiting, but heard nothing more. Finally, with a last troubled look at the darkened forest outside, she crept back to bed.

***

A bright light woke her the next morning, and when Caitlyn opened her eyes, she found that a shaft of sunlight had slid through the curtains and fallen across her face. She sat up, yawning, and for a moment couldn't understand why she was lying on soft Egyptian cotton sheets, instead of her sagging mattress in the cramped attic bedroom above the village chocolate shop. Then, as she looked around the spacious room decorated in muted shades of cream and gold, with the elegant furniture and luxurious en suite, she realised where she was: Huntingdon Manor. The events of last night came rushing back to her.

Glancing over at the twin bed next to hers, she saw Evie buried beneath the covers, still fast asleep, her frizzy red hair spread in a tangled mess across the pillow. Caitlyn started to rouse her young cousin, then changed her mind. Instead, she dressed hurriedly, splashed some water on her face, then retraced her steps to the window.

But when she pulled back the curtains, the scene which met her eyes looked nothing like the night before. Warm August sunshine filtered through the trees and shone softly on the lawns surrounding the manor house. Just beneath her, she could see Old Palmer, the head gardener, studiously clipping a box hedge with handheld shears, whilst a little black kitten played around his feet. Caitlyn chuckled as she saw the old gardener look furtively around, then bend down quickly and pat Nibs, tickling the kitten under his chin. She never thought she'd see the day when Old Palmer wasn't shouting at Nibs or chasing him off the rose beds, but it looked like James was right: the little kitten had managed to win even the crotchety old gardener over.

Suddenly seized by an urge to go down and join them in the morning sunshine, Caitlyn tiptoed to the door and let herself quietly out of the room. As she stepped out, she saw another figure also coming out of a room farther down the hallway. Light from the hallway window fell on a mane of big blonde hair and highlighted a curvaceous figure dressed in a clingy lime-green sundress. It was Pomona. Caitlyn broke into a smile but before she could call out to her cousin, Pomona turned and hurried off in the opposite direction.

Where's she going? Caitlyn hesitated, then followed. A few minutes later, they turned a familiar corner and Caitlyn watched her cousin approach a heavy wooden door decorated with iron studs. The Fitzroy Portrait Gallery. This time, however, Pomona didn't hover uncertainly outside the door—instead, she bent down and fumbled with the lock. A minute later, she pushed the heavy door open and slipped inside.

Caitlyn followed and stepped into the room after her cousin. Dust motes danced in the sunshine slanting through the row of windows, and the air smelled musty. Everything looked exactly the way she had seen it last: the row of oil paintings— portraits of the Fitzroy ancestors—hanging along the long wall facing the windows, the pieces of furniture covered in white sheets, the heavy, oppressive atmosphere...

Pomona was moving between the pieces of covered furniture, lifting each sheet and peering underneath. She glanced up as she heard Caitlyn step into the room and grinned.

"Hey! I thought you and Evie went back to Tillyhenge last night."

"We meant to... but my car died so we had to walk back here and stay the night."

"Ooh... I'll bet James was pleased," said Pomona with a grin.

Caitlyn blushed slightly. "I didn't see him, actually. Mosley let us in and showed us to our room." Quickly, she changed the subject. "Anyway, what are you doing?"

"Checking this place out! What does it look like?"

"But how did you get in? I thought the door is always kept locked."

"Yeah, I got the key off Mosley last night before I went to bed. I asked James at dinner and he said I was welcome to come up anytime."

"But what do you want to see?" asked Caitlyn in confusion.

"Aww, come on, Caitlyn—I can't believe you're asking that! This room is just full of awesome stuff." She gestured to the white sheets around them. "This is all from the old Lord Fitzroy's occult collection. Aren't you curious? Aren't you, like, dying to see what kind of stuff he collected?"

"No, not really." Caitlyn gave an uneasy glance

around. She couldn't explain it, but something about the room always bothered her. There was a darkness here, a sense of things that shouldn't be disturbed.

Pomona, however, didn't seem to feel it. She lifted up another white sheet and squealed at the display cabinet underneath. "Omigod, check this out, Caitlyn: elf-shot amulets! These look like real mediaeval ones too, not cheesy replicas from some New Age shop."

"What's elf-shot?"

"They're tiny arrowheads that fell from the sky and they were used by elves and fairies, who use them to shoot at people and cattle. It causes this piercing pain in your body," Pomona explained. "But if humans get hold of elf-shots, they can be used as a charm against witchcraft! Especially if you bind them with silver in an amulet—people wore them for protection in the Middle Ages..." She peered through the glass. "Wow, I can't believe how many different kinds he's got here. They're really hard to find, you know—you can't just go out and buy them. At least, not the genuine, magical ones."

"What do you mean?"

"Well, a lot of magical objects are like that. Like hag stones too. You can't find them when you're actually looking for them—but they turn up when they want to, when you least expect it."

Caitlyn looked at her cousin. It always impressed her how much Pomona knew about the paranormal and the occult—although she really shouldn't have been surprised. After all, Pomona had been obsessed with magic and witchcraft ever since her teens. In fact, now that she thought about it, she should have known that a room full of mythical occult items would have been irresistible to her cousin.

Pomona had her nose pressed against the glass top of the cabinet. "Ooh, that one is so pretty—you could, like, just wear it for jewellery, you know? It would look really cool set in a choker, don't you think? I've got this Versace dress with a plunging neckline that would be just awesome with that..." She reached for the latch and opened the case.

"Pomie! What are you doing?"

"I'm just having a closer look—"

"No, no, don't take it out!" Caitlyn slammed the cabinet door closed again and frowned at her cousin.

"I'm sure James wouldn't mind—"

"It's not that. I just don't think you should be playing around with things in this room."

"Aww, you're no fun," complained Pomona, flouncing off to the other side of the room. She paused in front of a small oil painting on the far wall. Reluctantly, Caitlyn joined her, eyeing the painting warily. She knew the picture well: it showed four men on horseback, galloping across a dark landscape.

"What a cool painting! The Four Horsemen of the

Apocalypse," breathed Pomona, staring up at it avidly. "War on the Red Horse, Famine on the Black Horse, Plague on the White Horse... and Death on the Pale Horse."

Again, Caitlyn was reluctantly impressed by her cousin's instant recognition and knowledge of the painting's subject. "I hate that painting," she said with a shudder. "It creeps me out." She cast another uneasy glance around the room. "In fact, this whole room creeps me out. Every time I come in here, I just want to get out as soon as I can. There's... there's something oppressive about this place."

"I think you're imagining it," Pomona scoffed. "Besides, who cares if it's a bit creepy when there are all these goodies to see? There must be, like, ancient magical texts and treasures from folklore... and hey—!" She grabbed Caitlyn's arm excitedly. "Have you ever thought? You might find your answers here!"

"Answers?" Caitlyn looked at her quizzically.

"Yeah, the answers you've been searching for, about your mother and that runestone you were found with as a baby... I mean, wasn't that what brought you to England in the first place?"

Caitlyn's hands went unconsciously to her throat and her fingers felt for the flat, oblong stone strung on a piece of ribbon, which she always wore around her neck. "I... uh... yes, it was..." she stammered.

Pomona gave her an incredulous look. "Don't tell

me you've forgotten all about it?"

"No, of course I hadn't forgotten!"

"Well, then, how come you're not doing anything about it? How come you're not asking the Widow Mags—"

"I have!" said Caitlyn. "I've tried several times. She just shuts me down. She's even warned me that if I want to remain in Tillyhenge, she'll teach me how to work magic but I wouldn't be getting any answers from her."

"What about Bertha?"

"She just keeps changing the subject whenever I try to bring it up! The only thing she would tell me was that my runestone isn't like hers... You know she wears one around her neck as well, right? Well, when I first arrived in Tillyhenge, she told me that runestones are handed down in witch families, usually as a gift to a young witch when she is a little girl. And mine is similar to hers—in fact, the stone is the same—but the symbols are different."

"Yeah, I know—the marks carved on her runestone are just standard witches' runes, aren't they?" said Pomona. "I've seen hers. But your marks are different—I noticed that ages ago. Yours don't look like any witches' runes that I've seen."

"Yes, that's what Bertha said too. She said she had no idea what my symbols meant... and I think she was telling the truth; she wasn't just saying that to fob me off." Caitlyn shrugged. "But that's all she would say. When I tried to ask more, she just clammed up and refused to say anything else."

"Okay, so... you're gonna give up, just like that? Just 'cos they won't talk to you? Man, if my mother was missing and there was all this mystery about my past—and I was back in the village where I was born—well, I'd be, like, out there asking questions, looking for connections, trying to find answers!"

"I *have* found some answers," said Caitlyn defensively. "I mean, I know now that I'm descended from a long line of witches and... and I know the Widow Mags and Bertha and Evie are my family—"

"But you still don't know what those symbols on your runestone means," said Pomona, pointing to the necklace. "And you don't know why your mother left you... or what happened to her..." Pomona shook her head. "Jeez, Caitlyn, I don't know how you can be so complacent, just going along every day, not knowing the truth—"

"Because I don't want to know!" Caitlyn burst out.

There was a moment's silence, then Pomona's face softened and she said gently, "You think she's dead, don't you?"

Caitlyn looked down, fiddling with a fingernail. "I... I don't know. I mean..." She hesitated, then said at last in a small voice. "Yes."

Pomona touched her arm. "Caitlyn—"

Caitlyn raised her head again. "It would explain why she hasn't got in touch with me, why she hasn't tried to find me, in all these years..." She gave Pomona a sad smile. "It's... it's hard to explain but... for the first time in my life, I have a feeling, at last, of knowing where I belong. I feel... *happy*, you know? Content. Like I'm finally where I'm meant to be, doing what I'm meant to be doing... I know there are still questions to be answered and I do want to find out the truth... but I suppose... well, I suppose I've just let myself be lulled into a false sense of contentment." She sighed. "I know, in my heart of hearts, that my mother is probably dead... but I still don't really want to hear anyone confirm it, do you know what I mean? And... and to be honest, I'm not sure I'm ready to face the 'truth' about my past, whatever that is. I have a feeling it's something bad, something I'll wish I never knew." She gave a rueful smile. "You're going to say I'm being a coward, aren't you?"

"Caitlyn—"

"I just want to live in this cocoon a little while longer," she pleaded. "That's why I haven't been pushing very hard... I sort of... just wanted to take each day as it comes."

"Oh, honey... I'm sorry, I totally understand!" Pomona gave her an impulsive hug. Then she stepped back and looked at her. "But you know... you can't keep running away forever. You have to find out someday."

Caitlyn sighed. "I know."

Pomona was silent for a moment, then she said: "Listen—I just had an idea. James said I could come in here anytime and snoop around as much as I like." She grinned in anticipation. "You know, James said his father might even have a real selkie skin somewhere!" She held a hand out. "Why don't you give me your runestone and I'll see if it matches anything I dig up?"

Caitlyn hesitated. "Well, I…"

Pomona chuckled. "I'm not gonna lose it—promise!"

Caitlyn untied the ribbon and started to hand the runestone to her cousin. Her neck felt strangely naked and vulnerable without it—suddenly, she jerked her hand back.

"N-no, I think I'll keep it," she said. "Maybe I'll… I'll come and have a look around myself when I have a moment free."

Pomona shrugged. "Okay. Suit yourself. Hey, have you had breakfast yet? I'm starving! C'mon, let's go down…"

They made their way down to the Morning Room, where breakfast was normally served, and walked in to find Professor Thrope and Nathan Lewis already sitting at the table. Caitlyn was surprised to see both men looking very sombre—in fact, the professor looked downright haggard, as if he had barely slept all night, and Nathan fidgeted in his seat, seemingly filled with nervous energy.

"Morning!" said Pomona cheerily. Then her smile faded as she looked at the two men's faces. "Man, what's going on? You guys look like someone died or something."

Nathan gave her an ironic look. "As a matter of fact, someone has. Sir Henry was found dead this morning."

"Dead?" Caitlyn stared at them.

Professor Thrope sighed. "Yes, one of his staff was heading to the village and found Sir Henry's body on Dead Man's Walk."

"But... how did he die?"

Nathan shrugged. "It's a bit of a mystery. The police have been called—James is with them now, actually."

Pomona gasped. "The police? So they think Sir Henry was murdered?"

CHAPTER TEN

The sound of voices in the hallway outside interrupted them and, a moment later, James Fitzroy walked in, followed by Inspector Walsh of the local CID. Nathan sprang up, his face alert, and Caitlyn was reminded again that in spite of his easy charm and jokey manner, Nathan Lewis was an experienced journalist with a nose for a story. He looked keenly at the detective inspector now and said:

"So is it true, Inspector? Sir Henry was murdered?"

Inspector Walsh looked slightly annoyed and said, "Where did you hear that? The police haven't released any statement to that effect. There's no need to jump to conclusions, young man."

"Ah, but there must be some foul play

suspected," said Nathan shrewdly. "Otherwise, why would you be here? You're a detective, aren't you, sir? They wouldn't call CID unless they thought there was a crime involved."

"I happened to be in the area this morning," said Inspector Walsh noncommittally. "And since this death occurred in the same area as the one last week, it seemed prudent to conduct a more thorough investigation... which is where my experience comes in handy. But that does not necessarily mean that we think the death is suspicious. In fact, as far as I can see, Sir Henry died of natural causes."

"What did he die of?" Caitlyn asked.

"Probably a heart attack," said Inspector Walsh.

"Heart attack?" said Nathan in a disbelieving tone. "Didn't the tramp who was found dead last weekend. also die of a heart attack? And he was found on Dead Man's Walk too, wasn't he? Inspector, doesn't it strike you as odd that two men should die of a heart attack in the same place, within the same week?"

"No, not really," said Inspector Walsh. "First of all, it is not exactly the 'same place'. Dead Man's Walk is a very long path, starting at Tillyhenge, leading past both the Pritchard and the Fitzroy estates, and on through farmland to the next town. The tramp was found at the end of the path, near where it starts by the village; Sir Henry was found on the short section between the Pritchard and

Fitzroy estates. There's at least a ten-minute walk between the two locations. As for the cause of death, it is a bit of a coincidence, yes, but heart attacks are one of the most common causes of death, especially in older men. I'm sure if you looked at any public place—say a restaurant or a city square—you'd find several people having died of heart attacks."

"Yes, but this isn't a busy spot," Nathan insisted. "This is a lonely country lane, where people rarely go... Surely you can't just assume—you have to do a post-mortem to find out."

Inspector Walsh glowered at him. "I'd thank you not to tell me how to do my job, young man. A post-mortem will be conducted if it is deemed necessary. However, I must remind you that autopsies cost time and money—taxpayers' money—and we can't just request them willy-nilly without good reason. Sir Henry was an older man who was overweight and drank heavily. I called and spoke to his doctor this morning: apparently, he had been taking medication for heart issues. Now, without any evidence to suggest foul play, I am inclined to go with the simplest explanation, which is that he had a heart attack while walking back to his estate last night. That does not mean that we won't investigate thoroughly—" He gave Nathan a pointed look. "—but I am not expecting to find anything of a suspicious nature."

"So there was no injury at all?" Nathan persisted.

The inspector hesitated, and James answered for him.

"This is to be kept strictly confidential, Nathan... but there were some bruises on his arm which were slightly odd."

"Odd in what way?" asked Nathan quickly.

James glanced at the inspector for approval, then said, "They look like they could be bite marks."

Nathan whistled.

"Omigod! Sir Henry was attacked by the Black Shuck!" Pomona gasped. "That's why he had a heart attack—he died of fright!"

The inspector frowned. "What's this?"

"There's a lot of talk in the village about sightings of a big black dog in the countryside around Tillyhenge," James explained. "The locals think it's the Black Shuck—"

Inspector Walsh made an irritable sound. "I don't have time for this superstitious nonsense! There was a girl attacked last night, you know, on another country path not far from Dead Man's Walk. She was jumped on by a gang of men wearing masks. They took her money but she managed to get away. That's the fourth attack in the last few months by this gang and we still haven't been able to get a lead on them."

"Was the girl all right?" Professor Thrope spoke up for the first time. "Was she hurt?"

"No, she's fine. Nothing other than a few scratches and bruises," said the inspector. "She was lucky. I dread to think what else they might have done to her, if they hadn't been scared off."

"What scared them off?" asked Nathan.

The inspector shrugged. "Who knows? Some noise, perhaps... the girl wasn't very clear when I spoke to her this morning. She was rambling, in fact—talking about glowing red eyes. But before you jump on that as evidence of a supernatural creature—" He gave Pomona a stern look. "—let me tell you that it is hardly surprising and means absolutely nothing. Given that she must have been very traumatised, it is very likely that she thinks she saw something, which she didn't. Especially if her imagination was already over-stimulated by gossip and superstitions that she heard in the village. Anyway, the point is..." He paused for emphasis. "The reason I mention this is to show that I have enough to deal with from real-life criminals, without worrying about beasties from folklore."

"But the strange bruises—" Pomona protested.

"Those bruises can't have been caused by the Black Shuck," said Inspector Walsh impatiently. "If a so-called demon hound attacked Sir Henry, wouldn't you expect it to leave him with serious wounds? Those marks never even broke the skin."

"Maybe ghostly doggies have really soft teeth," suggested Nathan, grinning.

Inspector Walsh did not look amused. James gave his friend an exasperated look, then cleared his throat and asked the inspector if he would like a cup of tea.

"No, thank you. I have to get back to the station. However, I'd just like a quick word with Ms Le Fey—" He turned towards Caitlyn. "Lord Fitzroy tells me that you walked back to the Manor through the woods last night?"

"Yes, my car broke down in the parklands on my way out and we had to come back here—me and Evie," Caitlyn explained. "We actually walked along Dead Man's Walk."

Inspector Walsh looked at her thoughtfully. "Did you, now? And did you happen to see anyone?"

Only my vampire uncle. Caitlyn decided it was easier not to mention Viktor. "No, we saw nobody."

"Did you hear anything or notice anything unusual?"

"Well, I thought I saw..." Caitlyn hesitated, glancing around the group.

"Yes?"

"Er... nothing... It was probably just my imagination," said Caitlyn.

The inspector seemed satisfied with that, although Caitlyn saw Nathan look at her sharply. She was relieved when he followed James and the police out to the foyer, obviously keen to pump the inspector for more information. Silently, she helped herself to a simple Continental breakfast from the sideboard, then sat toying with her food and listening half-heartedly as Pomona chattered excitedly about the morning's events. Professor Thrope seemed preoccupied too, making polite responses to Pomona's remarks but not really participating in her enthusiastic discussion of whether Sir Henry could have been killed by a ghostly black hound.

Caitlyn finished her breakfast and excused herself, heading back upstairs to rouse Evie. On the way, she met Mosley and discovered that the efficient butler had already organised for a car breakdown service to come and tow her vehicle away.

"That's great," said Caitlyn. "Can they get it repaired right away?"

"I'm afraid they will need a bit of time to order the part that needs to be replaced," said Mosley. "So you will be without a vehicle for a day or two. Would you like me to call you a taxi to take you back to the village?"

"I can run Miss Le Fey back to Tillyhenge," said a deep voice behind them.

Caitlyn turned to see James approaching, obviously having overheard their conversation. Her heart lurched slightly at the thought of having to sit in the quiet confines of a car with him. She knew it was silly, but ever since that disastrous day when he had rejected her confession, she had been nervous of being alone with James. So much still hung unresolved in the air between them. Then she remembered with relief that Evie would also be there, and flushed when she looked up and saw that James had read her mind.

***

An hour later, as they drove into Tillyhenge, Caitlyn was surprised to see a large crowd gathered on the village green. From the agitated expressions on people's faces and the amount of hand-waving and shouting, they were obviously upset about something.

"Oh my Goddess, what's going on?" asked Evie from the back seat.

"There aren't any spaces here..." said James, scanning the nearby area. "Why don't you and Evie jump out and see what it's all about? I'll go and park on the other side of the green and come back to join you."

They did as he suggested, and the two girls approached the crowd eagerly. Caitlyn's curiosity turned to concern, however, as she realised that it was the Widow Mags's name being shouted by many of the villagers.

"...knew she was a witch! Didn't I always say? Hiding in that cottage with those sinful chocolates of hers... I always said no good would come of letting her stay in this village!"

"Me too... I warned everyone about her but no one would listen!"

"She's put a hex on Tillyhenge—called up this

111

beast to haunt us all!"

"Yes! And we have proof—my boy saw it with his own eyes!" cried a dark-haired, middle-aged woman. She grabbed the arm of a teenage boy standing next to her and raised his hand in hers, in a triumphant gesture. "Go on, Fred—tell them what you saw!"

Looking slightly embarrassed, the boy mumbled: "Was out walking in the woods behind the village late last night and passed the chocolate shop... saw this light in the kitchen window and... er... thought I'd take a look... just in case, you know... not that I was snooping or anything..." He flushed. "Anyway, I saw her... the Widow Mags... she was waving her arms around and chanting something... and there was this big black shape on the table in front of her, with a head and four legs—"

"It was the Black Shuck!" his mother cut in shrilly. "The Widow Mags was using her witch powers to call him!"

There were gasps and cries of fear from the crowd.

"Yes! And that's what killed Sir Henry," cried Mrs Gibbs, nodding vehemently. "I told him not to go on Dead Man's Walk but he wouldn't listen to me. Oh, I knew something terrible would happen to him—I knew it! And then this morning, when I heard that he was dead, I just knew that the Black Shuck had got him." She leaned forwards and waved a finger. "The Widow Mags as good as murdered him!"

CHAPTER ELEVEN

"THAT'S RUBBISH!" Caitlyn burst out.

Everyone stopped talking and turned to look at her. Caitlyn suddenly found herself facing a circle of hostile faces. Evie drew closer, eyeing the crowd nervously.

"Caitlyn... don't..." she whimpered.

Caitlyn ignored her and said in a loud voice: "The Widow Mags has nothing to do with Sir Henry's murder... and anyway, the police aren't even sure it's murder. They still think he could have died from natural causes—"

"There was nothing natural about Sir Henry's death," said Mrs Gibbs grimly. "Just as there was nothing natural about the death last weekend. I don't care what the police say—we know the truth: they were both killed by the Black Shuck!" She

H.Y. HANNA

turned and pointed to the teenage boy. "And we have a witness here who saw the Widow Mags conjuring the demon hound."

"You don't know if that's what he saw," said Caitlyn. "It might have been something else completely—"

"Are you saying my boy is a liar?" demanded the dark-haired woman.

"No! Of course not... just... well, maybe he made a mistake. Maybe he got confused—"

"I know what I saw," insisted the boy. "I saw that evil witch doing black magic."

"She's not an evil witch!" Caitlyn said hotly.

"What is she then?" said Mrs Gibbs. She gave a contemptuous sniff. "Are you going to tell us that she's a 'good witch'?"

"She's... she's..." Caitlyn faltered, not knowing what to say. Her grandmother and Bertha had always made it clear that they had no wish to "come out" to the rest of the village. Sure, there were gossip and rumours—and even the occasional "magical incident" that got a bit out of hand—but they had always avoided openly acknowledging their witch heritage. To the world at large, Bertha was still just a herbalist and the Widow Mags was just a—rather eccentric—chocolatier. Caitlyn didn't feel that it was her place to reveal their true identities. But she couldn't bring herself to deny it either; to do so seemed like a betrayal of her grandmother's integrity and her own heritage—as if the truth was something to be ashamed of.

"Why are you defending the Widow Mags anyway?" asked the dark-haired woman. "What's she to you? You're not even from here—you only came a few months ago. We don't need outsiders meddling in our business."

"She's the Widow Mags's granddaughter!" someone shouted from the back of the crowd. "Her long-lost granddaughter from America."

There were loud whispers and murmurs going around the crowd now and Caitlyn felt even more hostile gazes trained on her.

The dark-haired woman narrowed her eyes. "Is that true?"

Caitlyn raised her chin. "Yes, it's true. The Widow Mags is my grandmother."

"So that's why you're defending her!" Mrs Gibbs hissed. "Because you're a witch too!"

Caitlyn took a step back. "I—"

"I beg your pardon?" came an icy voice.

They turned to see the tall figure of James Fitzroy at the back of the crowd. The villagers parted respectfully as he strode into the circle, and a sense of calm slowly replaced the previous atmosphere of hysteria. Mrs Gibbs looked at him eagerly and said:

"I'm so glad you're here, Lord Fitzroy! This girl is—"

"I'm well aware of Miss Le Fey's relationship with the Widow Mags," said James, his voice cold with anger. "I also heard what you said to her and I find it reprehensible that you should treat her in such a hostile manner."

Mrs Gibbs looked taken aback. "But... if she's a witch—"

"Don't be ridiculous—of course she's not a witch!" James snapped. He looked around the crowd, taking in all the villagers in his gaze. "You should be ashamed of yourselves for the way you're acting! Are we in mediaeval England? This is the twenty-first century, for heaven's sake! People do not believe in witchcraft anymore—we know it doesn't exist!"

Caitlyn squirmed. Part of her was filled with warmth at the way James was speaking up for her, but another part of her cringed at his continued denial of magic. And wasn't she adding to the deception too, by remaining silent? Was it right of her to let him defend her this way when she knew that what he was saying wasn't actually true? How could she hope to ever convince him to believe the truth about herself, when she let him perpetuate the lie to others?

All around her, the villagers were dropping their eyes, looking shamefaced, and giving each other sheepish looks. All except for Mrs Gibbs, who pursed her lips angrily. But she didn't dare say anything else. Giving Caitlyn and Evie a furious look, she turned and stormed away. Slowly, the rest of the villagers began dispersing as well.

"Thank you," said Caitlyn awkwardly, looking up at James.

"If anyone says anything else to you or the Widow Mags—or to you and your mother..." James added to Evie, "I want you to let me know. I will not allow bigotry and paranoia to rule this village." His normally warm grey eyes were hard and angry.

Caitlyn swallowed, feeling like a terrible hypocrite, but she murmured a reply, along with Evie. A few minutes later, James left them and Caitlyn trudged back to the chocolate shop alone.

She arrived at *Bewitched by Chocolate* to find the shop empty, as usual, and the Widow Mags in the kitchen at the back, busily making a new batch of ganache fillings for her chocolate truffles.

She went up to the old witch and said without preamble: "One of the boys in the village said he saw you conjuring something last night... is it true?"

"What do you mean?"

"He said he saw you chanting and waving your arms—and there was a dark animal shape on the table in front of you."

The Widow Mags scowled. "That little sneak! I knew he was spying on me through the window, no doubt, so he could go back and tell that meddling mother of his..."

"So... you *were* conjuring something?" asked Caitlyn hesitantly. "What was it he saw?"

The Widow Mags gave her a long look, then got

up and crossed over to the old-fashioned walk-in pantry. She swung the door open and gestured inside. Nervously, Caitlyn approached and peered in, then bit back a yelp of surprise as an enormous black shape loomed in front of her. She clutched a hand to her chest, calming her breathing as she realised that it was just a chocolate sculpture—a dark chocolate sculpture of a big, black bull.

"It's Ferdinand," said the Widow Mags. "Jeremy Bottom asked me to make a chocolate sculpture of him for the farm's Open Day next week. When Bertha dropped me back after the doctor last night, I didn't feel like sleeping, so I decided to tackle the sculpture. Took me till past midnight but it came out fairly well."

She spoke casually, but Caitlyn could hear the pride in her grandmother's voice as the old witch ran an assessing hand over the head of the chocolate bull. It was certainly something to be proud of. Although not quite life-size, it was wonderfully life-like, from the fine detail of the curled tufts of fur between the bull's ears to the smooth lines of muscle on the thick neck and powerful shoulders... and most of all, those big, liquid eyes, so like the real Ferdinand. Caitlyn had a soft spot for the gentle bovine giant who loved pats and cuddles, and who, until recently, had been lonely for company.

"It's beautiful," said Caitlyn, eyeing it admiringly. "I can't believe that silly boy mistook a chocolate sculpture for a phantom monster!"

"Well..." The old witch gave a raspy chuckle. "He wanted to see witchcraft so I gave him some witchcraft! I cast a little Animation spell to bring it to life for a bit. Didn't need to do all that arm-waving and chanting, of course, but I thought I might as well put on a good show."

"Grandma!" said Caitlyn in exasperation. "You know the villagers are terrified of you already. Why do you have to stir them up even more?"

The Widow Mags looked defiant. "He shouldn't have been spying on me. Why shouldn't I have a little fun?"

"Because now the whole village thinks that you called up the Black Shuck and set it on Sir Henry—they're accusing you of murder."

"What nonsense!" scoffed the Widow Mags, waving a dismissive hand.

"You might think it's nonsense but a lot of the villagers believe it. They're scared by the recent deaths and by all this talk of a ghostly demon hound—so they're looking for someone to blame. And it doesn't help when you go around provoking them on purpose! You know they're already prejudiced against you; you don't want to give them any more reason to think ill of you."

"They can think what they like," snapped the Widow Mags. "I don't care."

"You should care! You live in Tillyhenge too—they're your neighbours, your customers... and some of them could even become your friends. Can't you at least try to meet them halfway?"

"You sound just like Bertha," said the old witch irritably. "Now, are you helping me with a new batch of caramel or not? And you'd better not let it burn this time!"

Caitlyn gave the chocolate sculpture one last look, then sighed and followed her grandmother back to the kitchen table.

CHAPTER TWELVE

That night, as she got ready for bed, Caitlyn paused in front of the mirror and stared at her reflection. In particular, her eyes were drawn to the runestone around her neck. Slowly, she reached up and untied the ribbon, then lowered the oblong piece of stone into her hands and tilted it this way and that, watching the light trace the strange symbols carved onto the surface.

What do they mean? Ever since she was a little girl, she had sat like this, turning the runestone over in her hands and wondering about the significance of those engraved marks. It was one of the mysteries from her past which had always tormented her—one of the reasons she had come to England. Now, she thought of what Pomona had said earlier that day and felt ashamed of how easily she had given up. Her cousin was right—no matter how much she wanted to, she couldn't just hide in this "cocoon of complacency" forever.

But where was she going to find answers? What she had told Pomona was true: she had tried time and time again to ask the Widow Mags and Bertha about her mother and had got nowhere. Then it hit her. *Of course!* Caitlyn sat bolt upright. Why hadn't she thought of it before? She could ask Viktor! Surely, he must know something?

It seemed unbelievable now that she had never thought of turning to the old vampire—although maybe it was because she had never really looked at Viktor in a serious light. He had become an integral part of her new life, yes, but he had remained a surreal, fantastical, even comical figure—like the invisible friend you had as a child, who you talked to and shared a private world with, but who didn't belong in the "real" world, with your real friends and family. Viktor was always there, in the background, flitting about in his fruit bat form, and yet most people in Tillyhenge and at Huntingdon Manor didn't even know of his existence. And even though he and the Widow Mags seemed to be old acquaintances, Caitlyn rarely saw them together and neither spoke much about the other.

In fact, now that she thought about it, she wasn't even sure if Viktor was really her uncle. He had introduced himself as such and called himself her "guardian uncle"—but now she wondered what that title really meant. That was another thing she was going to ask him... She glanced at her watch on the bedside table. It was nearly midnight but, on an impulse, she grabbed a cardigan, slipped it over the oversized T-shirt that she wore for sleeping, then shoved her feet into a pair of soft-soled shoes and left the room.

She tiptoed down the spiral staircase and past the Widow Mags's closed bedroom door, through the kitchen, and out into the rear garden behind the cottage. This was a traditional cottage garden, with a stone path between two overgrown beds stuffed with herbs, flowers, and other cottage garden plants. At the other end, the garden opened out onto the edge of the forest. She knew that Viktor often hung around there (often literally, in his fruit bat form) and she hoped that she might catch him tonight.

Caitlyn paused as she stepped out of the garden, letting her eyes acclimatise. The moon was still full and bright, letting her see a fair distance, despite not having a torch. The forest spread out in front of her, a sea of trees merging together as they flowed up the slope, like a dark green blanket draped across half of the bare hillside. She strained to see, looking for a familiar shape or a movement— anything that might be a sign of the old vampire— but she saw nothing. Then, as her gaze travelled upwards to the top of the hill, where she could see the faint outline of the ancient stone circle, she saw something that made her catch her breath.

A dark, wolf-like shape appeared briefly next to the stones... *No, not a wolf—a dog*, she realised. A huge black dog. It was lit sharply by the light of the moon, then it turned and disappeared over the crest of the hill. A moment later, Caitlyn heard that familiar chilling howl.

The Black Shuck?

She had to find out. Without pausing to think, Caitlyn rushed up the hill. It was steep and she was panting hard by the time she reached the crest. To her right, the forest hugged the side of the hill, the trees becoming thinner and more sparse as they neared the top. Straight in front of her, on the exposed ridge, stood the misshapen boulders which made up the Tillyhenge stone circle. And beyond them, the hill sloped down the other side, levelling off into the open land which formed the parklands around Huntingdon Manor. The manor house was faintly visible, outlined by the moonlight, with a few windows still lit and glowing.

But there was no sign of that dark canine shape. Caitlyn hesitated, then walked forwards, stepping into the stone circle and weaving between the boulders, peering around and behind them. In the pale moonlight, with the shadows lending shape and feature to their craggy surfaces, the stones looked even more like the frozen warriors that they were said to be. *And it's almost midnight... the "witching hour"... the time when they are meant to come to life*, thought Caitlyn with a smile. After all the things she had seen since arriving in Tillyhenge, she wouldn't have been surprised if the boulders really did rise up stiffly and assumed the form of ancient English knights.

A noise behind her made her stiffen. Slowly, she peered over her shoulder. Was there something there, behind that boulder? Gathering her courage, she whirled around. A dark blur moved between the boulders... around her... behind her. Caitlyn whirled again, but she couldn't see where it had gone. She swallowed, suddenly feeling terribly vulnerable. She realised how stupid it had been of her to come up here alone...

Then something emerged from behind a boulder.

Caitlyn's heart thudded in her chest. A huge black dog stood before her. It was the size of a small pony, with shaggy black fur and eyes that glowed red above its pointed muzzle. It opened its mouth in a lazy pant and Caitlyn saw the gleam of long, white fangs. The Black Shuck might have been a phantom hound, but there was nothing ghostly about its teeth! It stared at her with keen interest, then slowly began to advance.

Caitlyn felt a surge of panic. She wanted to run but her feet refused to move. *Anyway, don't they say you shouldn't run from dogs? It only excites them and makes them chase you more*, she thought frantically, as the hazy memory of a Dog Safety pamphlet from some pet welfare society came back to her mind. What else had it said?

"Stand still, cross your arms, and ignore the animal until it goes away"...

Oh wonderful. Perfect advice when you're facing a demon dog: cross your arms, ignore it, and hope it goes away.

Caitlyn swallowed as the Black Shuck came even closer. She stood rigid as she saw it stretch its neck towards her, then something brushed her body and she heard the sound of loud sniffing.

Gulp. She hoped she didn't smell tasty.

Shifting her weight, she began to take a step backwards. The Black Shuck emitted a low growl. Caitlyn froze, then placed her foot back where it had been.

"N-n-nice doggie..." she croaked. What was she going to do? She couldn't stand here all night... Then she thought of what Nathan Lewis had said at dinner. It was ridiculous, but what did she have to lose? She took a deep breath and said in a firmer voice: "Er... n-nice doggie... SIT!"

The huge black dog cocked its head, looking at her quizzically. Then it lowered its haunches and sat down.

Caitlyn stared in disbelief. Then, on a hunch, she reached down and picked up a fallen twig. Waving it above her head, she threw it as far as she could. The Black Shuck sprang up and bounded after the twig. *Well, whaddya know? Even monsters like to play Fetch.*

Caitlyn turned to run in the opposite direction, but faltered to a stop as she found the Black Shuck in front of her again, holding the twig in its mouth. *How did it get back here so fast?*

The big black dog dropped the stick and looked at her expectantly. Caitlyn snatched the twig up and flung it over her shoulder as hard as she could, but she had barely taken a few steps when the Black Shuck was in front of her once more, with the stick in its mouth and its tail wagging eagerly.

I don't believe this. It's the middle of the night and I'm stuck on a hill playing a game of Fetch with a demon dog.

Caitlyn wondered what to do. She couldn't hope to win on speed—obviously, the Black Shuck could move with supernatural momentum—no matter how far she threw the stick, it always retrieved it and returned to her before she could run away. So she had to slow it down some other way. This time, she picked up the stick and, instead of just tossing it as far as she could, she aimed for the narrow space between two of the boulders. The black dog sprang after the flying stick and disappeared between the stones.

Caitlyn turned and started to race down the hill but, in her panic, she tripped and stumbled. The next moment, she was flat on her face, on the ground. There was a rustling behind her and she jerked around, rolling quickly to her feet. But instead of a black phantom hound, she found herself staring at an older man with enormous side-burns.

"Professor Thrope!" Caitlyn cried in surprise.

"Did you see it?" he asked eagerly. "The Black Shuck—it's up here somewhere!"

"Um... yes ..." Caitlyn stammered. "It was... it was over there..." She pointed to the circle of stone boulders.

The professor rushed over and looked around the stones, then returned a moment later, his face creased with disappointment. "It's gone! Oh, I can't believe I missed it. What did it look like?"

"Like... um... like how the legends describe it. You know... a big black dog with red eyes."

"And what was it doing?"

"Um..." It was weird standing here, calmly discussing a mythical creature. She was used to people being disbelieving or contemptuous of magic and the paranormal—not treating it like a perfectly normal daily occurrence. They might have been discussing a friend's spaniel! Caitlyn wondered how much to tell him. She decided that even a cryptozoologist probably wouldn't believe her if she said the Black Shuck had been playing Fetch.

"It was just... er... sniffing around." Then something compelled her to add, "It... it wasn't really as scary as I'd expected. I mean, it did look pretty fierce at first but then—"

"You see?" said Professor Thrope triumphantly.

"That's what I was saying at dinner last night: I think the legends have grossly distorted the truth. The Black Shuck isn't an evil monster preying on the unwary—it is more likely a guardian hound who appears to escort lone travellers safely to their destinations."

"But... what about the recent deaths?" asked Caitlyn.

"The deaths have nothing to do with the Black Shuck!" Professor Thrope snapped. He caught himself and added in a calmer voice. "I'm sorry. Forgive me... It's just that I get so frustrated when people seem intent on demonising these poor beasts, when humans have done far worse!" He scowled and waved a fist. "Violent gangs and serial killers have hurt far more people than any basilisk or manticore... and yet people still jump to assume the worst as soon as they think of any mythical creature. But just because something is ugly doesn't mean that it's monstrous!"

Wow. I wonder what he's like when he's giving his student lectures. Talk about being passionate about your subject! Caitlyn thought as she eyed the other man curiously. She noticed that he was dressed in old-fashioned striped pyjamas and a faded dressing gown. The clothes were worn and torn in places, and his hair was unkempt. He looked like he had been dragged not just out of bed but through a hedge backwards as well.

"What happened to you?" she asked, indicating

his appearance.

"Eh? Oh..." He looked down at himself and gave a sheepish laugh. "I couldn't sleep—I suffer from insomnia, you know—so I went downstairs to get a book. Well, I was in the Library when I heard it—this wonderful, eerie howling. I just knew it wasn't from an ordinary creature! I rushed outside and saw it—a great, big, black dog—standing at the edge of the formal gardens. By the time I got there, it had already started to climb the hill. I tried to follow as fast as I could, but I guess my haste was my undoing. I tripped and rolled part of the way down the hill again before I could stop myself..." He sighed. "By the time I'd picked myself up and climbed up here, I'd lost it. Then I saw you lying there..." He looked curiously at her in his turn. "What are *you* doing here?"

"Oh... er... I have insomnia like you so I was out... um... getting some fresh air," said Caitlyn lamely. She turned and pointed down to where a thatched-roofed cottage was faintly visible, nestled at the base of the hill. "I live down there—it's the Widow Mags's cottage."

"Ah yes... the eccentric old lady with the fabulous chocolates," said Professor Thrope with a smile.

Caitlyn looked at him uncertainly, wondering if cryptozoologists were sympathetic to witches too. After all, if you believed in the existence of sea serpents and unicorns, surely witchcraft was only a step away? But after her experience in the village green earlier that day, she wasn't sure she wanted to risk another scene of fear and revulsion.

"Er... yes, she's my grandmother," she said. "I'm staying with her at the moment. The front of the cottage serves as a chocolate shop."

"I must come by some time. Those chocolates we had after dinner were delicious!" He gave her a conspiratorial grin. "And if they *are* enchanted, well, I hope some of that magic rubs off on me and helps me on my next expedition."

Caitlyn chuckled. She found herself liking the eccentric old academic. Especially after the hostility she had faced today, it was a relief to meet someone who didn't freak out at the mention of the supernatural. Once again, she was tempted to confide in him—then she stopped herself. He could've just been joking—people made jokes about magic all the time. After all, it was easy to laugh about things that you didn't believe were real.

"It's late—we should get back to bed," said Professor Thrope. He put a solicitous hand under her elbow. "Shall I escort you back to your cottage?"

"Oh no, it's straight down the hill here... I'll be fine. Honestly, it's silly for you to come down all the way—you'd have to climb back up again. You can watch me, if you're really worried, but I've often come out by myself at night."

"Very well, my dear. I will just stand here and—" He paused, his eyes going to her throat.

"Is something the matter?"

"Forgive me but... that stone around your neck—where did you get it?"

"Um... it was given to me as a baby," said Caitlyn, reaching up self-consciously to touch the runestone.

"Ah... and do you know if those engraved marks mean anything?"

"No... I mean, I don't know... Why?"

He gave a self-deprecating laugh. "Oh, it is probably nothing. Just an old man's overactive imagination—"

"No, please, tell me!" said Caitlyn, putting a hand on his arm.

He looked surprised at her urgent tone. "Well, Lord Fitzroy kindly let me view his father's occult collection in the Fitzroy Portrait Gallery this morning. There are the usual gory artefacts, of course—the Hand of Glory and dried cats and such—but there are also some fabulous old texts on the bookshelves. Really, I was beside myself with excitement when I saw them! It will take me days to go through them all—I think I shall have to make a special trip back—but there could be first-hand accounts of cryptid sightings, dating all the way back to mediaeval times!" He waved his hands, his spectacles beginning to fog up in his excitement. "Just imagine, descriptions of mermaids and kelpies and maybe even a sea serpent—"

"Yes, but what does all this have to do with my

runestone?" asked Caitlyn impatiently.

"Eh? Oh... oh, yes, your runestone... well, when I pulled out one of the volumes, I noticed something jammed at the back of the shelf, behind all the books. It was a roll of parchment. I'm no expert and you'd have to get it tested, of course, but it did look very old ... although in remarkably good condition. And there was writing on the parchment. Actually, I'm not sure if it *was* writing, as I couldn't read it—and it didn't look like any language I know—but the way those symbols were arranged, I was sure they carried a certain meaning..." He indicated Caitlyn's runestone again. "When I saw those marks in your stone, they reminded me of the symbols on that parchment. They're very similar."

"Is the parchment still there?" asked Caitlyn breathlessly.

"Oh yes. I wasn't sure quite what to do with it—Lord Fitzroy wasn't around to ask, and I felt uncomfortable leaving it lying around—so I thought the safest thing was to put it back. It had obviously been tucked back there, unfound, for years—maybe even decades. The shelf is the topmost one in the bookcase by that painting of the Four Horsemen; you need to use the stepladder to reach it, so I suppose most people wouldn't have bothered to go up there. Only the more obscure books were placed up there—I would have never found it myself if I hadn't climbed up to reach the volume on sea serpents. *The Legend and Lore of Sea Serpents,* it was called. Marvellous book! If you have time, you must read it. Chapter twelve, in particular, is most enlightening. Well, the hypothesis that sea serpents could have several stomachs, like a ruminant, is probably a bit far-fetched but I think the ideas put forth about cryptid digestion are very thought-provoking and bear further discussion—" He broke off and gave a rueful laugh. "Forgive me, my dear. I'm sure you don't want to stand here in the middle of the night, listening to me prattle on."

"Oh, no—it's very interesting. But yes, maybe we could continue another time," Caitlyn agreed with a smile.

Bidding him goodnight, she started making her way back down the hill towards the Widow Mags's cottage. And in spite of her earlier words, she had to admit that there was something reassuring about knowing that she was being watched over as she walked back home.

CHAPTER THIRTEEN

Caitlyn woke up early the next morning, and her first thought was of the events of the night before. Now in the bright light of day, she couldn't quite believe that she had been standing on the hill, playing Fetch with a phantom dog... Seriously, the Black Shuck? The demon hound who was an omen of death? Maybe she'd tripped and fallen when she arrived at the top of the hill and smacked her head against one of the boulders... and dreamt the entire episode.

But she hadn't dreamt about meeting Professor Thrope—she could still clearly remember everything he had said. She thought of the parchment he had mentioned. Could there really be a connection to her runestone? There was only one way to find out. She had to get to the Manor library and compare the marks on her runestone with the symbols on the parchment.

Springing out of bed, Caitlyn washed and dressed hastily, then—with a hurried "good morning" to the Widow Mags, who was busy making chocolate truffles at the kitchen table—she rushed out the back of the cottage and headed up the hill again. This time, she barely paused when she reached the top, and spared the stone circle only a passing glance, before she plunged down the other side, towards the elegant Georgian manor house in the distance. Ten minutes later, she was greeting Mosley as he let her into the front foyer.

"Lord Fitzroy is currently engaged," said Mosley. "He is in a meeting with Inspector Walsh and Sir Henry's widow."

"Oh, is she still here?" said Caitlyn in surprise.

"Lady Pritchard was very distressed by the news of her husband's death—she felt too unwell to leave her bed yesterday and Lord Fitzroy has made her welcome to stay as long as she wishes. She seems better this morning, however, and Inspector Walsh was keen to speak to her, as he has not had a chance yet to interview her properly." Mosley flicked his wrist, shooting back the cuff of an immaculate sleeve and glancing at his watch, then said apologetically: "I'm afraid they have only just gone into the Library and may still be some time."

"Oh, that's all right. I'm not actually here to see James—I mean, Lord Fitzroy," said Caitlyn.

Mosley gave a discreet cough. "I believe your cousin Miss Sinclair is still in bed."

Caitlyn grinned. "I could have guessed that. Don't worry, I wasn't looking for her either. No, actually, I was hoping to have a look in the Portrait Gallery, if that's okay—?"

"Certainly. Lord Fitzroy has made it clear that *you* are welcome in all areas of the Manor, any time you like."

His tone hadn't changed and his expression remained inscrutable, but Caitlyn couldn't help her cheeks reddening slightly.

"Would you like me to show you to the Gallery, Miss Le Fey?"

"Oh no, that's fine...I know the way."

Caitlyn made her way through the formal rooms of the ground floor, heading for the back stairs. The staff were going about, dusting and polishing, checking flower arrangements and re-positioning furniture, in preparation for the official public opening at 10 a.m. Like many country houses and stately homes in the UK, Huntingdon Manor was too large and grand to be used strictly as a private residence in modern times, and so several sections had been opened to the public for guided tours and visits. In fact, in the short time since it had opened, it had become a hugely popular tourist attraction in this part of the Cotswolds, and there were even plans now to convert the old coach house into a restaurant.

These were some of the many projects and ideas that James had instigated since he inherited the title, and Caitlyn knew that while several of the older staff and village residents had resented the changes, most had come to appreciate the new opportunities and injection of life into the estate. In fact, James seemed to have won over everyone in the village and surrounding lands. From his lack of airs and graces, and willingness to "muck in" and help his tenant farmers, to his generosity and thoughtfulness as a landlord, everyone loved him. *And the women are probably all* in *love with him too*, Caitlyn thought with a wry smile. Then her smile faded as she thought of the scene in the village green yesterday, and she wondered if James would continue to hold the villagers' respect and affection if he kept defending her and the Widow Mags.

The sound of voices broke into her thoughts. She was approaching the back stairs and she noticed two men standing beside the alcove which held one of the downstairs public toilets. Her eyes widened as she recognised Nathan Lewis... and the scrawny old man beside him. It was Viktor! The journalist had a hand clamped around the old vampire's arm and was eyeing him suspiciously.

"...not until you tell me what you're doing here, old chap, skulking around the Manor like this. Who are you?"

Viktor drew himself proudly to his full height. "I am Count Viktor Konstantin Alexandru Benedikto

Dracul, of the Megachiroptera Order, Ancient Guardian of the Other Realms and one of the last natural-born vampires."

Nathan blinked. "I beg your pardon?"

Viktor made a tetchy sound. "Are you hard of hearing, young man? I said I am Count Viktor Konstantin Alex—"

"I heard you the first time," said Nathan hastily. "I just didn't... Ah!" Something dawned on his face. "Have you strayed away from your group?" He loosened his grip on Viktor's arm and looked at the old vampire more kindly. "If you tell me which nursing home you're at, I can ask Mosley to find your group for you. I thought James said the public weren't allowed in until ten o'clock... but I suppose they make an exception for geriatric visitors—"

"Geriatric? Nursing home?" spluttered Viktor. "How dare you! I may be in my sixth century but I am certainly not in my dotage yet! Vampires have been known to live for millennia—especially those, like me, who follow a fruitarian diet. Of course, if you are one of those sanguinivores from the Vampyrus order..." He made a face and shook his head, clucking his tongue. "They hardly live more than a few hundred years. Too much blood in the diet, you know—all that sodium."

"Er... right." Nathan looked slightly befuddled. "Well... I'll walk you back to the front of the house, shall I?" He started trying to steer Viktor up the corridor.

"Oh no, I cannot go yet—I have to find my teeth."

"Your teeth?"

"Well, technically they are fangs—the upper canines, to be precise. I think I might have dropped them somewhere here..." Viktor bent over and scanned the floor, teetering slightly.

Nathan caught him before he fell over. "Whoah! Okay, look... I really think we need to get you back to your group. Have you got a walker?"

Viktor bristled. "A walker? Why would I need a walker? I find your manners most insulting, young man."

"I just didn't want you to fall and break a hip."

"I have the most superior sense of balance," said Viktor loftily. "It is an extension of my bat form. And in any case, even if I were to break a hip, it would not matter—my vampiric regenerative abilities would heal it within a few days."

"Yes, but you're not *really* a vampire," said Nathan impatiently. "They're fictitious creatures and their abilities are just imaginary traits made up by storytellers."

"They are certainly not imaginary traits!" cried Viktor, affronted. "I grant you, many of the claims made in human books and films are a load of garlic—nonsense like having no reflection in the mirror and turning to ash in the sunlight—but there is no question that we vampires have supernatural abilities. For example, we are gifted with heightened sensory perception..." Viktor leaned towards the journalist. "Aha! I can hear the blood rushing in your veins."

"Er... actually, that's the toilet flushing," Nathan said as they all heard a *whooshing* sound.

"Hmph! I have had quite enough of your rudeness, young man!" huffed Viktor, spinning away and disappearing in a puff of mist just as a maid stepped out of the toilets carrying a bucket of cleaning equipment.

She looked at Nathan apologetically and said: "Oh, were you wanting to use the lavatory, sir? I hope I haven't kept you waiting long."

"No, no, although my old friend here might—" Nathan turned to where Viktor had been standing and looked in astonishment at the empty space. He looked quizzically around, pausing as he saw Caitlyn farther up the corridor.

"Did you see where he went?" he called out to her.

"Er... where did who go?" said Caitlyn, walking over to join him.

"This decrepit old chap—nutty as a fruitcake, thought he was a vampire, can you believe it?" Nathan chuckled. "But I have to admit, I kind of took to the old boy. He was a great character. He seemed very frail too—I wouldn't want anything to happen to him."

"I think I saw him heading back towards the front of the house," Caitlyn lied. "Don't worry—I'm sure he'll be fine."

"Really? He must move faster than I thought. Well, I hope he gets back to his group okay." Nathan waited until the maid had disappeared around the corner, then leaned close to Caitlyn and said, "I'm glad to have bumped into you, actually—I was coming to find you today."

"Me? Why?"

"I wanted to hear what you didn't tell the inspector yesterday."

"What do you mean?"

"When he asked if you heard anything or noticed anything unusual, when you were on Dead Man's Walk, you started to say you saw something—then you brushed it off and said it was just your imagination." He looked at her shrewdly. "But it wasn't, was it? You did see something. What did you see?"

CHAPTER FOURTEEN

Caitlyn hesitated. "I... I thought I saw a pair of red eyes."

Nathan raised his eyebrows. "The Black Shuck?"

"I... yes, I think so."

Caitlyn waited for the contemptuous look and the disbelieving laugh, but to her surprise, it didn't come. Instead, Nathan said seriously:

"And you think the Black Shuck could have been responsible for Sir Henry's death?"

Caitlyn stared at him. "Don't tell me you believe in the legend?"

Nathan shrugged. "Anything is possible."

"But... but I thought you didn't believe in the paranormal. Just now when you were talking about Vi—I mean, when you were laughing at that old man thinking that he was a vampire—"

"Yes, well, that was clearly a case of senile delusion," said Nathan, chuckling. "I mean, it's *obvious* that old fellow isn't a vampire."

Little do you know, thought Caitlyn with an inward smile.

"But this is completely different," Nathan continued. "Mind you, I'm not saying that some supernatural hound from folklore is roaming the countryside; that would be ridiculous. But I do think it's possible that a wild beast was responsible for Sir Henry's death. Not a 'demon dog' but a wolf or panther or some other large predator that's escaped from a private zoo collection. It would explain the other death too—the tramp."

"But... if that's the case, wouldn't they have mauled their victims more? From what I've heard, both Sir Henry and the tramp hardly showed any signs of injury, other than a few scratches and bruises—surely if you'd been attacked by a wolf or a panther, you would have been ripped to shreds?"

Nathan shrugged. "Maybe the animal got interrupted and scared off before it could do serious damage. Anyway, the point is, these men didn't just drop dead from a heart attack or other natural causes, no matter what Inspector Walsh says. There are too many strange coincidences. I have a journalist's instinct for these things and I'm telling, you, something isn't normal here." He leaned towards her. "I did some digging around yesterday afternoon—spoke to several people in the village, asked lots of questions... there were several things, you know, that Walsh didn't mention."

"Like what?"

"Well, for one thing, there were paw prints found in the mud around the bodies of both men. Huge paw prints."

"Couldn't they have been from a local dog? A mastiff or Great Dane, perhaps, or some other giant breed?" asked Caitlyn. "Have you seen James's English mastiff, Bran? He's enormous!"

"Yes, I've met Bran, and as big as his paws are, they're no match for these prints. The villagers described them as literally as big as dinner plates."

"Maybe they were exaggerating."

"Maybe. But they weren't exaggerating the fact that the paw prints were there. Too many people saw them. And there was another thing: both men showed signs of having been dragged."

"Dragged?"

Nathan nodded. "Yes, as if something had grabbed them with its teeth and dragged them through the undergrowth. That would fit in with those strange bruises that James mentioned—the ones on Sir Henry's arm." He gave a mock shiver and said, grinning, "Conjures up a pretty gruesome image, doesn't it? Either it's a savage wolf or panther on the loose, or a huge demon hound attacking its victims and trying to drag them away."

"I don't think the Black Shuck is like that," Caitlyn blurted.

"What do you mean?"

Caitlyn thought of the playful creature she had encountered on the hill last night. Okay, maybe "playful" was going a bit far, but the Black Shuck certainly hadn't been the bloodthirsty monster she had expected. Professor Thrope's words came back to her, about the black dog being a guardian, not a killer, and she said:

"What if the Black Shuck has been... well... misunderstood?"

Nathan threw his head back and laughed. "Misunderstood? You mean the poor demon hound is really a lonely pup who's just wandering around at night, looking for a friend?"

Caitlyn flushed. "I'm just saying that maybe the legends got it wrong—maybe the Black Shuck doesn't have malicious intentions."

"And what about all the reports through the centuries of a ghostly black dog attacking lone travellers at night?"

"Well, maybe it was just in the wrong place at the wrong time. Just like with Sir Henry and the tramp. Yes, I know it was seen nearby on both occasions, but maybe that was coincidence. Everyone has been so focused on the Black Shuck that they just assumed it must be the connection between the two victims, but nobody has considered if there might be some other common link."

Nathan looked at her with new respect. "Hmm... That's a good point. So what are you suggesting:

that it was murder?"

Caitlyn shifted uncomfortably. "Well, I don't—"

"No, no, I think you're onto something. And I think the police suspect something too—otherwise, why would they be back here questioning Lady Pritchard this morning?" His gaze went over Caitlyn's shoulder. "Ah! Talk of the devil!"

Caitlyn turned to see Lady Pritchard walking slowly towards them. She looked pale, with dark circles under her eyes, and her shoulders were slumped dejectedly. She seemed to collect herself as she saw them and gave them a wan smile.

"Hello... I'm looking for the Ladies. I was told they're at the end of this corridor—?"

"Yes, just through there." Nathan pointed at the alcove, then added, "I'm very sorry for your loss, Lady Pritchard."

Caitlyn echoed his words and Sir Henry's widow murmured her thanks.

"It's just so hard to believe that he's gone," she said with a forlorn look. "Henry was such a... a... well, a great presence, if you know what I mean."

"Had he had a heart attack before?" asked Caitlyn.

"Yes, a few years back. And the doctors did tell us that he was at risk of having another one... but he'd been taking his medication every day, you know."

"Perhaps it wasn't a heart attack," said Nathan in a casual voice.

Lady Pritchard looked at him sharply. "What do you mean?" She gasped. "Do you mean... do you think these stories about the Black Shuck could be true?"

"Well, I don't know about a ghostly black hound—personally, I think the 'Black Shuck' is more likely to be some escaped wild animal—but that wasn't what I was implying. No, what I meant was, there is also the possibility of foul play... Do you know if your husband had any enemies?"

"That's what the police have been asking me," said Lady Pritchard with a sigh. "And like I told Inspector Walsh, I don't know! I mean, Henry didn't see eye to eye with a lot of people and, you know, he could be a bit... er... blunt sometimes, but surely nobody would want to kill him just for disagreeing with them?"

"Is there anyone in particular who 'disagreed' with him recently?" asked Caitlyn.

Lady Pritchard frowned. "Inspector Walsh asked me that as well. In fact, Henry had a terrible scene just last weekend with Derek Swanes, our estate manager. He ended up firing him."

Caitlyn felt a prickle of interest. "Really? Why?"

"Henry said he caught Swanes fiddling with the accounts and embezzling money from the estate, but Swanes said it was all a mistake and—oh, they had the most dreadful row. I could hear it all the way from upstairs."

"So Swanes was angry about being fired, eh?"

said Nathan, giving Caitlyn a meaningful look.

"Oh, he was livid!" said Lady Pritchard. "He kept threatening to make Henry regret it. I came down just as he was leaving and I was really quite frightened by his manner. But Henry just laughed and said 'good riddance'." She sighed, then frowned and added, "But I don't think it's Swanes. I mean, he came back to see Henry the day before yesterday—it was just before we came over for dinner, actually—and he seemed very contrite. He apologised for his behaviour and said his temper had got the better of him; he even brought Henry a bottle of his favourite sherry. And Henry agreed not to press charges and said he would give Swanes his last month's wages. They had a drink together and parted quite amicably, actually." She glanced towards the alcove. "I'm sorry—you'll have to excuse me, but I really must use the loo."

As soon as the door had shut behind her, Nathan said: "Hmm... interesting. So despite Inspector Walsh's protests, the police *are* treating this as a suspicious death. Why else would they be asking Sir Henry's widow if he had any enemies? They must be wondering if anyone has a motive for wanting to harm him." A shrill ringing sounded suddenly from his pocket and he drew out his mobile phone. "Bugger! Sorry, I've got to take this call."

"It's okay. I was on my way upstairs anyway. I'll see you later," said Caitlyn, giving him a wave.

As she ascended the back stairs, she couldn't help thinking that Nathan Lewis was a great guy: fun, urbane, intelligent, and quite good-looking too... why couldn't Pomona go for someone like him, instead of Thane Blackmort?

At the thought of her cousin, Caitlyn wondered if she should pop into Pomona's bedroom—then quickly decided against the idea. She had already been delayed by the encounter with Nathan (and Viktor!) and the chat with Sir Henry's widow... if she got stuck with Pomona as well... at this rate, she wouldn't reach the Portrait Gallery until nightfall!

She decided to go and hunt for the parchment first. Then she could find Pomona and tell her cousin all about her discovery. She felt a thrill of excitement. Was she about to find some answers at last?

CHAPTER FIFTEEN

The Fitzroy Portrait Gallery looked as gloomy and oppressive as it always did and Caitlyn had to steel herself as she walked in. Making her way between the mounds covered in white sheets, she crossed the long room to where a series of bookcases lined the far wall. *Now, which one did Professor Thrope say it was?* she wondered, pausing beside the wall of books. *He'd said he was looking at a book on sea serpents. On the topmost level of the bookcase by the Four Horseman painting...*

Moving down the row of bookshelves, she stopped at last in front of an imposing bookcase of dark oak. Looking up, she scanned the spines of the leather-bound volumes: *A History of Magical Phenomena; The Magus; Understanding Mediaeval Magick; Witches, Wizards and Warlocks: A*

Comparison... ah! There! *The Legend and Lore of Sea Serpents.* She stretched up but her fingertips could barely touch the shelf—it was too high for her to reach.

Glancing around, Caitlyn spied a wooden stepladder mounted on wheels tucked into the corner of the room. She hurried to wheel it over and position it under the shelf, then mounted the creaking wooden steps until her head was level with the top row of books. Carefully, she gripped the sea-serpent book and tried to pull it out. It was wedged tight—there were too many volumes on this shelf and every book was jammed into place. She wriggled it vigorously but it would not come. Heaving a sigh of frustration, she sat back on the top rung of the stepladder. Then she had a thought: *Wait a minute... I'm a witch, aren't I? Surely the point of learning magic is to help situations like this?*

Turning back towards the bookcase, she stretched a hand towards the wedged book and closed her eyes, concentrating hard. She didn't know an appropriate spell but it didn't matter—the Widow Mags had told her that there was no need to chant an incantation to work magic. Spells were useful, yes—especially for novice witches who needed a verbal guide to help them focus—but the power lay not in the words themselves but in the force of the will behind them.

Now, Caitlyn tried to visualise the sea-serpent book slipping effortlessly out of its place in the row... smoothly, silkily... sliding forwards and out... leaving an open gap behind it... She flexed her fingers, reaching to touch the book, then her eyes flew open in surprise. She stared at the book in dismay. Well, it was certainly smooth and silky, alright—it had been turned into gleaming milk chocolate!

Oh rats! What was she going to do now? She had to change the book back. But first, she wondered if it would be easier to pull out now. She tried again; the chocolate melted slightly beneath her fingers where she was gripping the spine, but this time it slid out when she gave it a tug, leaving a small gap between the adjoining volumes. *Yes!* Caitlyn peered into the narrow space. *Was that...?* She thought she could see the faint outline of a roll of paper. Carefully, she reached into the gap and felt around. Her fingers encountered something dry and papery and she heard a rustling sound. Excited, she gave it a yank, then winced as she heard the sound of tearing.

She took a deep breath and told herself to slow down. Hitching herself higher to get a better angle, she tried again. It was an awkward position and she could feel the stepladder rolling back and forth with her movements. *I should have put the brakes on the wheels before climbing up*, she thought with chagrin. *Otherwise, if I shove or jerk too hard, the ladder could easily roll away from under me...* Taking a deep breath, she tried again, pulling the parchment as gently as she could, and was rewarded at last when she felt it shift beneath her fingers. *Ah! It's coming!* But just as she was drawing it out, she heard the sound of heavy footsteps in the corridor outside.

THUD. THUD. THUD.

They were growing louder, and Caitlyn threw an apprehensive glance over her shoulder, wondering who was approaching. The Gallery door was slightly ajar and, a moment later, a bundle of black fur darted into the room.

"Mew!"

Nibs! Caitlyn sagged with relief. The little black kitten was followed a few seconds later by a lumbering English mastiff: James's dog, Bran. The heavy padding sound had been his footsteps. He came in now, his head lowered, his forehead wrinkled, and his baggy face intent as he sniffed something along the ground.

"Nibs! What are you doing here?" said Caitlyn as the kitten scampered over to her. "No—wait, don't climb up here!"

But it was too late. Nibs had already jumped up and was rapidly making his way up the stepladder. A moment later, Bran arrived at the bottom and tried to climb up too.

"Woof!" he said, wagging his tail. "Woof! Woof!" Then he placed a heavy paw on the bottom rung of the stepladder and heaved himself up.

Caitlyn yelped as the mastiff's weight caused the

stepladder to roll sideways. She had been perched precariously on the top rung, and now she clutched madly at the bookshelf as she reeled backwards, falling through the air.

"*Aaahhhh!*"

The next minute, the breath was knocked from her body as she was caught in strong arms.

"*Oomph!*" James Fitzroy staggered backwards but he didn't drop her. Caitlyn blushed furiously as she wondered how much she weighed. Oh, why couldn't she be a slender, petite slip of a girl who weighed nothing more than a feather?

"Are you all right?" came James's deep voice near her ear.

"Y-yes... thank you," Caitlyn mumbled as James set her down gently. She stepped back, adjusting her clothes, her face red.

"What happened?" asked James.

"Nibs climbed up and I think Bran wanted to join us too, but when he put his weight on the ladder, it rolled sideways... and I lost my balance and fell."

"What were you doing on the stepladder?"

"Oh... um... I was checking out a book that looked interesting on the top shelf... and then I saw something tucked behind it and I got curious..."

"This?" said James, pointing to a roll of parchment lying on the floor next to the bookcase. Caitlyn realised that she must have dropped it when she had lost her balance. James bent to retrieve it, then paused as he saw the other thing that had fallen to the floor: a slim volume of a book, made completely of smooth milk chocolate. "What on earth is this?" He picked up the book as well and straightened, looking at it quizzically.

Caitlyn hesitated, debating whether to tell James the truth. Would he believe her this time? "It's... it's a book made of chocolate," she said lamely.

James frowned. "I can see that—I'm just wondering where it's from. I don't remember buying any chocolate in the shape of a book." He turned the brown volume over in his hands. "And I've never seen such fine workmanship either—look at the detail! You could almost believe that this was a real book that had been turned into chocolate. Is this one of the Widow Mags's chocolate sculptures?"

Caitlyn took a deep breath. "I made it," she said.

"*You* made it?" James looked at her admiringly. "My word, you really *are* coming on as a chocolatier, aren't you? I didn't realise your chocolate-making skills were so good."

"No, that's not what I—" Caitlyn hesitated, then took the coward's way out. "Um... yes, the Widow Mags has been spending a lot of time training me."

"Well, she's doing a fine job." James laid the chocolate book down on the bottom rung of the stepladder and turned his attention to the roll of parchment he had picked up.

Caitlyn had to restrain herself from grabbing it out of his hands. Instead, she watched with bated breath as he slowly unrolled the yellowed paper.

She wasn't sure what she had been expecting to see—some gilt-edged scroll, perhaps, with mediaeval illustrations and an ancient inked message in beautiful calligraphy—but she was disappointed to find herself looking at a crinkled piece of parchment, with a few symbols carelessly scribbled across the surface.

James stared at the parchment for a moment, then recognition dawned on his face. "Oh... this old thing!"

"You know it?" asked Caitlyn. "What is it? What does it say?"

"I don't know what it says—I never figured it out."

"What do you mean? Is it like a secret message that you have to decipher?"

James laughed. "Perhaps... but it's more likely to be just gibberish."

"Gibberish?"

James smiled at her. "Yes. One of my earliest memories was of coming to Huntingdon as a child one summer... This must have been—oh, about twenty-five years ago—when I was six years old... We didn't live here, you see—my mother preferred our townhouse in London—so my father used to come up to the estate by himself from time to time. But I do remember that summer... it might have been the summer my sister was born and my mother was busy with the new baby... so my father took me out of the house for a while to get me out of her hair... And he brought me here. There was a young man—my father's colleague, I think; somebody he was working with—who was here too. I can't remember the man's name, but he was great fun. He used to be closeted in meetings with my father all morning, but in the afternoons, if he had some time free, he'd spend it with me."

James gave her a wry look. "My father was quite an austere figure—very much the stern, traditional patriarch—and he never had much time for me. So it was a wonderful novelty to have an adult willing to play with me and spend time with me. And this chap was fantastic! He taught me to play chess, showed me how to read a compass and how to light a fire using a flint... and he used to tell me stories; he had the most incredible imagination! He'd recount tales about powerful spells and magical curses, about meeting vampires and hunting witches—" James caught himself as he realised what he'd just said. Then he cleared his throat and continued: "Anyway, one wet afternoon, when we couldn't go outside, he suggested a game—an imaginary quest where I had to search for a magical hidden treasure. And he created several 'clues' which were hidden all over the house and would lead me to the treasure. One of these 'clues' was an ancient scroll with magical symbols..." James held up the parchment.

"You mean... it's just a prop?" said Caitlyn.

"I'm afraid so. I remember watching him make it.

He got some parchment paper from my father's office, crumpled it up several times to get it nice and wrinkled, then smoothed it out and used an old-fashioned feather quill and ink to write some symbols on it. But I don't think they meant anything—he was probably just drawing random shapes and squiggles."

"Oh." Caitlyn couldn't keep the keen disappointment out of her voice.

James looked at her curiously. "You seem very upset. Did you expect them to mean something?"

Caitlyn hesitated, her hand going to her throat, where her runestone was tucked out of sight beneath the collar of her shirt. For a moment, she was tempted to confide in James, to tell him about her search for answers. But something held her back. Maybe it was his refusal to believe in magic and witchcraft... or the fear of another scene like the one when she had tried to convince him that she was a witch. She dropped her hand back to her side and gave him a forced smile.

"I guess my imagination ran away with me. I thought maybe they really were magical symbols that spelled out a message." She looked at him hopefully. "But are you sure? I mean, just because your friend scribbled them for fun doesn't mean that they didn't have a meaning."

James shook his head. "Trust me, I checked. When I was at Oxford, I came to visit my father here during one of the breaks between the terms, and I remembered the parchment and wondered if it was still there, at the back of the shelf, where I'd left it as a boy... It was. So, out of curiosity, I took it back to Oxford with me, and showed it to a couple of professors in the University, to see if any of the language experts and cryptographers there could decipher it. None of them could." He chuckled. "In fact, one of them sent the parchment back to me with a rather irate note telling me not to waste his time with gibberish."

"But... if it was just gibberish, why did you put it back behind the shelf?"

James shrugged. "I don't know, really. I was going to throw it away and then..." He gave her a whimsical smile. "I suppose it's a bit like when you go back to a place you loved as a child—a beach or a patch of woods or even a house you used to live in—and you find something that your younger self had made, like a treehouse or a makeshift raft or even a stone with a crack that had an old knife stuck in it, which you used to pretend was the Sword in the Stone..." He gave a self-deprecating laugh. "And you know it's silly but you put everything back the way you found it, just... in honour of your childhood memories, I guess. This was a bit like that. So I brought it back here, tucked it out of sight at the back of the shelf, and haven't thought about it since." He looked thoughtfully down at the parchment for a moment, then held it out to her. "Would you like to have it?"

"Don't you want it?"

James gave her a dry smile. "Well... as the quote says, 'when I became a man, I put aside childish things'. I think maybe it's time I stopped trying to hang on to the past. If you don't want it, I'll put it in the bin."

Caitlyn took the parchment hastily. She didn't know why, but for some reason, she couldn't bear the thought of James throwing it away. Folding it carefully, she tucked it into her back pocket. Then she groped around for something to say as an awkward silence descended over them. She recalled what Nathan had said earlier and asked:

"So... um... is Inspector Walsh opening an investigation into Sir Henry's death?"

James looked relieved at the change of subject. "Yes, he came to see Lady Pritchard this morning. He wanted to ask her about Sir Henry's business affairs and whether he might have had any enemies."

"So the police *are* treating the death as suspicious after all?"

"Well, I think the results of the post-mortem on the tramp who was found dead last week changed Inspector Walsh's mind. He got the report last night and it shows that the tramp had been poisoned by digitalis."

Caitlyn raised her eyebrows. "Digitalis?"

"Yes, it's a compound found naturally in foxgloves, which stimulates the heart, causing it to pump harder—it's used to treat conditions like heart failure. But it's a very powerful chemical and even a slight overdose can kill you." James grimaced. "I remember being in the garden with my mother as a little boy and being warned not to touch the foxgloves. People mistake the leaves, sometimes, for comfrey, you know, and try to make tea from it. And actually, there was a terrible case several years ago: a man in Sheffield committed suicide by eating foxglove leaves."

"Wow... I've heard that they're poisonous but I had no idea they were that lethal," Caitlyn said. "I've seen foxgloves growing in gardens everywhere in England! In fact, I think the Widow Mags has some—"

"Oh yes, they're very popular, especially in traditional cottage gardens. And they grow wild too, here in the countryside. You often find them in shady spots under trees and beside country lanes. The flowers are very pretty. As long as you don't eat any parts of the plant, you're fine."

"D'you think the tramp could have eaten some by mistake?"

James shook his head. "The examination showed traces of undigested chocolate in his stomach—the last thing he ate—and when they analysed the chocolate fragments, they found that they were laced with digitalis."

"You mean... someone deliberately injected some chocolates with digitalis poison—and then gave them to the tramp? That's horrible!"

"Well, it's also possible that the chocolates were intended for someone else and the tramp found them and ate them by mistake," James pointed out. "It will be interesting to see what Sir Henry's post-mortem turns up."

"So Inspector Walsh has agreed to do a post-mortem on Sir Henry after all?"

"Oh, yes, definitely. In fact, I think it might have been done as a rush case this morning. Lady Pritchard was very resistant to the idea—it's understandable, of course; no one likes the idea of someone cutting up their loved one's body. But since this is now a murder investigation, she has no choice in the matter."

Mention of Sir Henry's widow reminded Caitlyn of the conversation she had just had and she said: "Did Lady Pritchard tell you about their estate manager who was fired last weekend? He seems like someone with a grudge against Sir Henry."

"Yes. In fact, Inspector Walsh just left to go and question Derek Swanes now—"

A loud crunching sound made them both look around. They found Bran standing by the stepladder, drool dribbling from his lips as he chewed something with great relish, whilst Nibs perched on one of the upper rungs and watched him with interest. Fragments of chocolate were littered around the mastiff's huge paws.

"Aargh, Bran's eating the chocolate book!"

Caitlyn groaned.

"What?" James bit off a curse. He rushed to the dog's side and tried to prise the mastiff's jaws open. "Drop it, Bran—drop it!"

But it was too late. The mastiff swallowed, then opened his mouth in a wide doggie smile, bits of chocolaty drool still clinging to his jowls.

"Damn!" said James.

"What's the matter?" asked Caitlyn, surprised by the vehemence of his reaction.

"I need to get Bran to the vet—he may need treatment for poisoning."

"Don't worry, that chocolate hasn't got any digitalis!"

"No, no... I wasn't thinking that... Chocolate, by itself, is poisonous to dogs. It contains a substance called theobromine which can cause vomiting, seizures, cardiac problems... even death." He eyed Bran, who was sitting, leaning against the stepladder, panting amiably at them. The mastiff looked the picture of health. James sighed. "It might be okay, since Bran is such a large dog—the amount might not be lethal—but I can't take the risk. I've got to get Bran to the vet immediately."

"I'm sorry," said Caitlyn, mortified. "It's my fault—"

James gave her a quick smile. "Oh, no, it's probably *my* fault for not thinking and leaving the chocolate book where Bran could reach." He bent down and gave the mastiff's collar a gentle tug.

"Come on, boy... let's go."

The mastiff heaved himself to his feet, then ambled slowly to the Gallery door. Nibs sprang off the ladder and scampered after his big friend, and they followed behind the kitten. As they were about to step out, however, they nearly collided with Mosley.

"Ah, sir... Julian Pritchard, Sir Henry's brother, has just arrived," said the butler.

"I can't see him now, Mosley. I must take Bran to the vet as a matter of urgency. Can you tell him it's inconvenient and ask him to return later today—or tomorrow?"

The butler hesitated. "He's very insistent on seeing you, sir."

"Well... I can see him as soon as I get back from the vet, if he's happy to wait here." James glanced at his watch. "I remember Jeremy Bottom saying the vet was going to be over at his farm this morning, so if I'm lucky, I could catch him there... which means I could be back in about twenty minutes... assuming Bran is all right."

"I'll sit with Mr Pritchard until you get back, if you like," offered Caitlyn impulsively.

James gave her a grateful look. "That would be great. Thanks."

CHAPTER SIXTEEN

A few minutes later, as James roared off with Bran in his Range Rover, Caitlyn followed Mosley to the Drawing Room. There, she found a short, florid man in an expensive pinstriped suit waiting impatiently. He had a passing resemblance to Sir Henry but none of the older man's presence and charisma. He did seem to have the same sense of self-importance, though. He flicked a wrist, glancing at an expensive Rolex watch, then said in a loud, nasal voice:

"About time!" His gaze went beyond Caitlyn and he frowned. "Where's Lord Fitzroy?"

Caitlyn looked at Mosley but the butler seemed to be waiting for her to speak, so she gave Julian Pritchard an apologetic smile and said:

"I'm afraid he has something urgent that he

needs to deal with—but he'll be here soon. Um...
would you like a drink? I mean, tea—would you like
some tea?" she hastily amended, reminding herself
that she was in England.

Pritchard gave an impatient huff. "Oh, all right—
I'll have a cup. But I haven't got all day!"

Caitlyn glanced at Mosley, who inclined his head
as if to her unspoken instruction, and she couldn't
help thinking that somehow, she seemed to have
fallen into the role of hostess, her actions
resembling those of the lady of the Manor. Pritchard
must have got the same impression because he
glanced at her and said:

"You Fitzroy's wife?"

"Oh no!" Caitlyn flushed. "No, no, I'm just... er...
a friend."

"Hmm... speaking of wives, my sister-in-law is
here, isn't she? That's really why I came. I... er...
wanted to offer my condolences to my brother's
widow. Went over to Pritchard House first but she
wasn't there. Staff told me she was staying here."

"Yes, she stayed the night after the dinner, and
then yesterday, after she heard the news about Sir
Henry, she felt too unwell to go home."

Pritchard turned and called to Mosley, who was
just about to leave the room. "Oi, you! Tell Sherry
that I want to see her."

Mosley stiffened at the man's rude manner but
his voice was bland as he said: "Lady Pritchard is
resting in her room. I am not sure she is up to

seeing anyone."

"What is she, an invalid?" scoffed Pritchard. "You go and tell her that I'm here."

Mosley's lips tightened but he nodded and left. Caitlyn cleared her throat and said:

"I'm very sorry about your brother."

"Oh yeah." Julian Pritchard made a face. "Never thought the old boy would cark it so soon. Still, I always knew Henry had a dodgy ticker—knew it was going to get him some day."

Caitlyn was taken aback by the man's callous manner towards his brother's death. Then she reminded herself that maybe this was the British way. Didn't they believe in keeping a "stiff upper lip" and never showing emotion in public? Maybe Julian Pritchard was really devastated about losing his brother and crying inside. She glanced at the man's face. *Hmm... or maybe not.* His smug indifference irked her and provoked her to say:

"Actually, there is some uncertainty over the cause of death. The police are still investigating."

He scowled. "What do you mean? I thought it was all cut and dried. Just need to set a date for the funeral."

"Oh no—I don't believe Sir Henry can be buried until his body is released after the post-mortem."

"*What?*" Julian Pritchard sprang up from the sofa. "They're doing an autopsy? What the bloody hell for?"

"Well, since it's unclear what Sir Henry died

from, I suppose they want to make sure that there hasn't been any foul play."

"Of course there wasn't any foul play!" snapped Pritchard. "What do they think this is—some sodding TV show? My brother just died of a heart attack; end of story." He narrowed his eyes. "Is this that stupid woman's idea? Henry's wife has always been a hysterical sort. I suppose she's been bleating to the police and telling them wild stories—"

"No, actually, Lady Pritchard was very against the idea of an autopsy. And she hasn't been hysterical at all," Caitlyn added, annoyed. "In fact, I think Lady Pritchard is holding up really well, considering the shock she's had."

Pritchard gave a derisive laugh and mimicked her voice: "'Lady Pritchard'? I knew her when she was plain Sherry Holt. She's nothing more than a small-time actress who landed on her feet because she met my brother in some pub and he took a fancy to her. She only ever married him for the money—" He broke off as he heard steps approaching the Drawing Room, and Mosley reappeared a moment later, escorting Sir Henry's widow.

Seeing the woman again, Caitlyn couldn't help thinking how uncharitable Julian Pritchard was about his sister-in-law. Lady Pritchard looked ill with grief: she was ghostly pale, almost white, and there were even darker shadows under her eyes than when Caitlyn had last seen her. If anyone ever embodied the classic image of a woman mourning her husband, she did.

"Oh, Julian—isn't it awful?" she cried, raising a hand to her mouth and giving a muffled sob. "I can't believe Henry is dead!"

"Um... yes, yes..." Pritchard looked horrified at the thought of having to deal with an emotional woman. "Jolly bad luck. Well, can't be helped, can't be helped... Just want to get the estate settled as quickly as possible now, eh? Have you spoken to the lawyers yet?"

Lady Pritchard looked doubtful. "I don't know if we can do anything while the police are still investigating—"

Julian Pritchard made an angry noise. "What the bloody hell do they think they're doing? What's there to investigate? Men die of heart attacks all the time."

"They're saying it might not be a heart attack," said Lady Pritchard breathlessly. "Oh, Julian—they're saying Henry might have been murdered!"

Her brother-in-law gave a forced laugh. "Why would anyone want to murder old Henry?"

"Well, the police were asking me if Henry had any enemies. They said people are often murdered by someone wanting revenge... or someone who stands to gain from their death... you know, like inherit the estate. Oh, except... it can't be that, because in that case, the main person who benefits is you, and you wouldn't murder Henry," said Lady

Pritchard ingenuously.

Wouldn't he? Caitlyn wondered as she turned to look at Julian Pritchard. His cold attitude towards his brother's death took on a new significance—and his horror and anger about the autopsy too. Someone who had murdered Sir Henry certainly wouldn't want his body examined by a forensic pathologist...

Julian Pritchard gave a nervous laugh. "Quite right, Sherry—quite right. And if the police suggest that, I hope you'll tell them so. Now listen..." He changed the subject abruptly. "Did Henry reject Blackmort's offer?"

Lady Pritchard looked at him blankly for a moment. "You mean... for the sale of that strip of land? I seem to remember Henry saying that he was going to refuse—"

"Yes, yes, I know, but had he given an official reply yet?"

"I...I really don't know—"

"I don't think so," Caitlyn spoke up, recalling the conversation at dinner. "One of the reasons Sir Henry was so keen to get back that night was because he said he had a meeting the next morning with the Blackmort representative. He was planning to give them his answer then. This was after you'd left the table," she added to Lady Pritchard.

"Ah, good..." Julian Pritchard rubbed his hands, looking pleased. He turned to his sister-in-law. "You know how to get hold of this rep?"

Lady Pritchard looked vague. "I suppose Henry would have the details somewhere in his study— Oh! I just realised: the man would have come for the meeting yesterday morning and Henry wouldn't have been there," she said in consternation.

"I'm sure your staff told him the news," Caitlyn assured her. Then she thought of something. "By the way, do you know if the tramp who died last week had been on your property?"

Lady Pritchard shook her head firmly. "No, I never saw him."

"Never mind the sodding tramp," said Julian Pritchard. "Listen, Sherry—why don't I drive you back to Pritchard House and then we can have a look in the study together?" He gave his sister-in-law a patronising smile. "You probably wouldn't understand about this, but this deal with Blackmort, it's quite important. Wouldn't want to miss a great opportunity just because of bad timing, eh? Come on..." He reached for her elbow.

"But..." Lady Pritchard looked bewildered as her brother-in-law started trying to steer her towards the door.

"Um... don't you think you're being a bit impatient?" said Caitlyn, disgusted by the man's manner. "Lady Pritchard has had a bad shock and isn't feeling very well. I don't think you should rush her—"

"She looks fine to me," snapped Pritchard. "And when I want you sticking your nose in my family's affairs, I'll ask you."

Caitlyn was speechless, taken aback by the man's rudeness. She watched helplessly as he manoeuvred Lady Pritchard out the door. A few minutes later, she heard the sound of a loud motor starting. She went to the window; the Drawing Room overlooked part of the front lawn and driveway, and she was just in time to see a flashy red sports car with the licence plate *"BIG 805S"* reverse with a squeal of its tyres, gun its engine a few times, then roar away down the driveway.

CHAPTER SEVENTEEN

"Holy guacamole, this place is packed!" Pomona looked around the village pub in wonder. "I don't think I've ever seen it this busy. And it's not even lunchtime yet."

Looking around, Caitlyn agreed. The Tillyhenge village pub was like many of its kind, with low ceilings, exposed wood beams, and dark wood furniture in cosy corners. At this time of the day, it was normally empty, with perhaps only one or two of the regulars having a quiet pint. Today, however, almost every table was full and the queue for orders stretched around the bar. She could see one of the barmaids hurrying to and from the kitchen hatch, bringing out platters of food, and Terry the landlord behind the bar counter, pulling pints with gusto and barely managing to keep up with the orders.

He glanced up, caught sight of them across the room and gave them a cheery wave. Caitlyn smiled back. She liked Terry, not only for his good-natured, down-to-earth manner, but also for the fact that he was one of the few villagers who wasn't prejudiced against the Widow Mags. In fact, Terry's great fear wasn't witches—it was drug dealers—and he patrolled his pub with an eagle eye, convinced that drug cartels were waiting to infiltrate his pride and joy at any moment.

Pomona grinned and nodded towards a table near them, where several middle-aged ladies had their heads together, talking earnestly. "Aha! They're all here for the gossip."

Caitlyn followed the direction of her cousin's gaze and caught a snippet of the conversation: the women were avidly discussing Sir Henry's death and the Black Shuck. In fact, as they pushed through the crowds and made their way past various other tables en route to the bar, she found that the ghostly black hound was the subject of almost every conversation. Like most small villages, Tillyhenge thrived on gossip—the more melodramatic the better—and there hadn't been anything as exciting as the Black Shuck for a long time. Now, it seemed like every local resident—and several from other villages too—had gathered in the pub to exchange theories, hearsay, and speculation.

And from what Caitlyn could hear, it sounded like the stories were getting wilder and more outlandish with each telling. By the time they'd got to the bar, she'd heard the Black Shuck being variously described as a demon flying through the night sky, a monster the size of a bear, a ghost hound invading your home, and an evil black mist which could enter through your nostrils.

"Jeez, where do people get their crazy ideas?" laughed Pomona. "You'd never think you were in the twenty-first century, listening to these villagers talk."

Caitlyn wasn't really surprised. Tillyhenge had a reputation for magic and witchcraft—in fact, it was this quirky identity that helped it stand out amongst the other villages in the Cotswolds and attract tourists. So the locals were used to being immersed in folklore and superstition, and seemed to embrace the association much more readily than most.

"You know, it's kinda weird how everyone's so quick to jump on a mythical creature as the culprit and never consider that the killer might be human," said Pomona.

"Well, you seemed to believe it was the Black Shuck too when you were talking to Inspector Walsh this morning," Caitlyn reminded her.

"Yeah, but that was before you told me about the estate manager—and that jackass brother! I think they're both much more likely to have killed Sir Henry than some phantom dog. They've both got, like, the perfect motives. Besides, a demon hound wouldn't need to use poison to kill people—it could just scare everyone to death!"

"We don't know for sure that both men were killed by poison," Caitlyn reminded her. "James says the police have only had the post-mortem results for the tramp so far and they're still waiting to see the report on Sir Henry—"

Pomona waved a hand. "It'll be poison. I'll betcha anything you like. And I'll bet they'll find chocolate in his stomach too."

"I could have told you that without an autopsy. We all had chocolates after dinner, remember?"

"Except that professor guy and Mrs Gibbs."

Caitlyn gave her cousin an incredulous look. "You don't think she poisoned Sir Henry?"

Pomona laughed. "Nah, she's a prissy old cow but she's not a killer. Anyway, why would she want to murder him? Man, she was like his 'BFF' all through dinner, agreeing with everything he said—hey!" Pomona pointed over Caitlyn's shoulder and grinned. "Guess who's just walked in?"

Caitlyn turned to look. Mrs Gibbs and a few other village ladies had just entered the pub. They paused inside the entrance, scanning the room, and Mrs Gibbs's eyes narrowed as she spied the two girls at the bar. She gave Caitlyn a cold stare, then followed her cronies to a table on the other side of the room. Caitlyn shifted uncomfortably, trying to ignore the woman's blatant hostility, and she was grateful when Terry appeared on the other side of the bar counter at that moment. He held up an empty pint glass and looked at them expectantly.

"What can I get you, ladies?"

"Can we have two lemonades... and what's the lunch special today?" Caitlyn asked.

"There's homemade steak and kidney pie, and the usual fish 'n' chips... or there's always a ploughman's."

"A what?" Pomona looked at him in confusion.

"A 'ploughman's lunch'," Terry explained. "Traditional packed lunch for British farm workers." He smacked his lips. "Nice wedge of crumbly, farmhouse cheddar wrapped in a cloth, some pickled onions, a good hunk of bread—the thick, crusty kind, mind you—and an apple to finish it off."

"That's it?" said Pomona, looking horrified. "That's all they have for lunch?"

"Well, people add all sorts of extras these days, like roast ham and hard-boiled eggs, and even some fancy salad, but nothing beats the simple, old-fashioned version, I reckon."

"Um... I think I'm gonna give that a pass," said Pomona. "I'll have the pie."

"Me too," said Caitlyn.

"Pies are going to take longer, though," Terry warned them. "Got a whole backlog of orders to get through."

Caitlyn glanced around the pub. "Yes, you're really busy today, aren't you?"

The landlord wiped some sweat from his forehead. "Aye, you could say that again! Place is mobbed. Haven't been this busy since the Fitzroy's gamekeeper was found murdered up on the hill and Tillyhenge was in the news—half of England must have come to gawk at the stone circle that time." He looked around the room. "Probably the same this time. Half of these are from out of town: nosy residents from other villages, and tourists who want a bit of titillation..." He squinted at the crowded tables. "Reckon there's a reporter or two here too. The press are always sniffing for a story."

"It's great for business, though, isn't it?" said Caitlyn with a smile.

"Aye, you're right. Don't mind where they're from, as long as they pay for their pint... Though there's one or two that I wouldn't mind seeing the back of. Him, for instance..." Terry nodded towards a table in the far corner.

Caitlyn followed the direction of his gaze and saw a thin middle-aged man with a receding hairline, sitting by himself. He was nursing a beer and staring at the tabletop, a bitter expression on his face.

"Derek Swanes," said Terry with a meaningful look. "The Pritchards' ex-estate manager."

"Oh! So that's Swanes," said Pomona, eyeing him with disappointment. "Man, I was expecting him to be a lot more, like, seedy, you know? That guy doesn't look like he could murder anyone!"

179

"I wouldn't put it past him," said Terry darkly. "Never liked Swanes—don't know what Sir Henry was thinking, hiring him to manage the estate. Always had a dodgy look about him. Wouldn't have been surprised if Swanes was mixed up in drugs! Looks just the type, doesn't he? All skinny and shifty-eyed. Told my missus, I did—you have to be extra careful with these skinny customers. They say drug dealers are all skinny types. On account of the constant stress, evading the authorities, you see?"

"Er... yes..." Caitlyn exchanged a grin with Pomona behind the landlord's back.

"But don't worry, I've got Rocco on the case," said Terry with a proud smile. "Not that he's a proper sniffer dog, mind, but he's a clever little mite. I reckon he'd know which customers were up to no good."

Caitlyn glanced across the room to where a little brown-and-white terrier was trotting, stiff-legged, between the tables, pausing every so often to sniff a leg suspiciously, and she laughed to herself. It had been a match made in heaven when Terry had offered to adopt the terrier, after its owner had been arrested for murder in Tillyhenge recently. The pub owner had found the perfect partner to share his paranoia and the dog had found the perfect owner to let him indulge in his pugnacious tendencies.

"Anyway, I'd best get your order in. Take a table and the girls will bring your food round."

They thanked him and, carrying their drinks,

went off to search for a spot. They were lucky that a couple were just vacating a table near Mrs Gibbs and her friends, and they sank into the chairs gratefully. As she leaned back in her seat, Caitlyn realised that they were also not far from Derek Swanes. She eyed the man curiously, wondering if he really could be mixed up in the recent deaths. Pomona was right—he looked like a weak, ineffectual sort of man—not the type who would have the guts to plan a murder. But then, appearances could be deceptive, couldn't they?

"You think it's him?" asked Pomona, reading her thoughts.

Caitlyn shrugged. "I don't know. He looks bitter enough and I suppose he could be nursing a grudge, but he just doesn't look like he could murder anyone. Also, he wasn't at that dinner. Assuming that Sir Henry *was* poisoned, how could Swanes have had a chance to—"

"Hey!" Pomona snapped her fingers. "Didn't you say that Sir Henry had a meeting with Swanes just before the dinner party?"

"Yes, that's what Lady Pritchard said. Swanes came to apologise for his behaviour."

"Did they, like, eat or drink anything together?"

Caitlyn knitted her brow, trying to remember. "I think Lady Pritchard said they had a drink. Actually, I just remembered—she said Swanes had brought Sir Henry a bottle of his favourite sherry. As a sort of apology gift, I guess."

Pomona jiggled excitedly. "That's it! I'll bet that's when he poisoned him. It's the perfect setup! You bring a bottle and you say: 'Hey, sorry I messed up. Let's have a drink together, to show there's no hard feelings...' And then that gives you a chance to spike the other person's glass."

"I suppose... but then, did Swanes murder the tramp too? Why would Swanes want to kill him?"

"Maybe the tramp found out about Sir Henry's murder and Swanes killed him to silence him."

Caitlyn shook her head impatiently. "No, that would only work if he was killed *after* Sir Henry—but he was killed almost a week before."

"Okay, similar scenario; maybe the tramp found out what Swanes was *going* to do—like he overheard him planning it or something—"

"But the tramp never went to the Pritchard estate," Caitlyn protested. "I asked Lady Pritchard when I saw her this morning and she was definite that he hadn't been there. Personally, I think it's more likely to be Sir Henry's brother. Not just because he was such a jerk but because he seems to have a much better motive."

"You mean greed?"

Caitlyn nodded. "He looks like the type that will do anything for money. And he obviously really likes to spend it—I noticed that he was wearing all sorts of expensive watches and things, and he drove a really swanky sports car that must have cost a small fortune."

"Yeah, but that sounds like he's already pretty rich—so why would he wanna murder Sir Henry?"

"Maybe he's living on credit and needs more money to support his lifestyle... or maybe he's got big debts... or... or..." Caitlyn sat up excitedly as an idea occurred to her. "Maybe he's been bribed to do it!"

Pomona looked puzzled. "Bribed?"

"Well, bribed is probably the wrong word. Incentivised, induced... basically, somebody offered him a lot of money to bump his brother off." Caitlyn leaned closer and said, "Blackmort."

Pomona's face darkened. "What do you mean? What's Thane got to do with anything?"

"You heard Sir Henry at dinner that night—he was refusing to sell that piece of land that Blackmort wanted really badly. But with him dead, now there's no one standing in the way of the deal going through."

"So? That doesn't mean that Thane Blackmort hired someone to kill him!" snapped Pomona. "Man, I'm so sick of everyone dumping on Thane all the time. Just 'cos the guy's rich and powerful, and a bit mysterious, doesn't mean that he's evil!"

Caitlyn paused, surprised by Pomona's angry defensiveness. She hesitated, then changed what she was going to say. "Uh... well, I suppose not. Maybe it wasn't from Blackmort's side then. Maybe it was Julian Pritchard himself getting impatient and greedy. I mean, he seemed really desperate this morning to get hold of Blackmort's rep—he practically bullied Lady Pritchard into going back to Pritchard House with him, so that she could contact the rep for him—and I'm sure he's getting some kind of extra kickback for selling that land."

She glanced at Pomona's stormy expression and added hastily, "In fact, now that I think about it, it can't have been Blackmort instigating things because if it had been, Julian Pritchard wouldn't need Sir Henry's wife to contact the rep for him, would he? He would just be in touch with them himself. So yeah, that was a stupid idea."

Pomona looked slightly mollified and said, "It could be Pritchard doing it on his own. Although I still don't see where the tramp comes in with him either."

Caitlyn gave her cousin a sideways look and said casually, "Maybe you should ask Nathan what he thinks when you get back to the Manor—he seems to have some pretty good ideas."

"Mmm... I'd rather talk to Professor Thrope. That guy is fascinating, and he always has the best stories."

"Don't you think Nathan's a really nice guy, though?"

"Nathan? Yeah, he's all right..." said Pomona. Then she looked at Caitlyn sharply. "Wait a minute... are you trying to set me up with him?" She laughed. "Honey, I appreciate the thought but he's not my type. He's too... decent, you know? I like 'em a little dark and dangerous." She winked. "Anyway, you should be focusing on your own love life. Speaking of which…"

She leaned forwards suddenly with a conspiratorial smile, her bad mood forgotten. Caitlyn watched as Pomona reached into her pocket and pulled something out.

"Check out what I found in the Fitzroy Portrait Gallery this morning!"

CHAPTER EIGHTEEN

Caitlyn looked down at the item in her cousin's palm. It looked like an irregularly shaped stone, with a hole in the centre. "What's that?"

"It's a hag stone!" said Pomona, her eyes gleaming. "A really old one, by the look of it."

"What's a hag stone?"

"They're these rare stones you find—usually by a beach or a river—which have a natural hole in the middle. Like from the movement of water, or something. You hear about them a lot in European folk magic."

"I've never heard of them."

Pomona rolled her eyes. "That's 'cos you never read the right books! Hag stones are said to protect against malevolent witchcraft and the black arts. People used to, like, hang them in their homes and on the farm, to protect themselves and their animals. I think there are English fishermen who still tie hag stones to their boats, to repel witches and keep evil spirits away."

"Well, it's not repelling me," said Caitlyn dryly.

"That's 'cos you're a good witch! It's not just witches, anyway. It can protect against any kind of negative force. People used to hang hag stones at the end of their beds, to protect them from the Night Hag."

"The what?"

"The Night Hag—she's a succubus witch who comes while you're sleeping. That's why you get nightmares, see? The Night Hag sits on your chest and sucks the life force out of you—*What?*" Pomona demanded, frowning.

"Sorry..." Caitlyn chuckled. "It's just such a funny image. Seriously, is there anything this stone doesn't do? Let me guess, it cures diseases too, right?"

"Yeah, it does! It's supposed to have healing properties if you rub the stone against a wound or a broken bone. And it's also supposed to let you see into the Otherworld. Legend says that if you hold it up and look through the hole, you'll be able to see fairies and spirits and things concealed by spells..." Pomona broke off and scowled. "Okay, you don't have to look so snarky. Jeez, Caitlyn, I would have thought that you of all people would show some respect for these old folk legends about witchcraft and magic."

"Sorry," said Caitlyn, abashed. "You're right, Pomie. I guess old habits die hard—you know I was always really sceptical of these occult objects and superstitions."

"Yeah, but you're a witch now! You know magic exists!"

Caitlyn put her hands up in a defensive gesture. "You're right, you're right! I... I've never had your easy faith, Pomona. I don't know how you can just believe things when you don't have any proof—"

"Because I feel it with my heart, even if I don't see it with my eyes."

Caitlyn hung her head, feeling shamed by Pomona's simple words. She also realised guiltily that she was doing the very thing that she'd accused James of. And she had far less excuse than him to be sceptical.

"You're right. I'm sorry," she said quietly, giving her cousin a contrite look. "So... what else do hag stones do?"

Pomona grinned, regaining her good humour. "Okay, okay... so this is the bit I was coming to: hag stones are also meant to have been used in fertility and love spells. See, they say the hole represents the Sacred Vagina of the Great Goddess and if you find a tree branch that fits exactly in it, that represents the Penis which—STOP LAUGHING!"

"Sorry! Sorry!" Caitlyn gasped, clapping a hand to her mouth and trying to stifle the giggles. "But... aww, come on, Pomie—you have to admit, that's hilarious!"

Pomona's lips twitched. "Well, okay—I did think that sounded a bit cheesy... but you never know! The hag stone definitely has magical powers. I mean, it found me."

"What do you mean?"

"Well, I was walking around the Portrait Gallery, just looking at random stuff, right? There's a whole bunch of glass cabinets in one corner of the room... and then I saw it, the hag stone... It just appeared on the top shelf in one of the glass cabinets."

"What do you mean, 'it just appeared'? It must have been in there the whole time and you just didn't see it."

Pomona shook her head vehemently. "No, I'm telling you—it wasn't there before. I'm positive! I know 'cos I walked past that cabinet twice and I stopped to look through the glass at everything inside it. There was definitely no hag stone. And then, the third time I passed it, I saw it immediately. Which fits what the legends say perfectly!" she added excitedly. "It's just like the elf shots. They say you don't find hag stones—the stones find you. You could spend all day combing a beach and, like, never find one... and then when you're not looking, one turns up on your doorstep."

Caitlyn lifted the hag stone out of Pomona's hand and held it in her palm. It felt unusually heavy for a stone of its size. The surface of the stone was smooth, as if polished by centuries of moving water, and around the hole in the centre, there was a slight iridescent sheen. In spite of herself, Caitlyn felt a thrill at the thought that she could be holding a magical stone.

"I'm surprised James let you bring it out," she commented, holding the stone up to the light to see it better.

"Well..." Pomona gave her a mischievous look. "Actually, James wasn't around so I just... sorta helped myself."

Caitlyn lowered the stone and stared at her cousin. "But... all the cabinets are locked."

Pomona winked. "Locks are no big deal if you know how to pick them."

"Pomie!" Caitlyn said, aghast. "That's... that's like stealing!"

"It's not stealing! It's not like I'm not gonna return it! I'm just... borrowing it for a bit. I just wanna have a chance to look at it properly. And besides—" She broke off suddenly as there was a commotion by the door.

"YAP-YAP-YAP-YAP!"

Rocco the terrier was rushing, teeth bared and fur bristling, towards a huge English mastiff who looked down at him in bewilderment. It was Bran. Behind the mastiff, two men were just entering the pub, the taller one having to duck his dark head in the low entrance. Caitlyn's heart gave its customary jolt at the sight of James Fitzroy.

"Ah! Inspector Walsh! Lord Fitzroy!" said Terry,

beaming. Then he waved a hand at the terrier, who was still dancing around the bigger dog, barking nonstop. "Oi! Rocco! Stop that!"

"YAP-YAP-YAP-YAP-YAP-YAP-YAP-YAP!"

Caitlyn winced. She couldn't believe how one small dog could make so much noise. Terry bent down and scooped up the terrier, then carried it— still squirming and yelling threats at Bran—behind the counter and out to the back of the pub. Everyone breathed a sigh of relief as the yapping was muffled behind closed doors.

Bran lumbered slowly across the room, his jowly face set in its usual placid, amiable expression. Caitlyn was pleased to see that the mastiff looked completely well. James had been with the vet longer than he'd expected that morning—in fact, he hadn't returned until lunchtime, and Caitlyn had only caught a glimpse of his Range Rover arriving back at the Manor as she was preparing to leave with Pomona. So she hadn't had a chance to ask him how Bran was, although she had guessed that everything was all right from the cheery wave he had given them as they'd driven past.

Now, she started to raise a hand in acknowledgement as James and the Inspector advanced into the room. But Pomona leaned across and hissed:

"Quick! Hide it! Hide it!"

Caitlyn realised that she was still holding the hag stone. Hurriedly, she shoved her hand beneath the table. But the two men hadn't noticed them anyway; in fact, James and the inspector seemed to be only intent on the man at the table in the corner. Derek Swanes watched them nervously as they approached him and sprang to his feet as they stopped by his table, his defensive voice carrying across the pub:

"...can't arrest me! I've done nothing wrong! I never saw that bloody tramp... and I didn't touch Sir Henry either!'

"Mr Swanes, I'd just like you to answer some questions," said Inspector Walsh. "This is not an arrest. It is not even a caution. I am simply asking you to help with an investigation."

Swanes calmed down slightly. "Well, all right," he said sullenly. "Just so long as you know that I'm only doing this as a helpful witness, right? Not as a suspect!"

"You can use my office, if you like, Inspector," said Terry, who had returned to the room. "That's nice and private."

Everyone watched avidly as the inspector escorted Swanes out of the rear door, after the landlord. James called to Bran and was about to follow them when one of the villagers intercepted him and asked:

"Is it true, sir, that Sir Henry was poisoned?"

James hesitated, then—obviously deciding that it would be all over the village grapevine tomorrow anyway—said: "Yes, the post-mortem report has just confirmed that. He was poisoned by digitalis."

There were gasps from various tables and a hubbub of excited whispering rose around the room.

"Was the poison in chocolates too?" someone else yelled from the back of the room.

James hesitated again. "I believe so, but I am not at liberty to discuss the details of the autopsy. I'm sure Inspector Walsh will release a statement to the press this afternoon and you'll be able to find out more then."

He had barely disappeared through the rear door, with the mastiff at his heels, when someone hissed loudly:

"I knew it! I knew those chocolates were to blame!"

Caitlyn stiffened as she recognised the voice. It was Mrs Gibbs. She turned to see the belligerent woman standing up at her table, addressing the rest of the room.

"I was at the dinner party with Sir Henry on the night he died," said Mrs Gibbs, her chest swelling with importance. "And I saw him eating chocolates with my own eyes—chocolates provided by the Widow Mags!" Her voice turned shrill and accusatory as she looked around the tables. Everyone's attention was riveted on her and she flushed with pleasure. "Ohhh yes, I'm sure I don't need to tell you about the chocolates made by that witch! They are full of dark magic, bewitched to

tempt you and seduce you and... and make you feel
all manner of sinful things when you taste them! Of
course, I didn't touch them," she added self-
righteously. "I was strong and resisted, despite the
heavy pressure from my companions to corrupt
me."

Pomona spluttered with indignation and started
to say something, but Mrs Gibbs continued
dramatically:

"And little did I know what a lucky escape I
had... Even I, in my worst imaginings, did not think
the chocolates could be imbued with POISON!" She
gave a mock shudder. "To think that I too could
have been murdered by that evil witch—"

Caitlyn felt her temper flare again, but before she
could say anything, Pomona sprang up.

"That's such a loada crap!" she yelled. "I was
there too that night and I ate some chocolates. We
all did: me and Caitlyn and James and his friend,
Nathan, and Sir Henry and his wife... so if those
chocolates were poisoned, how come the rest of us
haven't died?"

"Well, I..." Mrs Gibbs stammered. "I... I...
wouldn't know how a witch's mind works! You
should go and ask the Widow Mags yourself. She...
she must have hexed them so that they affected Sir
Henry only," she said, finishing triumphantly.

"Aww, for cryin' out loud!" said Pomona in
disgust. "You're just prejudiced against her and
making stuff up!"

"I am speaking the truth as I see it," said Mrs Gibbs, pulling herself to her full height.

The door to the pub swung open again and Caitlyn heard gasps across the room as a hunched old woman with fierce eyebrows, a hooked nose, and wild grey hair stepped in. *The Widow Mags!*

CHAPTER NINETEEN

The old witch was accompanied by a good-looking man with a weather-beaten face, dressed in typical farmer's gear of overalls and green rubber boots, who Caitlyn recognised as local dairy farmer, Jeremy Bottom. He was smiling and saying:

"...no, no, I have to buy you a drink—it's the least I can do to say thank you for that brilliant chocolate sculpture of Ferdinand. That's going to go down a real treat on the Open Day, I can tell you—" He broke off as he became aware of the unnatural silence that he had stepped into.

Everyone in the pub had stopped talking and was staring at the new arrivals, many of them with fear in their eyes. This was partly because of what Mrs Gibbs had been saying but also partly because the Widow Mags hardly ever ventured out into the village. She grew much of her food in her own cottage garden and vegetable patch, and relied on Bertha to bring the rest of the supplies. Once in a while, she was reluctantly persuaded to leave the chocolate shop for a physiotherapist appointment in the nearest town, but other than that, the old witch remained ensconced in her chocolate shop. So while everyone in the village knew of her and talked about her and maybe had even glimpsed her at a distance, few had been brave enough to venture into *Bewitched by Chocolate* and so most had never met her in person.

Now, they were staring at her with fear and fascination. The Widow Mags looked around, her gaze proud and unflinching, then—ignoring the stares—she hobbled slowly across the room. After a moment's hesitation, Jeremy followed her. They were met at the bar by Terry, who had returned from the back room. Caitlyn held her breath, watching to see what the landlord would do. She knew that a lot of the people—especially Mrs Gibbs's table—were hoping that he would refuse to serve the old woman.

"Ah, Widow Mags... haven't seen you in a while," said Terry with an easy smile. "How's the chocolate-making going?"

Caitlyn felt some of the tension leave her shoulders and she heard an uneasy murmur of conversation start up again around her. But before she could relax completely, a shrill voice rang out across the room.

"You have some nerve, coming in here like this." Mrs Gibbs had taken a few steps towards the bar and was standing with her arms akimbo, staring at the Widow Mags, her chin thrust out out aggressively.

"Now, now..." said Jeremy hastily. "*I* invited the Widow Mags in here to buy her a drink—"

"Jeremy, how could you do that?" hissed another woman at Mrs Gibbs's table—a thin, sour-faced woman with a vague resemblance to the good-looking farmer. "I told you never to associate with that woman! It's bad enough that Chris has to mix with that scatty granddaughter of hers at school, without you encouraging her to come into the village as well!"

"And I told you that I'm not listening to your superstitious nonsense, Vera," said Jeremy. "The Widow Mags has just as much right to come into the village as anyone else—"

"Not if she's a murderer!" hissed Mrs Gibbs. "No one is safe in Tillyhenge while we let a witch practise black magic here. She ought to be locked up and the rest of her heathen family too! That Bertha—how do you know what evil potions she's concocting in her herbal shop? And the granddaughters... including that one there!" She whirled and pointed a finger at Caitlyn.

"You leave my granddaughters out of it," the Widow Mags growled.

But Mrs Gibbs ignored her. Jabbing a finger at Caitlyn, she continued in an accusing voice: "This girl seems to have an unholy influence over Lord Fitzroy—how do we know what she's done to him?"

"Yes!" cried another voice. A tall, attractive woman in her early thirties with an upturned nose and brassy blonde hair rose from another table. Caitlyn's heart sank as she recognised Angela Skinner, the owner of a dress boutique in the village, who had made no secret of her contempt for the Widow Mags. Angela had been badly humiliated when she had tried to vandalise the chocolate shop a few months ago and had been even more furious when a cruel prank she'd tried to play on Caitlyn had backfired on her. She had been quiet lately, but Caitlyn knew that the other woman was just biding her time, hoping for any chance to get back at her. Now, she narrowed her eyes and pointed a finger at Caitlyn, saying:

"Yes, that girl is a witch too! James—I mean, Lord Fitzroy has been completely different ever since she arrived in Tillyhenge. She must have bewitched him, cast some kind of evil spell on him, and—"

"I... I didn't do anything of the kind!" cried Caitlyn, furious and indignant.

"Oh no?" Mrs Gibbs asked. "I was at that dinner and I saw how Lord Fitzroy looked at you. No man could be enthralled like that by natural means. You have used black magic to possess his mind and bind him to you—"

"Aww, for crying out loud—that's not black magic, you stupid woman!" shouted Pomona. "It's called love! Haven't you ever heard of people falling in love?"

Oh God. Caitlyn blushed furiously, squirming with embarrassment. She knew that Pomona was only trying to help, but this was almost worse than being accused of malevolent witchcraft. Her feelings for James were intensely private—she didn't even like discussing them with her cousin—and now their relationship was being dissected in front of the whole village...

"Love?" Angela gave a scornful laugh. "Lord Fitzroy's got his pick of beautiful, sophisticated girls from all over England. Why would he fall for a fat little frump like her?" She gestured to Caitlyn. "Look at her! With a bum like that?"

Caitlyn flushed even brighter red and had to resist the urge to sit down quickly, so that the table could hide her hips.

Pomona glared at the other woman. "You got a problem with hips? Why don't you get your skinny ass over here and I'll show you what real booty looks like!"

Several people tittered and Caitlyn squirmed even more. The whole thing was turning into a nightmare, like one of those awful daytime TV talk shows with cheesy melodrama galore.

"Pomona... forget it..." she said weakly, trying to

tug her cousin's hand. But the American girl ignored her. She was livid now and begging for a fight. Before she could speak again, however, Mrs Gibbs hissed:

"That's not love! At least not wholesome, natural love." She turned to Caitlyn and jabbed a finger in her face. "You can't hide what you're doing, you trollop—employing the dark arts to seduce Lord Fitzroy so you can use him to protect you and your grandmother. That's what you did the other day, wasn't it? You bewitched him to defend you and humiliate me in the village green! But I know your game! I'm not afraid of you! A righteous woman like me will always win over sluts like you...!"

The woman's hateful voice filled her head. Caitlyn stood trembling, the blood pounding in her ears, but she was so angry she found that she couldn't speak. Her hands curled into fists and she felt something hard dig into her palm. It was the hag stone. Suddenly, she wished fervently that the stone's powers were real, that it really could be used to repel negative forces. Even as the thought formed in her mind, something burned her hands and she flinched and jerked backwards, dropping the hag stone on the table. She saw it glow iridescent green for a moment, then fade back to normal. It all happened so quickly, she wondered if she had imagined it.

Caitlyn glanced up, wondering if anyone else had seen it, but it looked like everyone's attention was still fixed on Mrs Gibbs and Pomona, who were yelling at each other like two demented fishwives.

"...then I'll tell all the papers—see if I don't!" Mrs Gibbs waved a fist.

"Ahh, SHUT UP!" yelled Pomona.

"—and she won't be able to hide then or run to Lord Fitzroy for protection because I'll make sure that everyon-*mm-mmm... mm-mmm... mmm-mm... mmm!*"

Mrs Gibbs's eyes bulged as her lips suddenly clamped shut, sealing her mouth and preventing her from saying anything other than: *"Mm-mmm-mmmmm-mm!"*

Everyone in the room stared. A few got up and came closer, peering at her curiously. Several people started talking at once in hushed, scared tones.

"What's happened to her?"

"Is she having a seizure?"

"Somebody call Inspector Walsh!"

"Oh my God, her mouth's been glued shut."

"Don't be ridiculous! How can anyone's mouth be glued shut?"

"Well, look at her! Isn't that what it looks like?"

"I had a cousin who got this kind of skin tumour—dermatofibromas, it was called—when your skin doesn't stop growing. Maybe it's something like that."

"No tumour grows that fast!"

"I think it's black magic... I think she's been

hexed!"

Several heads turned to look at the Widow Mags but at that moment, Inspector Walsh rushed into the room, followed by James and the villager who had gone to call them.

"What's going on? Where's the emergency?" asked the detective.

Mrs Gibbs staggered up to him and began gesticulating wildly while making hysterical muffled noises through her lips.

"Mm...mmm! Mm... mmm... mmmmmm... mm!"

Inspector Walsh frowned at her. "I'm afraid I can't understand you, Mrs Gibbs. You'll have to speak clearer."

"Mmmm... mm... mm...mmmm! Mm! Mm!"

The detective looked at her irritably. "Madam, is this some kind of a joke?"

Mrs Gibbs's face went crimson and she began hopping up and down with frustration. "Mm... mmm! Mm... mmm... MMMM... MM... MM!"

"Sir, it's the witch! She's put a hex on Mrs Gibbs and sealed her lips," shouted one of the villagers.

"What nonsense!" said the inspector. "If this is all part of some elaborate prank, I am not amused and I will be arresting all those involved!"

"No, sir, it's the truth! Ask anyone here—we all saw it happen! Mrs Gibbs was talking and then..."

Unnoticed by the rest of the crowd, the Widow Mags hobbled quietly over to where Caitlyn and Pomona were standing.

"What have you girls done?" she demanded in an urgent undertone.

"Huh?" Pomona said blankly.

The Widow Mags gestured to Mrs Gibbs. "That woman—what have you done to her?"

"What do you mean? We haven't done any—"

The Widow Mags cut her off. "Where did you get this?" she asked harshly, pointing to the table.

Pomona followed her gaze. "That? Oh, it's a hag stone" Her eyes widened. "Omigod... are you saying that the hag stone is doing that to Mrs Gibbs?" She whooped. "That is so cool!"

"Pomona!" said Caitlyn, slightly shocked.

"Hey, the stupid woman had it coming to her. She deserved it."

"Hag stone magic is not something to be played with lightly," said the Widow Mags. "There is great power imbued in those stones, which could cause terrible harm if unleashed with the wrong intentions." She reached for the stone. "We must break this spell."

"Aww... do we have to?" said Pomona, glancing back at Mrs Gibbs, who was still dancing around in front of an increasingly irate Inspector Walsh. "This is so much fun to watch."

The Widow Mags gave her a severe look.

"Oh, all right..." said Pomona sulkily.

The Widow Mags picked up the stone and closed her fingers over it, chanting softly under her breath all the while. The stone glowed red... then gold...

then green... a whole kaleidoscope of colours... but Mrs Gibbs still remained unable to speak.

"It is resisting me," said the Widow Mags. Her hands were clenched around the stone, shaking slightly, and beads of sweat appeared on her brow. "What we need to do is cover the stone... envelop it with something, to muffle its power... a padded box or a bag lined with fleece..."

Caitlyn's eyes alighted on her glass of lemonade.

"What about if it's submerged?" she asked the Widow Mags.

The old witch's eyes lit up. "Yes! That would be even better. But we would need a thick liquid— water or similar would not be dense enough."

Caitlyn grabbed her glass and closed her eyes, concentrating hard. When she looked again a few seconds later, she was delighted to see that the glass was now filled with thick hot chocolate.

"Here," she said, shoving the glass towards the Widow Mags.

The old witch tossed the hag stone into the molten chocolate. There was a loud hiss as it touched the liquid, as if the hag stone was burning hot—although no steam rose from the glass. Then it sank into the creamy brown depths and disappeared.

A second later, Mrs Gibbs gave a loud gasp, opening and closing her mouth like a goldfish. Caitlyn released a breath that she hadn't realised she had been holding, and an excited hubbub rose in the room as everyone tried to work out what had happened.

"*You!*" cried Mrs Gibbs, turning to point an accusing finger at the Widow Mags. "It was you, wasn't it? You hexed me!"

Caitlyn felt a rush of indignation. She wanted to shout: "*The Widow Mags saved your life, you stupid woman!*" but before she could open her mouth, Inspector Walsh said testily:

"Mrs Gibbs, that is quite enough! If you thought that your ridiculous pantomime would convince me that there are supernatural forces at work, you are sadly mistaken, and frankly, madam, I am losing patience with these ludicrous accusations. Unless you can show me a real offence, I ask you to cease these complaints—or I shall have you arrested for public disturbance and wasting police time!"

"You...! You...!" Mrs Gibbs spluttered, her face practically purple with suppressed rage. She looked wildly around the room, then with a strangled cry, she stormed out of the pub.

CHAPTER TWENTY

Caitlyn felt drained and exhausted after the events of the day, and as soon as she'd washed up after dinner and Pomona had left to go back to the Manor, she excused herself and went to bed. She wondered if her cousin would return the hag stone (now rinsed of all chocolate) to the Portrait Gallery as soon as she got back, like she'd promised. Thoughts of the Gallery reminded Caitlyn of the piece of folded parchment that she had tucked into her pocket that morning. Getting back out of bed, she padded across the attic bedroom to where her jeans were slung across the back of the chair beside the ancient chest of drawers. She extracted the paper and returned to bed, propping herself up against the pillows. Slowly, she unfolded the parchment, frowning at it in the dim light from the bedside lamp.

A sense of disappointment washed over her again as she remembered James's prosaic explanation for its existence. To think that it was nothing more than a silly prop used in a child's game! She had been so sure that it had some special significance, that those scribbled marks and symbols meant something... Then she paused. *Wait.* Even though it *was* just a plaything, surely the fact that the symbols matched those on her runestone *did* mean something? The coincidence was too strange to ignore. Why would that young man have picked *these* symbols to use? How could he have known about them? Even if he was just doodling them in a careless fashion, he had to have known the symbols from somewhere...

She reached up and carefully untied the runestone from its ribbon around her neck, then held it up next to the parchment to compare. *Yes.* They were a match. Not all the marks—it was not the identical pattern of symbols engraved on the runestone—but enough to see that these marks were from the same source; the same "language", if you like.

But what do they mean? wondered Caitlyn in frustration. Then she remembered Viktor; she hadn't had a chance to speak to him about her mother yet—when she had seen him with Nathan Lewis that morning, there hadn't been any opportunity to talk privately, and she hadn't seen him again all day. The old vampire might also know what the symbols meant, or at least something about them. *Tomorrow*, she thought.

Folding the parchment carefully back up, Caitlyn placed it on her bedside table, then switched off the lamp and lay down. Sleep didn't come easily, however. Instead, she lay awake, staring into the darkness, while her mind whirled around, thinking about her runestone... the symbols on the parchment... the mysterious young man who had scribbled them... the Fitzroy Portrait Gallery... her mother... Viktor... Her thoughts swirled, then sank slowly at last, like snowflakes settling on a windowsill, and she felt herself drifting away...

An eerie howling sounded from outside her window. Caitlyn jerked up, wide awake again.

The Black Shuck!

Flinging back the covers, she rushed to the window and looked out. Despite it being only a few weeks to September and the official start of autumn, the nights were still balmy and she had left the window open to let in the evening breeze. Now, she leaned out precariously as she scanned the woods around the back of the cottage. Was the demon hound there? The howling had sounded close. She hesitated, then turned and flung on some clothes before hurrying downstairs. The Widow Mags's bedroom door was firmly shut and Caitlyn remembered that her grandmother had taken one of Bertha's herbal tonics after dinner. It was to help her arthritis, but it usually meant that the old witch also slept sounder than usual.

Caitlyn tiptoed past, then through the kitchen and out the back door, feeling a sense of déjà vu wash over her. Hadn't she gone through this exact sequence only two nights ago? Only this time, she didn't rush up the hill; she paused at the edge of the garden and strained her ears to listen. There was nothing for a moment—nothing except the night sounds of the woods: the murmur of the wind through the trees, the sharp bark of a fox, the call of an owl... and then...

She heard it again: that eerie, mournful howl. It seemed to be coming from deeper within the trees. Without stopping to think, Caitlyn plunged into the woods. The moon was still full and bright, but here under the canopy, it was dark—although it was better than the night after the dinner party, when she had been wandering with Evie in the Fitzroy parklands. The trees here seemed to be spaced farther apart and have less dense foliage on their branches, so more of the moonlight filtered through. At any rate, Caitlyn found that her eyes adjusted quickly and she was able to walk fairly confidently along the track between the trees.

She couldn't really understand what had compelled her to rush into the forest. She knew that she was being foolhardy—after all, she was unarmed, wandering in the dark, searching for a ghostly hound which some believed to have attacked and even killed two men. And yet somehow she didn't feel scared, only excited and full of anticipation. It was as if she wanted to prove something to herself—to confirm that her experience that night at the top of the hill hadn't been a hallucination or a figment of her imagination. Was the Black Shuck the monster that everyone claimed it was? Or was it the inquisitive, playful creature that she had met?

A rustling up ahead made her slow her steps and peer cautiously into the undergrowth. Was that...? *Yes!* Her heart gave a lurch of recognition and delight as she saw a large, shaggy black hound step out from between the trees. The Black Shuck's eyes glowed red, just like the legends said, but there was no malice in them. Instead, there was an expression of intelligence and empathy and—Caitlyn was surprised to realise—anxiety. The demon dog gave a soft whine, exactly like a pet who was worried about something and looking to its owner for reassurance, then it turned its head and looked at the shadows which led deeper into the forest.

There was something out there that was bothering the big black dog, Caitlyn realised. Something it was worried about. Even as she had the thought, the ghostly hound turned and trotted purposefully off, deeper into the forest. She hesitated a second, then hurried after it. She hadn't gone a few steps, however, when she heard a louder rustling ahead of her. It was coming from the left this time, at an angle from the path that she and the Black Shuck were on, and it was accompanied by voices. Male voices.

"Careful!"

"Where is it? I can't see it."

The next moment, she heard a shout, a menacing growl, and a wild rustling—someone crashing through the undergrowth—and then there was a blur of motion around her. She whirled in confusion, stumbling forwards, and cried out in surprise and alarm when something—someone— collided with her, knocking the wind out of her. She was flat on her back, in the undergrowth, and blinded by a light shining in her eyes. She blinked and put up a hand to shield her face, then gasped as she found herself staring up into the barrel of a hunting rifle.

"Caitlyn!"

The gun was swiftly lowered and someone crouched down next to her. It was James Fitzroy. His grey eyes were wide with shock and concern.

"Caitlyn—are you all right? Are you hurt?"

"I... I'm okay," she said as he helped her to her feet. "Just a bit winded, that's all... something smacked into me."

James gave her a rueful smile. "I'm afraid that might have been me. I was running and couldn't see very well... I thought—but what are you doing out here in the forest?"

Before Caitlyn could reply, they heard a shout

nearby: someone calling James urgently. Caitlyn recognised the voice—it was Nathan Lewis. James hurried off in that direction and Caitlyn followed. They were soon met by the journalist, who raised his eyebrows at the sight of Caitlyn, but didn't waste time asking questions. Instead, he turned urgently to James and said:

"I think it's there... in the clearing, up ahead."

James nodded silently and started forwards. Caitlyn felt a flash of alarm as she saw him lift his rifle.

"James!" She darted after him and put a hand up to grab the rifle. "No... you mustn't shoot it!"

He looked at her, startled. "Caitlyn, this is a wild animal, a dangerous predator—"

"No, you're wrong. I think it's not—"

"THERE!" Nathan shouted suddenly behind them.

They all turned to look. Something was emerging from behind the fallen tree trunk in the clearing. James shoved Caitlyn behind him, shielding her with his body, and raised the rifle to his shoulder. His finger slid over the trigger. Caitlyn felt his muscles tense as the shape moved across the clearing... and then James gave an exclamation as he saw who it was.

"Professor Thrope?"

The cryptozoologist froze, then came forwards quickly, a finger on his lips. "Hush! You'll scare it away! The Black Shuck... it was just here... I saw it—"

"Bloody hell, Professor—what happened to you?" said Nathan, coming to join them.

Caitlyn saw that the cryptozoologist looked as dishevelled as when she'd last seen him at the top of the hill. His spectacles were crooked, his hair mussed, and his clothes torn in places. He had an air of nervous energy about him and he seemed to be unable to stand still, shifting his weight from foot to foot.

"I haven't got time to talk," he said hurriedly, turning away. "I have to go after it—"

"Absolutely not," said James, grabbing the older man by the arm. "I can't let you go into the forest like this. There's a dangerous animal loose and you could be killed."

"But I—"

"It's too late now to go any deeper into the forest. I think we'd better abandon the hunt and head back."

The cryptozoologist became agitated. He struggled against James's grip. "No! You don't understand—this is very important! It's my only chance—"

"I'm sure you'll see it again, Professor," said Nathan, patting the man's shoulder. "There have been so many sightings recently. The creature is obviously staying in this area. We'll have a much better chance of catching it in daylight."

"Yes," said James. "I'll organise a hunting party

in the morning and you're very welcome to join. But you're not going anywhere tonight."

His voice was quiet but there was a finality in his tone that was more authoritative than any loud posturing. Caitlyn saw the professor's shoulders sag in defeat. He sent one last yearning look into the forest, then sighed and turned around to follow them.

"We'll see you back to the cottage first," James said to Caitlyn.

"Oh no, you don't have to—" She saw the look on James's face and sighed, knowing that she'd have to give in to his old-fashioned chivalry. "Okay. Thank you."

"What were you doing out in the woods anyway?" asked Nathan as he fell into step beside her.

"Um... I heard a strange howling sound and came out to investigate."

"Alone? Didn't you think that it might be dangerous?" demanded James.

"Well, I... I wasn't really thinking," Caitlyn admitted. "But... I can't really explain it—but I just have a feeling that the Black Shuck wouldn't harm me."

James made a noise of exasperation, but Professor Thrope said eagerly behind them:

"Yes, yes! I have always said that I don't think the Black Shuck has malevolent intentions."

"I'm sure that's very comforting to the two men who are dead," said Nathan.

"But there's no proof that the Black Shuck was responsible for those deaths!" protested the professor. "This is yet another case of a cryptid being blamed, just because of blind fear and ignorance. Besides, I'd heard that the police are treating it as a murder investigation now and have a suspect—a human suspect?"

"Yes," James admitted. "The police do think it's possible that both men were the victims of foul play, and they *are* investigating... but they also haven't ruled out the possibility of a... a wild animal being involved—"

"But the Black Shuck isn't a wild animal!" said Professor Thrope. "It is a spectral hound—and it is not roaming the countryside, looking for its next meal."

"Well, what is it doing then?" said Nathan.

The professor hesitated, then shrugged. "I... I don't know... But that is why it is so important that I follow it and observe it!"

Before Nathan could answer, they emerged from the forest next to the Widow Mags's cottage.

"Oh Lord... what is that amazing smell?" said Nathan, distracted from the discussion and inhaling deeply.

James laughed. "Probably one of the Widow Mags's latest chocolate creations. It's almost impossible to come near this cottage and not be tempted in."

"I think it's the new salted caramel sauce recipe

that Grandma's been trying," said Caitlyn.

"*Salted caramel?*" Nathan clutched his chest in an exaggerated fashion. "Be still, my heart! Forget the Black Shuck, *I* would commit murder for some salted caramel sauce."

Caitlyn giggled. Then she looked shyly at the men. "Would... would you like to come in for a drink?"

"Now? No, it's late and I'm sure you'd like to get to bed," said James.

Caitlyn laughed. "I don't think I could sleep a wink right now—I'm too keyed up! But I think a cup of salted caramel hot chocolate might help..."

Nathan's eyes glazed over. "Homemade hot chocolate?"

Caitlyn nodded. "The thick, rich, dark kind—not that watery, sugary instant stuff."

"Say no more!" Nathan pushed James aside with mock violence. "You can go home, mate. I'm accepting the lady's invitation."

CHAPTER TWENTY-ONE

James had been in the cottage several times, although usually in the front shop area, and Caitlyn couldn't remember if he had ever spent time in the kitchen. Now, she felt herself blushing slightly as she invited him to sit down at the long wooden table. It seemed somehow a much more intimate gesture—a sense of domestic familiarity—and she would have felt terribly awkward and shy if it hadn't been for the presence of the other two men. She was grateful to have the excuse of busying herself collecting mugs and the ingredients for the hot chocolate drinks.

"Oh, not for me, thank you," said Professor Thrope. "If it's not too much trouble, can I have a coffee instead?"

"You're turning down homemade hot chocolate?"

Nathan gaped at him. "Have you been hit on the head, Professor?"

The older man chuckled. "It sounds unbelievable, I know, but I'm not a fan of chocolate."

"It's no trouble at all," Caitlyn said with a smile. "But I'm afraid we only have instant coffee—"

"That'll be fine. With a bit of sugar would be lovely."

Caitlyn began to make the drinks, conscious of James's eyes on her as she moved about the kitchen. Suddenly, she wished that she had taken a bit more time selecting what to wear when she had rushed out earlier. She had just grabbed whatever was to hand—an over-sized T-shirt and some leggings—and thrown it on with careless haste. Now, she realised to her horror that she had put the T-shirt on backwards. And her leggings... they were old and faded... did they make her bottom look hideously big? She tugged surreptitiously at her T-shirt, wishing that it was even bigger and extended down farther... all the way to the floor would have been good!

"Um... so how come you guys were out hunting the Black Shuck?" she asked, hoping to distract James from his observation.

"We were in the Library and I heard something outside the window," said Nathan. "I looked out and—bugger me!—there was this huge black dog with red eyes slinking past. It was heading for the back of the property, towards the forest, and it was moving fairly fast, as if it knew exactly where it was going."

"Yes, yes, I saw it from my bedroom window!" said Professor Thrope. "I came down right away—I could hardly believe my luck—a real, live sighting of a cryptid! I lost the Black Shuck the other day but I was determined to get closer this time." He frowned at Nathan. "I did not see you and Lord Fitzroy, though, when I went out."

"We must have been ahead of you. I called James as soon as I saw the creature and he grabbed a gun and we rushed out in hot pursuit."

"How come *you* didn't worry about the danger then?" asked Caitlyn, setting some milk on the stove to heat up. Then she crossed back to the long table and carefully chopped up a thick slab of rich, dark chocolate.

"There were two of us—and we had a gun," said James. "Besides, while I fully support gender equality, there are still some situations where men do have superior advantage in strength and size."

"I suppose," Caitlyn conceded.

"Ah, only if you're a tall, muscular example of manhood like James... not if you're a weedy little ferret like me," said Nathan, striking a comical pose and pretending to flex his biceps.

James grinned and called his friend something rude, which had Caitlyn laughing as she crossed back to the stove and poured the chopped chocolate into the simmering milk. She stirred slowly as the chocolate melted in oozing swirls, then she added some of the salted caramel sauce that the Widow Mags had made earlier in the day. The rich, buttery aroma of the caramel mingled with the intense, bittersweet fragrance of the dark chocolate and permeated the whole kitchen.

"Are you trying to kill us slowly?" said Nathan with a groan. "I think I'm going to start drooling like Bran."

Caitlyn chuckled. "It's coming, it's coming! Would you like whipped cream on top?"

"I can't believe you even need to ask that question."

Caitlyn laughed again, then looked at James and the professor. Both nodded.

"You don't like chocolate but you have whipped cream with your coffee?" said Nathan to the cryptozoologist.

The older man laughed. "I know. I'm strange. But actually, the Viennese drink their coffee like this. It's called a *café mélange*. And trust me, once you taste it, you'll never go back to boring straight coffee again."

Caitlyn stirred the mixture on the stove until it was a smooth, rich, dark mahogany liquid, then carefully poured it into three mugs. The kettle that she had set to boil was also whistling and she hurriedly took this off the stove and poured hot water into a fourth mug with some instant coffee powder and sugar. Then she found a small bowl of fresh whipped cream in the fridge, leftover from the day's baking, and spooned some of that across the top of each mug.

"Here, let me help you," said James as she started to lift the mugs and carry them over to the table.

He'd barely got up when the door to the kitchen opened and the Widow Mags shuffled in.

"So this is what all the noise was," she growled.

"Oh, I'm sorry, Grandma—did we wake you?" asked Caitlyn, setting Nathan's and the professor's drinks in front of them.

"Caitlyn has kindly been making us a nightcap," James said with a smile. "Hot chocolate, with some of your delicious caramel sauce. We'd love you to join us."

The Widow Mags's face softened and she said gruffly, "I'm still working on that caramel sauce recipe. It's not quite right... so you're tasting a recipe failure."

"Bloody hell, if you call this a failure... Send all your duds to me!" said Nathan, raising his mug in a toast and taking a big swallow.

The professor did likewise—then jumped up and spat the drink from his mouth, spilling it all over the table. Everyone stared in astonishment.

"It's chocolate!" he cried.

"Oh... gosh, I'm really sorry! I must have switched the mugs by mistake and put the wrong one in front of you," said Caitlyn. She picked up the mug nearest to her. "This must be the coffee. I couldn't tell because of the whipped cream on top." Hurriedly, she placed the correct drink in front of the professor.

"Bloody hell, Professor—when you said you weren't a fan of chocolate, you really meant it," said Nathan with a laugh. "I've never known anyone to hate it so much they'd spit it out!"

The cryptozoologist flushed. "Er... no, it wasn't that... it was... er... very hot." He looked apologetically at Caitlyn. "I'm so sorry for the mess. If you give me a cloth, I'll clean up the table."

"Don't worry—it's no big deal," said Caitlyn, grabbing a rag from the sink and quickly wiping the table.

Professor Thrope was looking really embarrassed now. He glanced at the Widow Mags and said hurriedly, "Please don't think that's any reflection on your chocolates, madam. I'm really quite mortified. The... er... heat of the drink took me by surprise and it was purely a reflex reaction... I didn't mean to be rude."

The Widow Mags gave him a long look, but all she said was: "I'm not that easily offended."

They finished the rest of their drinks in an awkward silence, occasionally punctuated by stilted conversation. The Widow Mags's presence seemed to have a sobering effect—especially on Nathan and Professor Thrope, who didn't know her well and watched her a bit warily. Caitlyn felt a bit bad for her grandmother. It wasn't the old witch's fault that her appearance was so intimidating, and her natural reserve—built up from enduring years of hostility from the villagers—meant that she wasn't used to making new friends easily or engaging in casual chitchat. Caitlyn wished that Pomona was there—her bubbly American cousin would have put everyone at ease in no time with her vivacious manner and outrageous comments. She herself didn't have the social confidence to lead the conversation, and besides, she always felt slightly shy and self-conscious whenever James was around.

Finally, the men thanked her for the drinks and stood up to take their leave. As they were trooping out the back door, James paused and said to Caitlyn:

"Oh yes—I've been meaning to let you know that your car has been repaired. They've delivered it back to the Manor... would you like me to bring it down to the village for you?"

"Oh no, I don't want to give you extra work—I can come and pick it up myself tomorrow morning."

"You can bring that kitten back with you," the Widow Mags spoke up suddenly. "Wouldn't want to impose too much at the Manor and not do our part in looking after the little mite."

Caitlyn hid a smile. She could remember how crotchety and unreceptive the old witch had been the first time she had brought Nibs to the chocolate shop... but it hadn't taken long for the little kitten to worm his way into the Widow Mags's heart! And now, although she would never admit it, the Widow Mags missed the naughty ball of fluff when he went to stay at the Manor and looked forward eagerly to his return.

CHAPTER TWENTY-TWO

The car started with a deep, throaty purr the first time she turned the ignition and Caitlyn smiled at Nibs, sitting in the cat carrier on the passenger seat next to her.

"Now that's sounding a lot better, isn't it?"

"Mew!"

Cailtyn released the handbrake and was about to start down the driveway when Mosley came hurrying out of the front door of the Manor.

"Miss Le Fey! Miss Le Fey!"

Caitlyn rolled down her window. "Yes?"

"I've just had a phone call from your aunt: there's been a problem with one of her shipments for her distributors, which she must see to immediately. She was wondering—now that you've got the car—if you could help her by taking your grandmother to the doctor's follow-up appointment this morning?"

"Oh, of course. What time is the appointment?"

"Ten o'clock."

"Sure, no problem."

The butler hesitated, then said: "I beg your pardon, madam—but I noticed that you walked over alone from Tillyhenge this morning?"

"Yes...I came over the hill, from the chocolate shop. Why?" Caitlyn looked at him in slight surprise.

He gave a polite cough. "I hope you'll forgive the presumption but I wanted to urge you to take care when walking alone. There has been another attack on a young woman, you see."

"Really? When?"

"It happened late last night—I just heard the news from the staff this morning. She was walking alone through the woods at the back of Tillyhenge and she was jumped on by a gang of men."

Caitlyn drew her breath in sharply. "Is she all right?"

"She managed to get away, although not before she was... er... manhandled quite a bit. She's at the hospital now, I believe, but I don't think her injuries are serious. The police are investigating, of course. They believe it's the same gang who attacked the girl last week. They're hoping, this time, the victim can give them enough information to track down the culprits and make an arrest."

"God, I hope so…" Caitlyn swallowed, thinking of the poor girl who had been attacked. "Thank you for telling me, Mosley, and for your concern. It's really sweet of you." She gave him a smile. "And I will be more careful—I promise."

The butler retreated back to the house and Caitlyn let the car roll forwards. As she drove around the curve of the driveway, she glanced at the petrol gauge and noticed that it was nearly on empty. The GP clinic was in the neighbouring town—Tillyhenge was too small to have its own village doctor—and she would need to have ample fuel to get there and back. She decided she'd better fill up the car before picking up the Widow Mags. Caitlyn glanced at her watch: it was just after nine; she could easily fit in the detour.

Ten minutes later, she pulled into a small petrol station at the side of the motorway. As she manoeuvred the car into place next to the pumps, she spotted a red sports car parked on one side of the forecourt. It looked familiar… Then she caught sight of the number plate: **BIG 805S**. Of course! It was Julian Pritchard's car. She looked instinctively around but could not see the man anywhere.

Not that you want to run into him, she thought darkly. The less she saw of that vain, greedy, obnoxious jerk, the better. But as she was returning the nozzle to the pump and screwing the fuel cap back on, she noticed a thin man with a receding hairline getting out of a rundown Volkswagen which had just pulled into the station. It was Derek Swanes.

Caitlyn paused, suddenly alert. The two men who were suspects in Sir Henry's murder... both here at the same time... was it a coincidence?

She started to follow them into the station building—then she remembered Nibs. The cat carrier was too big and cumbersome to lug along, but she couldn't leave the kitten in the car either. Even here in the shade and with the windows down, there was a risk that Nibs could overheat. She bit her lip, then—making a split-second decision—she opened the carrier and reached in to scoop the kitten out. He had been dozing, lulled by the movement of the car, and now he yawned and looked around sleepily. Caitlyn tucked him carefully into the side pocket on the outside of her large canvas shoulder bag. He fit snugly into the space, like a joey in a kangaroo pouch, and curled up happily, tucking his head between his paws.

"Don't purr too loudly," Caitlyn murmured as she heard a soft rumbling coming from her bag. She slung it over her shoulder, shut and locked the car, then walked as nonchalantly as she could towards the station store.

Inside, she made her way slowly to the counter, pretending to browse some of the shelves along the way, whilst her eyes scanned the area. It was a fairly large store, with chillers displaying drinks along one wall, rows of shelves filled with grocery and hardware sundries down the middle, a rack of magazines by the windows, and along the far wall, a counter with a self-service hot drink dispenser, next to a long narrow table and some tall plastic stools. Two men were sitting side by side on the stools, their heads bent together: Julian Pritchard and Derek Swanes.

Caitlyn went up to the counter and paid for her petrol, then asked about a hot drink.

"You pay here, luv, and I give you a cup, then you go and help yourself," said the lady behind the counter in a bored voice. She indicated the dispenser on the far wall. "Coffee and hot chocolate from the machine, and there's hot water for tea. Teabags in the box on the left."

Caitlyn handed over some money, received a paper cup in return, then turned towards the far wall. She paused beside the magazine rack and eyed the men thoughtfully. They looked engrossed in conversation and were paying no attention to the elderly couple standing by the dispenser. Derek Swanes had never met her face to face, so he wouldn't recognise her anyway. As for Julian Pritchard... he was the type of self-centred man who probably never paid much attention to others and only noticed them in ways which were directly relevant to himself. She didn't think that he would remember her from their brief conversation yesterday and, for the first time, she was grateful that she didn't have Pomona's kind of glamorous good looks, which always drew men's attention.

Still, it didn't hurt to be too careful. So she rummaged in her bag, trying not to jostle Nibs too much, and pulled out a pair of sunglasses and a floppy cotton hat that she kept folded up at the bottom. She put these on. The hat wouldn't hide all of her red hair but it would make it less noticeable. Slowly, casually, she began to walk over. She was pleased to see that the elderly couple by the dispenser were still fiddling with the buttons, obviously struggling to figure out how to work the machine, and it gave her a great excuse to stand next to the two men as she pretended to wait in the queue.

"...will go the police! You'd better make it worth my while to keep quiet—I didn't sign up for murder and this is all getting way over my head!"

"Keep your voice down!" hissed Julian Pritchard. "Do you want the whole world to hear? I told you, you'll get your cut... but for now, you have to sit tight. Do nothing, just wait for this thing to blow over—do you hear?"

"It's all right for you," said Swanes sulkily. "You're not the one being hauled by the police out of pubs and being treated like a murder suspect in front of the whole village!"

Pritchard gave a sarcastic laugh. "What? Worried about your good name?"

"It's not my name I'm worried about—it's my freedom."

"Well, you shouldn't have been so stupid as to have left a trail of evidence behind you, should you?"

Swanes cast a nervous look around. "I can't stay here—I need to get away."

"*No!* I told you, if you do anything, you'll just draw attention to yourself and really make the police suspicious. You have to sit tight."

"Well, I want half my money now, then. You promised—when the job was done, I'd get half immediately. Well, the job's done now. So... I want my money!"

Pritchard sighed in annoyance, then reached into his inner jacket pocket and pulled out a fat envelope. "I thought you'd start to get twitchy, so I came prepared. Here..."

Swanes grabbed the envelope and opened it to look inside. Caitlyn leaned over surreptitiously and caught a glimpse of a wad of notes.

"This... this isn't even ten percent!" said Swanes indignantly.

"It's more than enough to be going with," snapped Pritchard. "And you're not getting another penny until things calm down and I'm ready."

Swanes shoved his stool back angrily and Caitlyn had to jump quickly out of his way. He swore under his breath, then stormed out of the store. Julian Pritchard looked around. Quickly, Caitlyn ducked her head and scurried across to the dispenser machine, which was finally free. As she shoved a teabag into the paper cup and pushed the button for hot water, she watched Pritchard out of the corner of her eye. He drained his cup, made a face, then tossed it into the nearby bin and walked out of the store. A few minutes later, the red sports car roared off with a gratuitous gunning of the engines.

Caitlyn came out of the store, holding her cup of unwanted tea and staring down the motorway, where the red sports car was now a speck in the distance. She couldn't quite believe what she had overheard—it had sounded almost like a clichéd conversation from a bad B-movie! Had she really overheard Sir Henry's killers discussing his murder?

CHAPTER TWENTY-THREE

Caitlyn stood for a long time staring down the motorway, long after the red sports car was no longer in sight. Then she suddenly remembered the Widow Mags's doctor's appointment. She glanced at her watch and gasped, then ran back to her car. The extra time she had spent eavesdropping on Pritchard and Swanes meant that she was now very late. She jumped into the car, hearing a startled *"Mew!"* from Nibs as she tossed her shoulder bag onto the passenger seat and started the engine.

"Sorry, Nibs... sorry!" she said breathlessly as she spun the wheel and the car shot out of the petrol station, taking the turn onto the motorway with a squeal of the wheels. She drove as fast as she dared back to Tillyhenge and pulled in by the village green ten minutes later. Unfortunately, the narrow, cobbled lanes of Tillyhenge were not made for cars, and so she had always parked in the green and made the rest of the way to the chocolate shop on foot. Today, though, she groaned at the thought of the extra delay... then she saw two figures she recognised standing by the large oak tree on one side of the village green.

"Caitlyn!" Bertha waved, and began hustling the Widow Mags towards the car.

"I'm so sorry!" Caitlyn said, getting out of the car. "I got a bit sidetracked at the petrol station—"

"Never mind, if you leave now, you'll only be a little late," said Bertha in her calm, reassuring way. "That's why I thought we'd come out to meet you— save you having to go all the way to the chocolate shop to get Mother."

"They always keep you sitting in the waiting room for ages anyway," said the Widow Mags grouchily. "There isn't a single doctor who's ever on time!"

As it turned out, the old witch was right. They arrived only five minutes late but sat in the waiting room for another twenty minutes before they were seen. By the time they were finally escorted into the doctor's office, Nibs was waking up from his nap and poking his head out of the side pocket of Caitlyn's bag.

"Mew?"

"Shh!" Caitlyn pushed his head gently back down. "I'm not supposed to bring any animals into the clinic. Go back to sleep, Nibs! Just another twenty minutes..."

She sat down next to the Widow Mags and, after a moment's hesitation, placed her bag on the floor next to her chair. She was worried that Nibs squirming in the side pocket might draw too much attention if she kept the bag on her lap. Thankfully, though, the kitten seemed to have settled down again and she breathed a sigh of relief.

Beside her, the Widow Mags was grumpily answering a series of questions as the doctor listened to her chest with a stethoscope. Her usual GP wasn't seeing her today and, like many old people who disliked change, she was very put out.

"Dr Stanton asked me all these things last time," grumbled the old witch. "Why do we have to go through them again?" She leaned back and eyed the young doctor critically. "Are you sure you should be seeing his patients? You don't look old enough to be qualified."

The GP flushed. With his clean-cut good looks and mop of blond hair that flopped boyishly over his forehead, Dr Nichols did look very different from the usual stereotype of the grey-haired, bespectacled, middle-aged family doctor. He cleared his throat politely.

"Er... yes, I've been practising for a few years now, as a matter of fact. Dr Stanton is planning to retire soon and I shall be taking over his practice." He smiled at the Widow Mags, ignoring her look of horror. "Now, the purpose of your appointment today is to go over your test results. If you'll remember, the last time you were here, you had some blood tests done." He tapped on the keyboard at his elbow and glanced at the computer screen. "Ah... yes... yes... Well, it all looks remarkably good, I must say, for a lady of your age... your iron levels are good, your cholesterol is within range... hmm... your vitamin D levels are a bit low, though. Do you get out in the sun much?"

For a moment, Caitlyn thought the Widow Mags was going to snap: "None of your business!" but to her relief, the old witch muttered:

"I go out when I have to."

"Well, I think you need to make an effort to go out a bit more," said Nichols gently. "We're still having lovely summer weather—you should take advantage of that. You live in Tillyhenge, don't you? Beautiful countryside all around there. Great place for walks... up that hill... around the fields... And the village green is nice too—pick up a pint at the pub and sit at one of the wooden benches outside, hmm?"

Caitlyn winced slightly as she thought of the Widow Mags's last disastrous visit to the pub. "Uh... is it bad to be low on vitamin D?" she asked to change the subject.

"Well, you need vitamin D to absorb calcium and phosphate from your food," Nichols explained. "Otherwise you can develop bone density problems, which can be particularly serious in the elderly. You get a bit of vitamin D in your diet—oily fish, for example—but your body can actually make most of the vitamin D you need when your skin is exposed to sunlight. Of course, you have to be careful about the risk of skin cancer too... but a bit of sunshine is very good for you." He tapped on the keyboard again and something churned out of the printer on his desk. "I'd like you to start taking some vitamin D supplements as well. I'll give you the name of a brand I recommend." He rose from his chair. "Now, if you don't mind, I'd like to examine you and check your mobility... I have a special interest in arthritis, you see, and I have been trialling some new management techniques. That's why you were transferred to me. Dr Stanton thought I might be able to help you..."

"I'm not trying any new-fangled quackery!" said the Widow Mags suspiciously. "It's bad enough having to go to that physiotherapist every few weeks."

The young doctor smiled, undeterred. "Well, let's just have a look at your range of movement first, shall we?" He coaxed her up and led her into the centre of the room.

Caitlyn was impressed with Nichols's patience and good humour, although she supposed that dealing with cranky geriatrics was just a normal part of his job. She leaned back in the chair and looked idly around the room as the GP took the

Widow Mags through a series of exercises. It was a bright and cheerful office, with a sink in one corner, next to the examination bed, and a set of filing cabinets in the other. Several "thank you" cards decorated the top of the filing cabinets, the shelves on the wall, and the windowsill—it looked like, despite his youth, Dr Nichols was popular with his patients. There was even a half-open box of chocolates on the shelf by the window. Then she did a double-take as she saw something else on the shelf... a little black kitten picking his way between the cards, pausing every so often to sniff them curiously.

Nibs! What is he doing up there?

Caitlyn glanced quickly down at her bag and was dismayed to find it flopped sideways on the floor, the side pocket gaping and empty. *Oh rats.* The little kitten must have crawled out while she was preoccupied, and was now happily exploring the room. Caitlyn wondered if she could grab him before the doctor noticed. She stood up. Dr Nichols paused in what he was doing and looked at her enquiringly.

"Oh... uh... I was just admiring your cards... It must be very rewarding being a doctor... helping so many people..." Caitlyn babbled, pointing and crossing over to the windowsill.

"Ah." He gave an embarrassed laugh. "Er... yes, many of my patients are kind enough to show their appreciation."

He turned back to the Widow Mags and Caitlyn pretended to bend down and look at the cards more closely, whilst she moved closer to the shelf where Nibs was perching The kitten's tail went up as she came near and he uttered a happy *chirrup* of recognition.

Nichols looked up, startled. "What was that?"

"What was what?" said Caitlyn, hurriedly moving so that she stood between Nibs and the doctor, blocking the kitten from view.

"That sound... I thought I heard..."

"Hmm? I didn't hear anything," said Caitlyn brightly.

The GP gave her a doubtful look, then turned back to the Widow Mags. Caitlyn glanced back at the shelf, to find Nibs batting at the box of chocolates.

"No, Nibs... don't!" she hissed, rushing to grab him.

But the kitten ignored her. Before she could reach him, he gave the box another playful swat with his paw and sent the whole thing flying off the shelf. Chocolate bonbons scattered everywhere, rolling across the carpet and under the furniture.

"Nooo!" Caitlyn groaned, horrified.

"Mew!" cried the kitten excitedly, jumping down and chasing one of the bonbons as it rolled under the desk.

Dr Nichols turned and stared in astonishment.

"I... I'm sorry!" Caitlyn gasped. "He was supposed

to stay in my bag..."

She knelt down quickly to collect the scattered chocolates. Almost all the bonbons had fallen out of the box and were inedible now, having rolled across the dirty carpet. And these didn't look like cheap, mass-market supermarket chocolates either, Caitlyn noted with dismay—no, they looked like creations from a fancy chocolate shop. In fact, each bonbon was in the shape of a mushroom—a little toadstool—with the detail of the spots beautifully rendered on the rounded surfaces.

"Ah... don't worry about it..." said Nichols, coming over.

"I'm so sorry... I really am so sorry!" said Caitlyn, mortified. "I feel awful. These must have been a special gift from a patient."

"Er... it's okay," said the doctor with an awkward smile. "Probably better for me not to eat too much chocolate anyway."

"We'll bring you a box from my shop next time," said the Widow Mags gruffly.

The young doctor's smile widened. "Ah... I've heard a lot about your chocolates. I certainly wouldn't say no to that."

Caitlyn finished picking up the fallen bonbons, including the one that had rolled under the desk. Nibs was still trying to play with it and, recalling James's concern for Bran, she hastily snatched the bonbon out of the kitten's reach. She had no idea if chocolate was poisonous to cats too, but she wasn't taking any chances. As she was about to rise, she spotted a small pink card which must have fallen out of the box as well. She picked this up, glancing at the handwritten message which said: *"To my favourite doctor... from your Ticklewickle".*

"Oh, I'll take that," said Nichols, grabbing the card and stuffing it in his pocket, his face red. He cleared his throat, then said: "Animals aren't allowed in the clinic, you know, unless they're registered guide dogs or other therapy pets."

"Yes, I know," said Caitlyn sheepishly. "I'm sorry. We were late for the appointment and I didn't have time to drop Nibs off at the chocolate shop. And I couldn't leave him in the car on such a hot day..."

"Yes, well, as long as you remember for next time," said Nichols. He picked up the printout from the printer and handed it to the Widow Mags. "Here you go—you can ask for that supplement at the pharmacy. Any good chemist should stock it. And try some of those mobility exercises I showed you. Let me know how you get on... and I'll see you for a follow-up in about... say, three months?"

A few minutes later, Caitlyn followed the Widow Mags gratefully out of the doctor's office, a squirming Nibs held firmly in her arms. The receptionist and other patients stared in surprise at the sight of the kitten but Caitlyn didn't offer an explanation, just bundling the little cat out to her car as fast as she could.

"Mew!" said Nibs indignantly, his fur all ruffled

and standing up, as Caitlyn placed him back in the cat carrier. He pressed his nose against the bars of the carrier door and shoved, trying to get out again.

"Oh no... you've got up to quite enough mischief for one day," said Caitlyn severely. "I still can't believe you knocked all those chocolates to the floor! I nearly died. They were probably really expensive, from some fancy shop—"

"Those chocolates were homemade," the Widow Mags spoke up.

"How can you tell?"

The old witch gave her an impatient look. "I know chocolates. Those were made by hand, in a domestic setting. Very good mould used too—probably Belgian—very fine detail. I don't think I've seen a mould for bonbons in the shape of toadstools."

Caitlyn helped her grandmother into the car, then got in herself. As she drove off, she wondered if someone in the village was trying their hand at homemade chocolates, with the view to starting a rival chocolate business to challenge the Widow Mags?

CHAPTER TWENTY-FOUR

When they arrived back at the chocolate shop, it was to find Pomona in the kitchen, helping herself to some chocolate fudge that the Widow Mags had made yesterday and impatiently waiting for them.

"Where have you guys been? I've been waiting, like, forever!" the American girl said as they came in.

"I took Grandma to see the doctor," Caitlyn explained as the Widow Mags went out to the front to open up the chocolate shop. Then she leaned close to her cousin and added: "Pomie—listen to this!" Quickly, she told Pomona about seeing Julian Pritchard with Derek Swanes and what she had overheard at the petrol station.

"Holy guacamole... you think they were in it together?"

"Well, it sounded like it. I mean, they didn't

actually discuss the murder in detail, but Swanes talked about Pritchard promising him half the money 'when the job was done'. He also talked about not wanting to go to jail—he seemed really scared. He said 'I didn't sign up for murder'—"

"But that's practically a confession!" cried Pomona.

"Well, it depends on how you look at it. It could have other meanings too, like... either he didn't mean to kill Sir Henry but it happened by mistake... or there *was* some other crime that he was happy to commit—something that he *did* 'sign up for'—but now he's panicking because he's inadvertently become a suspect in a murder investigation and that was not part of the deal."

"You're over-thinking it," said Pomona, wrinkling her nose. "The guy talks about Sir Henry's murder, he talks about having done the 'job' and not wanting to end up in jail... what else do you need? I'll bet Pritchard got Swanes to poison Sir Henry, so that he could inherit the estate. In return, he promised Swanes a 'cut'—"

"But where does the tramp fit in, then?" asked Caitlyn. "Why would Pritchard and Swanes want to kill him?"

Pomona shrugged. "I told you—he probably saw something or heard something about their plans and they had to silence him."

"I guess... it just seems strange though. Like a piece of a jigsaw that doesn't quite fit in the space it's supposed to go in."

"Anyway, you gotta tell the police what you overheard."

"Yes, I was planning to call Inspector Walsh as soon as I got back." Caitlyn glanced at the time. "Or maybe after lunch. Another half an hour won't matter."

"Oh, lunch! That reminds me—James wanted to know if you're free for lunch tomorrow."

Caitlyn blushed. "With... with him?"

Pomona rolled her eyes. "No, with the Archbishop of Canterbury. Yeah, of course with him... and Nathan and Professor Thrope. He was thinking of a picnic on the lake, 'cos you know we missed out the last time they took the boats out—"

"Oh, you mean a group lunch!" Caitlyn stammered. "I... sorry, I thought... I mean..."

Pomona burst out laughing. "You thought I was talking about a date? Honey, James might be English, but I'm sure he can ask you out on a date himself, without needing me to act as a go-between. He's not *that* reserved."

Caitlyn's cheeks were flaming. "I wasn't really expecting... I mean..."

Pomona gave a long-suffering sigh. "I don't know what to do with you two. It's *obvious* to everyone that you're crazy about each other but you're just doing this stupid polite dance around each other all the time... it's driving me nuts! I swear, I'm gonna find a way to lock you two into a hotel room and throw away the key—"

"Don't you dare!"

"Well, then... you gotta sort things out. Why don't you guys just, like, *talk* to each other?"

"I've tried talking to James. He wouldn't listen!"

"So try again! Jeez, Caitlyn, I used to think you were pretty gutsy, but lately it seems like you just give up on things so easily... like that thing about your mother—"

"Oh, I found out something about that," Caitlyn interrupted, eager to get the subject off her relationship with James.

Pomona stopped. "Really? What?"

"Well, it's not about her exactly, but it's sort of related."

Quickly, Caitlyn told Pomona about finding the piece of parchment in the Gallery and the disappointing truth about its origin.

"...although I still think it's weird that the man used similar symbols to what's on my runestone when he was making up the parchment. Even if he was just randomly doodling stuff, he had to have known about those symbols in the first place, to use them—don't you think? That *must* mean something... I need to ask James if he can remember any more about the man."

"Can I see it—the parchment?" asked Pomona eagerly.

"It's upstairs in my room—come on, I'll show you."

The two girls trooped upstairs; Caitlyn pulled the parchment out from under her pillow and smoothed it out for Pomona to look.

"Are you *sure* that it's just random doodles?"

"Yes, James said he checked. It's not any language that's known in the world."

"In *this* world, maybe," said Pomona.

"What do you mean?

"Well, maybe the symbols are from a magical language... from the *Otherworld!* Listen..." Pomona's eyes were sparkling with excitement. "Remember when I was telling you about the hag stone and its magical powers? One of the things legend says is that if you look through the hole in the middle, you can see beings from the Otherworld... you know, things like fairies and demons or even things made invisible by a spell or enchantment."

"Yes, I remember you saying that... but that's just... well, it's just a folktale!"

Pomona gave her a look and Caitlyn ducked her head, remembering her cousin's chiding. Pomona was right—she should try harder not to be so instantly sceptical. She took a deep breath and said, "Okay... so supposing it's true?"

Pomona tapped the parchment with her finger. "So... maybe if we looked at these symbols through the hag stone, they would suddenly make sense!"

Caitlyn looked doubtful. "I suppose we could try. I could bring it over to the Manor tomorrow and we could get the hag stone back out of the Gallery—"

"Who needs to wait until tomorrow?" Pomona reached into her pocket and drew out something. Caitlyn caught a glimpse of smooth, grey stone with a hint of iridescent shimmer.

"Pomie! You said you were going to return it!"

"I *am* going to return it... eventually!" said Pomona, grinning. "But I'm just keeping it for a little longer; I mean, it's out already—what difference does one more day make?"

"You know what the Widow Mags said—that thing is dangerous! It's not some toy to play around with. What if it suddenly 'activates' again, like it did yesterday? And what if the Widow Mags isn't around to deal with it? You could end up hurting someone—"

"Who cares if they're prissy old cows like Mrs Gibbs?"

"Pomona!"

'Oh, all right. I'll put it back tonight," said Pomona with bad grace. "But first, I gotta try this!" She grabbed the parchment and spread it out on the bed, then took the hag stone and placed it over some of the scribbles.

Caitlyn felt her pulse quicken, and she couldn't help copying Pomona as her cousin leaned eagerly over to look through the hole in the stone.

Nothing happened. The parchment looked exactly the same through the hole.

"Maybe you gotta look at it from a bit farther back," said Pomona, picking up the parchment and holding it at arm's length, whilst with her other hand, she held the hag stone up to her eye, like someone holding an old-fashioned monocle.

"Anything?" Caitlyn asked.

Pomona shook her head in frustration. "No. It looks the same—but I was sure..." She tossed the hag stone to Caitlyn. "Here, you try."

Caitlyn sat down on the bed, with the parchment in her lap, and brought the hag stone up to her right eye. She squinted through the hole. Nothing. She tried the left eye. The symbols remained as unintelligible as ever.

"Sorry, Pomie. It was a nice idea but..." She gave her cousin a smile of chagrin.

But Pomona wasn't giving up that easily. "Maybe it needs to be activated," she said. "Why don't you, like, chant over it or something?"

"I wouldn't know what to chant."

Pomona heaved a loud sigh. "Well, meditate then... or wave your fingers over it... just do *some*thing!"

More to placate her cousin than anything else, Caitlyn turned back to the hag stone and stared at it. She took a deep breath and tried to focus her mind on the hole in the stone, to fade out everything else around her so that her world narrowed down to just that circle, through which she could see a few of the symbols on the parchment. The black marks blurred under her unblinking gaze...

And then something shimmered.

Caitlyn blinked. Had she imagined it? No, there it was again. A slight shimmering around the edges of the symbols. And then, for a brief second, the symbols themselves seemed to uncurl and reform into different shapes... shapes almost like letters...

"Caitlyn? Pomona? Where are you?"

Caitlyn jumped at the sound of the Widow Mags's voice. The hag stone fell out of her hands, bounced on the wooden floor, and rolled under her bed.

"Rats!" she muttered.

Pomona hurried out to the landing. "We're up here... in Caitlyn's room. We'll be down in a minute!" She returned to the room and asked eagerly: "Well? Did you see something?"

Had she? Or had it just been her imagination, because she had desperately wanted to see something—anything? "I... I don't know," Caitlyn answered.

"Well, try again!"

"I've got to get the hag stone... it fell and rolled under the bed." Caitlyn got down on her hands and knees to look under her bed. "This reminds me of the doctor's clinic this morning," she mumbled as she poked her head under the wooden bedframe.

"Why?"

"Because Nibs got out of my bag and started climbing all over the room... and he knocked a box of chocolates off the shelf and they all fell on the floor... and one of them rolled under the doctor's desk so I had to crawl under it to pick it up... oh God, Pomie—I felt so bad. All the chocolates had to be thrown away after falling on the floor and it was such a waste. The doctor was really nice about it, but you could see that they were homemade chocolate bonbons... like someone had taken a lot of time and effort to make them for him. They were a gift from a patient, I think... there was even a card and—*OH!*"

Caitlyn jerked up so quickly that she smacked her head on the underside of the bed. "OWWW!" She emerged rubbing her head ruefully.

"What?" Pomona looked puzzled.

"Pomie, I just realised something! When I was looking at the card, I kept thinking that there was something really familiar about the message, although I couldn't figure out what it was—"

"What did it say?"

"It said: '*To my favourite doctor... from your Ticklewickle*'."

"'Ticklewickle'?" Pomona pulled a face.

"Yes, and I just realised what that reminded me of: Sir Henry and his wife!"

"Huh?"

"That night at the dinner party, didn't you notice Sir Henry and his wife calling each other by these ridiculous pet names?"

Pomona shrugged. "I dunno... maybe... I wasn't really paying attention to them."

"Well, I was, and they were calling each other these really cheesy terms of endearment—"

"What, you mean like 'sweetie pie'—that sort of thing?"

"Oh God, much worse, Pomie! Stuff like... like... poopykins or something like that."

Pomona roared with laughter. "'Poopykins'? You've gotta be kidding me."

"Well, okay, maybe not that one—but something very similar. I'm not kidding. But the point is—the names were bordering on the ridiculous. It wasn't 'darling' or 'sweetheart', you know, the kind of thing you hear most people using. So... what are the chances that someone else who made Dr Nichols his chocolates would also use ridiculous pet names like that?"

Understanding dawned on Pomona's face. "You think... you think *Sir Henry's wife* sent the doctor those chocolates?" Her eyes gleamed. "Ahhh... they're having an affair!"

Caitlyn frowned. "Well... I don't know if we can jump to that conclusion."

"Why not? Come on, why else would she call herself '*your Ticklewickle*'? That doesn't sound like a normal doctor-patient relationship to me."

"Well, maybe... I don't know, maybe it's a joke or something... Or maybe she has a crush on him but we don't know if he returns her feelings."

"Did he look guilty?"

Caitlyn remembered the young doctor's flushed

face as he'd snatched the card out of her hands. "Yeah, he did, actually."

"They're having an affair," said Pomona. "Trust me, I know these things."

"You know..." Caitlyn thought back to the dinner party. "I just remembered that night at dinner, Sir Henry complained that his wife was always having migraines and the doctor was always coming over to their house for various things."

"There, you see?" said Pomona triumphantly. "She could just make up some medical condition every time and get her lover to come over, see her in her room, examine her in private... it's, like, the perfect excuse!"

Caitlyn gave her cousin a startled look. "They wouldn't be... you know... in her own house? With Sir Henry there?"

Pomona laughed. "You're such an innocent, Caitlyn. Why not? I'll bet that's part of the thrill—doing it right under her husband's nose. And he's probably, like, one of these old-fashioned English types... you know, where the couple don't share a bedroom... she's got her own suite and he's got his. It's the perfect set-up." Pomona leaned forwards excitedly. "And you know what? This gives her a motive to murder Sir Henry as well! I mean, you can't tell me that she married him for love. She must have been at least twenty years younger than him."

"That doesn't mean anything. There are people

who fall in love with someone much older than themselves," argued Caitlyn. "And she did seem to be really grieving his death."

Pomona gave a cynical laugh. "Sheesh, you're such a romantic! Yeah, I guess there are genuine happy marriages with a big age gap... but not in this case, honey. I'm telling you, Lady Pritchard married Sir Henry for his money."

Caitlyn frowned. "But the thing is, I don't think she gains a lot of money from his death—his brother inherits most of the estate."

They heard the Widow Mags calling them again from downstairs. Caitlyn suddenly realised that it was well past lunchtime and she was starving.

"We'd better go down," she said, getting to her feet. She folded up the parchment again and slid it under her pillow. "I'll look for the hag stone later. I think it's fallen into one of the cracks between the floorboards and I might need to shift the bed to get to it. But it'll be safe down there under the bed anyway."

CHAPTER TWENTY-FIVE

As it turned out, there was a sudden rush of customers after lunch: a big coach of Asian tourists had arrived in the village, and they were followed by more local visitors and residents of nearby towns, all keen on seeing the village with the "Black Shuck murders" that was being talked about so much in the press. The girls were kept busy boxing truffles, recommending chocolate bars, serving fudge brownies and fresh strawberries, and ladling out mugs of homemade hot chocolate all afternoon, whilst the Widow Mags stayed in the kitchen, tempering, mixing, melting, and moulding to meet the extra demand.

Caitlyn didn't manage to find a free moment to call the police until mid-afternoon and she was disappointed to learn that Inspector Walsh was away busy and couldn't come to the phone.

"You can relay the information to me," said the sergeant in a bored voice.

"I really wanted to talk to Inspector Walsh. Do you know when he'll be free?"

"No idea. He's in the interview room at the moment and could be there until evening."

"Is he questioning someone in relation to Sir Henry's murder?"

"That information is confidential, miss."

"But I need to know if he's questioning Derek Swanes or Julian Pritchard! If he is, I have information that could be crucial to the case. Please, can't you at least tell me that?"

There was a moment's hesitation on the other end of the line, then the sergeant said grudgingly, "No, he's not questioning those two men, but that's all I can tell you. Now, you can either give me the information and I will pass it on to Inspector Walsh, or you can call back tomorrow. I wouldn't try again today—the inspector's going to be tied up for a while."

What's going on? What is Inspector Walsh so busy with? Caitlyn wondered. She shifted her weight from foot to foot as she debated what to do. Somehow, it didn't feel right to hold back the information about Swanes and Julian Pritchard, just so she could speak to Inspector Walsh herself. It was too important to the investigation. Reluctantly, she gave the sergeant a quick account of seeing the two men together and their overheard conversation. But to her surprise, he showed no excitement or even curiosity over the information.

"That all?" he said, still in that bored voice.

"Yes... but did you understand what I said?" asked Caitlyn. "This could be proof that they were plotting to murder Sir Henry. It's the best lead yet on the case! Inspector Walsh needs to be told this at once. I know he's already questioned Swanes—I don't know if he's questioned Julian Pritchard—but he needs to find them both at once and question them about their alibis for that night."

"*Ahem*—we do not need members of the public telling us how to run our investigations," said the sergeant frostily. "As I said, I will pass this information on to the inspector and he will act as he sees fit. Thank you for calling."

Caitlyn hung up with a sigh of frustration, but there was nothing else she could do. She would just have to try and put it out of her mind for now. She could always call the station again tomorrow—perhaps first thing—and try to speak to Inspector Walsh then. Feeling cheered, she went back out to the front of the cottage, to rejoin Pomona in the shop. She found her cousin busily dealing with a queue of people all wanting to choose truffles from the display beneath the glass counter.

"I hate to say this..." said Pomona with a grin as she grabbed the tongs and began filling another box with chocolate truffles, "... but murder is great for business!"

Nibs was delighted as well, scampering around the shop, getting under everyone's feet and cheekily approaching every customer to say hello. Normally, Caitlyn tried to keep the kitten at the back of the cottage, but with things being so hectic, she soon gave up constantly trying to keep the naughty ball of fluff out of the shop. None of the customers were complaining about him anyway—if anything, most of them seemed to love him, fussing over him and obviously thinking that the "little black witch's cat" just added to the charm of the "enchanted chocolate shop".

It wasn't until the shop had closed for the day and Pomona had left to return to the Manor that Caitlyn realised she hadn't seen Nibs around for a while. He wasn't in the shop anywhere, and when she went into the kitchen, where the Widow Mags was carefully wrapping up some leftover ingredients to be stored in the fridge, she couldn't find the kitten anywhere either.

"Have you seen Nibs?" she asked the old witch.

The Widow Mags paused in what she was doing. "He was in here a few minutes ago..." She nodded towards the open door that led to the garden at the back of the cottage. "He's likely out in the garden."

Caitlyn cast a worried glance outside. She couldn't see the little kitten in the flowerbeds but she noticed that the back gate was slightly ajar. Nibs had been getting bolder and bolder lately, often leaving the cottage garden and venturing into the forest. There was so much in there to keep an inquisitive kitten occupied. With the long summer days, it was still a few hours until sunset; nevertheless, she didn't like the idea of the little cat being out alone in the woods.

"I think I'd better go and look for him," she said.

Soon, she was back on the familiar path leading through the trees—the same one she had been walking on the night before, when she had met the Black Shuck... just before James and Nathan had appeared. She found herself hoping that the ghostly hound hadn't been hurt in the fracas, then laughed at her thoughts. How could a demon dog be hurt? She should've been more worried about any humans getting hurt! In fact, come to think of it, Professor Thrope had been extremely lucky not to have been shot by mistake. The cryptozoologist always seemed to be turning up in the strangest places—which she supposed was part of his job. Still, he was lucky he hadn't been hurt so far, if not by the monsters he was chasing, then by the humans hunting the monsters!

A rustling in the undergrowth made her suddenly pause and peer through the bushes.

"Nibs? Nibs, is that you?"

"Mew!"

"Nibs... what are you doing there?"

There was no reply from the kitten. Caitlyn sighed and left the path, climbing in through the tangled undergrowth and crouching down to look for the kitten amongst the shrubbery.

"Nibs?"

Something dark moved behind a bush. Caitlyn was about to shout a gleeful "Aha! Gotcha!" and reach out to grab the kitten, when the leaves parted and she found herself staring into a pair of glowing red eyes.

She jerked backwards in alarm. It was the Black Shuck! She had never seen the phantom hound out in daylight before—although it was fairly dim here in the forest, so it was still well concealed.

"*Mew?*" A little ball of black fur suddenly popped out of the undergrowth a few feet from the Black Shuck. Nibs mewed again in delight at seeing her and started towards her. Then the kitten froze as he saw the dog.

The huge black hound lowered its shaggy head towards the kitten and Caitlyn held her breath. Would it harm Nibs? The black muzzle moved closer and closer... Then suddenly there was a hiss and the sound of spitting, followed by a growl of pain as the Black Shuck jerked back. It pawed its muzzle and Caitlyn saw three parallel lines of red, as if a tiny claw had swiped across the dog's nose. Nibs must have scratched it! The next moment, the Black Shuck turned with a soft whine and retreated, disappearing deeper into the undergrowth.

"*Mew!*" said Nibs, scampering up to Caitlyn.

She scooped the kitten up and checked him over: he seemed to be unharmed. In fact, it looked like it was the Black Shuck who had retreated with its tail between its legs. *The terrible demon hound terrorised by a little kitten*, thought Caitlyn with a smile.

Carrying Nibs securely in her arms, she walked swiftly back to the cottage. Inside, she found the Widow Mags sitting at the wooden table in the kitchen, sorting through some cocoa beans.

The old witch glanced up and said: "So you found him?"

"Yes... and I saw the Black Shuck!" said Caitlyn breathlessly.

The Widow Mags raised her eyebrows but said nothing, as if waiting for her to continue. Caitlyn hesitated a moment, then told her grandmother about her three encounters with the legendary phantom hound. It was a relief to finally be able to tell someone. She had wanted to tell Pomona several times but had always held back. She didn't know why—after all, Pomona believed in the paranormal more easily and passionately than anyone else. And she knew her cousin would never have laughed or scoffed at her suggestion that the Black Shuck was more playful canine than predatory monster. Still, Caitlyn had felt somehow reluctant to share her personal experiences. Now, though, she told the Widow Mags everything.

"Why do you think it keeps appearing?" she asked the old witch. "I mean, I just can't believe that it's involved in these murders... and yet it's true that the sightings only started around the time that the tramp was first found dead."

"Perhaps you should think about other coincidences."

"What do you mean?"

"The deaths of the tramp and of Sir Henry are not the only things that occurred at the same time as the appearance of the Black Shuck. There are other coincidences too—other simultaneous appearances."

"Simultaneous appearances?" Caitlyn frowned. "I don't understand..."

"Who else arrived in Tillyhenge at the same time as these sightings began?"

"Well... I don't know... there are several tourists and local visitors who come every day—I can't know them all... and then there's James's guests up at the Manor—Nathan and Professor Thrope—and Pomona, of course..." She shook her head. "But what do any of them have to do with the Black Shuck?"

The Widow Mags gave her a thoughtful look. "More than you realise. However, I understand what it is like to need to keep an identity secret and I shall respect that by saying no more."

And she refused to be drawn further, no matter how much Caitlyn cajoled and begged. Instead, she poured the beans into a small jute sack and secured it, then gestured to the pile of similar sacks and said briskly:

"I'm taking these over to Bertha—she's trying a new range of cocoa bean soaps. Perhaps you can help me carry them."

Obligingly, Caitlyn helped the Widow Mags shut up the chocolate shop, then followed her through the winding cobbled lanes to the other side of Tillyhenge, where Bertha's shop, *Herbal Enchantments*, was situated. Her aunt was just closing up the store as they arrived and she smiled at them as they walked in.

"Ah... the cocoa beans for the new soap! Thank you, Mother... Evie, dear, can you take them?"

"Ooh, Mum, can I have some?" asked Evie, hurrying out to collect the jute bags. "I found this brilliant spell online which helps you tap into the ancient magic of *Theobroma cacao*; they say it's really powerful for 'happiness spells' and even—" Her cheeks reddened. "—to sweeten another person's heart... and you can make a 'mojo bag' with it too! You just need to combine a cocoa bean with a pinch of borage and seven allspice berries, and put them all in a red flannel bag—"

"A 'mojo bag'? Whoever heard of such nonsense!" said Bertha. "Evie, how many times have I told you not to believe the things you read about magic online? There's all sorts of rubbish on the internet! People who have no real knowledge of what they're talking about, publishing all sorts of ludicrous spells and potion recipes—"

"I think the real magic is how you managed to get on the internet in Tillyhenge," said Caitlyn with a laugh. "I can't get reception on my phone half the time."

"The black spot over the village comes and goes," said Evie. "You get used to it if you live here. You just keep trying until you get through eventually."

"Well, I personally think it's a good thing in a way—forces you young people to go to a library, once in a while," said Bertha as she walked over to the shop door and flipped the sign from "OPEN" to "CLOSED".

"I didn't realise the shop opened so late," commented Caitlyn, watching her aunt.

"Well, we don't normally, but as I was about to close up, this poor chap appeared with the most dreadful scratch on his nose... Professor-something-or-other..." Bertha glanced at her daughter and smiled. "Evie said he's a guest at the Manor and that she met him the night she was at the dinner party."

Caitlyn stared at her aunt. "Professor Thrope?"

"Yes, that's right," said Bertha. "Anyway, I couldn't just leave him like that when he was obviously in so much discomfort. So I let him in and found some herbal salve for him to put on the scratches."

"Did he say how he got them?" Caitlyn asked breathlessly.

"Well, he said he fell down in the woods and

265

scratched his face on some brambles..." Bertha frowned. "Although I must say, I'd never seen bramble scratches look like that. They were so straight—almost parallel, you know—and if I didn't know better, I'd have thought that they were scratches from a cat or the claws of some other small animal."

Caitlyn felt her mind spinning as she struggled to accept a shocking idea. But it was all there: the strange way the cryptozoologist had always appeared after a Black Shuck sighting, his passionate insistence that the demon dog meant no harm, his strong aversion to chocolate... She glanced up and met the Widow Mags's eyes, and remembered what the old witch had said back in the chocolate shop kitchen: *"...who else arrived in Tillyhenge at the same time as these sightings began... other simultaneous appearances... I understand what it is like to need to keep an identity secret..."*

"Where is Professor Thrope now?" she asked Bertha.

"Oh... I suppose he's walking back to the Manor."

"He's taken Dead Man's Walk," Evie said with a shiver. "Even though Mum told him not to."

Bertha gave a helpless shrug. "Well, I can see why he would want to—it *is* the quickest way back, since it cuts through the woods at the back of the village, past the Pritchard estate and then through

Fitzroy land, before leading into town. And he did tell me that he's walked that path several times and knows it very well. It's just that... well, what with these recent deaths and the sightings of the Black Shuck, I think it's too—"

Caitlyn was out the door before her aunt had finished. She dashed down the lane, past the rows of thatched cottages, until she came to where the street petered out into a clearing at the edge of the forest. She knew that this end of the village—the opposite to where the chocolate shop was—backed onto the woods which surrounded the Pritchard estate, and the path which started here—the notorious Dead Man's Walk—led eventually to the track that she and Evie had been walking on the night of the dinner party.

Dusk was falling and she cursed her own stupidity for not grabbing a torch before leaving Bertha's shop. Well, there wasn't time to go back now, and in any case, she was sure Professor Thrope wouldn't have gone far. She was too impatient to confront him and find out if her extraordinary idea could be true. She started briskly down the path and she hadn't been walking five minutes when she saw the cryptozoologist's figure ahead of her.

"Professor! Professor Thrope!"

He turned. "Ah... Miss Le Fey..."

She paused, panting, in front of him. In the gathering dark, she noticed that he had a white bandage across his nose. He shifted uneasily as he saw her eyes on it.

"Er... what a coincidence—are you walking up to the Manor too?" he said brightly.

Caitlyn hesitated. Now that she was here, facing him, she wasn't sure how to broach the subject. She glanced at the bandage again and said, "Um... what happened to your nose, Professor?"

"Oh... this...?" He gave a forced laugh. "I... er... fell down when I was exploring in the woods this afternoon. There were some prickly bushes about and—"

"That's not really what happened, is it?" Caitlyn interrupted gently.

"Er... what... what do you mean?" he stammered.

"That scratch wasn't from a bush—it was from a little black kitten... *My* kitten, Nibs... I know, because I was there." She took a deep breath and said in a rush, "You're the Black Shuck, aren't you?"

CHAPTER TWENTY-SIX

Professor Thrope stared at her with an expression of mingled horror and panic. For a moment, Caitlyn thought he was going to vehemently deny it. Then his shoulders slumped and he said with a sigh:

"So you have discovered my secret."

"I should have seen it earlier—I don't know why I didn't! The way you always seemed to conveniently appear, 'chasing' the Black Shuck after it was seen... and the way you always refused to eat any chocolate: the night at the dinner party, and then again last night, with the hot chocolate drinks... it's because chocolate is poisonous to dogs, isn't it? That's why you spat out the drink!"

He looked sheepish. "Yes. I would have had a hard time explaining things if I ended up in hospital with theobromine poisoning. But it's usually quite easy to avoid chocolate, actually. And very early on, I discovered that the easiest way to explain my presence near the Black Shuck was to pretend that I was hunting for it. That way, I'd always have a ready-made excuse when people saw the ghostly dog... and then saw me soon after."

"Yeah, you were very good at it," said Caitlyn. "The way you always immediately said 'Have you seen it?' or something similar."

Professor Thrope gave a sad smile. "I have had years of practice. Why do you think I became a cryptozoologist? Sometimes the easiest way to hide is in plain sight, and by becoming a 'monster hunter', I could conceal my connection to my 'other self'. With my profession, nobody questioned why I was always dabbling in the supernatural."

"Can't you just not become your 'other self'?"

The professor sighed. "I wish it were that simple, my dear. You see, the curse of the Black Shuck has always run in my family. I am not the first—those stories of the big black dog from all over Britain are probably all sightings of various members of my family, my ancestors. And we have never had control over when the shape-shifting occurs. In a sense, it is like someone who suffers from migraines or seizures: they can just come over you with no warning, and you can go for long spells with no trouble, and then suddenly be prone to several attacks."

"Are you aware when you are the... the hound?"

"Not really. I mean, I have a hazy memory of things when I 'wake up' again as myself afterwards. It's almost like a dream, you know—some parts are incredibly vivid. For example, I can remember flashes from the night the tramp was killed... seeing him walking along the path... the way the moonlight shone on his face... the funny mushroom-shaped chocolates he was eating... seeing him stagger and collapse into a bramble bush... the way his head lolled back as I grabbed his arm with my teeth and—"

"Wait... if you can see all that... how do you know that *you're* not the one who killed him?" asked Caitlyn uneasily.

"No, no, the Black Shuck—I—would never harm anyone!" cried the professor. "I was grabbing his arm to try and drag him to someone for help. He was unconscious but still alive then, and I was trying to save him. It was the same with Sir Henry. But they were both too heavy—and they died before I managed to get very far. I had to leave them on the path."

"So that was the reason for those strange bruises on their arms, in the shape of teeth," Caitlyn said, recalling the police report.

He nodded. "It is part of the curse. When I am the hound, I feel compelled to find those at risk and guard them from harm. It is something I cannot control. Sometimes I wonder if that is what triggers the shifting—when there is imminent danger to someone nearby. And then it is as if an obsession comes over me and I cannot rest until I have found the person. I walk alongside them and try to stay with them, until the threat has passed." He sighed. "But often, the very person whom I am trying to protect is frightened of my canine form and thinks that *I* am the threat."

"It's hard not to be scared when people see the Black Shuck," said Caitlyn.

He gave her a sad smile. "It is the most terrible irony! I have often wondered why I can't shift into a unicorn or some other beautiful creature—one which has a reputation for benevolence—so I can do my duty better. But no, the curse dictates that I change into a huge black dog with glowing red eyes, a monstrous form which scares the very people I'm trying to protect. So sometimes they run from me and I fail to protect them... and sometimes I am forced to shift back into my human form before I am able to complete my mission—"

"Last night!" said Caitlyn. "That's what happened, wasn't it? When I saw you, you were on your way to that girl—the one who got attacked by the gang. That's why you looked so anxious. But then James and Nathan arrived and prevented you from going to her—"

"Yes," said the professor heavily. "I was forced to change and I could not argue with them without arousing suspicion. And in any case, in my human form, I do not have a clear idea of where to go, whom to protect... it is only when I am the Black Shuck and something—some instinct—tells me where to go. So I had to abandon my mission." He grimaced. "When I heard the news about the girl this morning, I felt dreadful. I had failed her. Perhaps I ought to have tried harder."

"You can't protect everyone out there," said Caitlyn gently. "You can't blame yourself. And you did save the girl last week, didn't you? The night that Sir Henry was killed, a girl was also attacked by this gang, but she got away because they were scared off by something. I remember Inspector Walsh saying he questioned that girl and she was rambling about 'glowing red eyes'... that was you, wasn't it?"

He had a grim look of satisfaction. "Yes, I was successful that time."

"Well, you saved her. And I'm sure you saved Mrs Parsons's niece—Evie said she told everyone the Black Shuck had walked alongside her when she was taking a shortcut through a field on the way home. So you've done lots of good! Don't be so hard on yourself."

The cryptozoologist gave her another sad smile. "Thank you, my dear... I only wish I could have done more to save those men." Then he took a deep breath and straightened his shoulders. "Now, can I offer you my protection and escort you to the Manor?"

"Oh, no, that's okay. I'm not going there, actually. I only came down this path to talk to you. I'll go back to the village now... Don't worry, it's only five minutes—I'll be fine."

"Very well. I will see you tomorrow then, perhaps... And... er... I wonder if I might ask you—"

"I'll keep your secret, Professor."

He smiled at her. "Thank you."

Caitlyn gave him a wave, then started retracing her steps back to the village. She thought of what he had said... the burden of carrying such a noble curse... the strangeness of being a different form of yourself... and having those vivid scraps of memory afterwards...

She frowned.

What was it Professor Thrope had said about the tramp? He had been describing what he saw: *"I can remember flashes from the night the tramp was killed... seeing him walking along the path... the way the moonlight shone on his face... the funny mushroom-shaped chocolates he was eating..."*

Caitlyn stopped walking. Professor Thrope's voice rang in her ears: *"mushroom-shaped chocolates"*. Toadstools were a kind of mushroom. In fact, they were the kind most commonly depicted in books and paintings, because of their cute appearance: the traditional image of a fairy sitting on a pretty red mushroom with white spots. They were also the type most commonly copied in arts and crafts, the kind that would be used for candy designs and chocolates moulds...

Could it have just been a coincidence? *No*, she decided. The Widow Mags had said that it was unusual to find chocolate moulds in that shape—it certainly wasn't the kind of thing that would be easily found in a shop here in the Cotswolds.

What were the chances that someone else had made mushroom-shaped chocolates?

So slim as to be not worth considering. Which meant that Lady Pritchard had made the chocolates that the tramp had been eating the night he died—the very same chocolates which had contained the digitalis poison. And yet she had denied ever seeing him. Caitlyn clearly remembered the way the woman had shook her head firmly and denied that the tramp had ever been on the Pritchard estate.

Why had she lied?

Because she can't afford for anyone to find out that she gave the tramp those poisoned chocolates.

Caitlyn's head swam as she realised where her thoughts were leading: *Lady Pritchard is the murderer.*

CHAPTER TWENTY-SEVEN

Caitlyn thought back to that night at the dinner party... yes, she remembered now! Lady Pritchard had pushed her plate of chocolates towards her husband as she had complained of a migraine. It would have been easy for her to conceal her own chocolates amidst the pile of bonbons that Sir Henry had heaped on her plate, and after she'd left, he would have eaten them, together with the others, and no one would have noticed. Meanwhile, she was safely tucked up in a guest room at the Manor, her alibi secure, as her husband collapsed and died on the walk home.

And then the next day... Caitlyn thought again of the woman's pale face and haggard appearance, with the dark shadows under the eyes and the listless manner. But what was it that Julian

Pritchard had said? He had sneered about his sister-in-law: *"I knew her when she was plain Sherry Holt. She's nothing more than a small-time actress who landed on her feet because she met my brother in some pub and he took a fancy to her. She only ever married him for the money..."*

If Lady Pritchard had been an actress, she would have been experienced with the use of make-up to create a desired image; it would have been easy for her to present the illusion of a grieving widow to the world—not just in the way she looked but also in the way she walked and talked... all she had to do was use her acting skills and theatrical experience to her advantage!

And furthermore, the woman had subtly dropped hints and made insinuations about the estate manager and about her brother-in-law, setting each one up to be a suspect. Oh yes, she had played her part perfectly! Her wide-eyed fear about the Black Shuck and then her supposed shock over her husband's murder; her innocent remarks about Julian Pritchard inheriting most of the estate, and her account of Swanes having a fight with her husband...

She had been clever. She never made a direct accusation and even pretended to defend the other men; for example, when she protested that Swanes was unlikely to hold a grudge since he'd returned to see Sir Henry the day of the dinner party. But while she was doing so, she made sure that everyone knew Swanes had brought Sir Henry a bottle of his favourite sherry—the perfect vehicle to poison him with...

Caitlyn blinked and came out of her thoughts to find herself standing in the middle of the path, with her fists clenched and her breathing rapid. Slowly, she unclenched her hands and wondered what she should do. She could go to the police with her theory... but it was late now and Inspector Walsh had probably gone home. She doubted that the station would contact him unless it was an emergency. She also wasn't sure she wanted to go to him without more concrete leads. Especially as— she winced as she remembered—she had just left a message for him earlier, insisting that Julian Pritchard and Derek Swanes were responsible for Sir Henry's murder. If she rang the station again now, contradicting herself with a different accusation, they would think she was either mad or playing a prank.

Besides, it would be her word against Lady Pritchard's and she had a bad feeling that she wouldn't win. The sympathies of everyone in the village were very much with Sir Henry's widow at the moment, whereas Caitlyn knew that because of her own connection to the Widow Mags and the recent, nasty scenes with Mrs Gibbs, many people viewed her with suspicion and distrust.

I need to confirm that Lady Pritchard really has a chocolate mould in the shape of toadstools. Just guessing that she was the one who gave the box of bonbons to Dr Nichols, based on that card, isn't enough—I need to see the mould in her house. And I also need to check that the chocolates that the tramp had been eating were made using the same mould, she thought. She had to speak to Professor Thrope again and ask him if he could remember more details of what the tramp's chocolates had looked like. He had only said "mushroom-shaped". She needed to know if they had been *toadstool* mushrooms.

Whirling, Caitlyn hurried up the path again. Twilight had really fallen now and it was hard to make out shapes in the increasing gloom. Then she saw him up ahead: he had left the path and was bent over some bushes at the side of the track.

"Professor Thrope! Professor—" Caitlyn broke off as she neared the figure and realised that it wasn't the cryptozoologist at all. "*Viktor!* What are you doing here?"

The old vampire straightened and said grouchily, "Looking for my fangs, of course! Confounded dentist—if only he had done his job... I told him they were not attached properly. I have been searching for two days, going all over the place... I've even been over to the neighbouring estate—"

"To Pritchard House?"

"Yes, and I must say, they have a terrific orchard there: apples and pears and even cherries—yes, proper English Morello cherries!—I simply had to stop and sample some. The apples were a bit early season but not bad at all... mmm, and the plums!" He smacked his sunken lips. "Wonderful, juicy red ones... Silly woman was turning them into plum chutney—they should be eaten fresh! Went in to tell her, you know, and was she grateful? Oh no, she had the audacity to call me a thieving old tramp and tell me to get out of the kitchen! Really! The nerve of some people—"

"Wait, Viktor... you went into the kitchen at Pritchard House?" Caitlyn suddenly had an idea. "Did you see any chocolate moulds while you were there?"

"Eh? Mould? What mould? There's no mould on the fruit if you pick them fresh and keep them clean."

"Never mind..." Caitlyn was thinking rapidly. If she could get into Lady Pritchard's kitchen and find a mould that had the exact outline of those toadstool-shaped chocolate bonbons, it would be the first piece of proof.

"Listen, Viktor—do you think you can remember where the kitchen is?"

"Of course I remember," the old vampire blustered. "Nothing wrong with my memory, I assure you—"

"Great. Can you take me there? Now?"

Still grumbling about his missing fangs, Viktor started to lead the way. Luckily, the moon was high in the sky, and although it was on the wane and no longer a perfect silver sphere, it was still putting out a strong enough glow to see by. Caitlyn remembered that Bertha had said Dead Man's Walk would pass right beside the Pritchard estate, before crossing into Fitzroy land—it was why it had been used by Sir Henry as a shortcut—and she wasn't surprised when, after several minutes, she saw a smaller track branch out and disappear into the trees on their right. Viktor turned and shuffled off down the offshoot and Caitlyn hurriedly followed. A few minutes later, she found herself stepping out onto the edge of a manicured lawn. They had come out just beside Pritchard House.

It was not as large and grand as Huntingdon Manor, of course, although it was still an impressive country house. It had probably once been a big farmhouse, which had been extended and modernised. They were facing the back of it, and what had once been the old kitchen or herb gardens had been re-landscaped in a formal style, with squares of grass and neat hedging between paved pathways. The largest section of lawn—the one they were standing beside—curved around the house and disappeared out of sight at the front.

"The kitchen is there, at the rear," said Viktor, pointing to a pair of double windows which were brightly lit.

Ducking low, Caitlyn scooted across the gardens until she came to the ornamental hedge closest to the house. She followed this as it circled around the side of the building, pausing when she heard a familiar voice coming from an open window. Slowly, she looked over the top of the neatly clipped hedge.

Viktor's bald head popped up next to hers and he peered myopically over the hedge as well. On the other side was a wide terrace which ran along the side the house. And leading onto the terrace was a pair of French windows. They were partially open and looked into a large sitting room, with a marble mantelpiece around a traditional fireplace and a three-piece sofa suite upholstered in expensive floral fabric. They could hear a woman talking on the phone and it was a familiar voice that Caitlyn recognised: Lady Pritchard.

"...thank you for the condolences, Mrs Gordon-Smitherington... Yes... yes... it has been very hard but I'm bearing up as best I can... No, the police have not released the body yet, I'm afraid... No, they haven't told me... yes... part of the investigation... No, not at all... Thank you... It was really very kind of you to call... yes, I will... Goodbye."

A minute later, Sir Henry's widow came into view. Caitlyn was struck by the change in her. Gone was the pale, broken woman with shadowed eyes and despondent manner; in her place was an attractive blonde with healthy, pink, flushed cheeks and bright blue eyes, who laughed cynically to herself as she walked over to the French windows. She made as if to close them, then changed her mind and stepped out onto the terrace.

Caitlyn froze. If Lady Pritchard came around the hedge, she was bound to see them! But to her relief, the woman walked along the terrace to the front of the house. She disappeared from view around the corner. Caitlyn bit her lip. It was risky to sneak into the kitchen now when she couldn't see what the woman was doing and didn't know if she might come back any minute. On the other hand, the longer they stayed huddled here, the greater the likelihood that they might be discovered too.

She turned to the old vampire by her side. "Viktor—listen, you stay here. I'm going back to the kitchen—I'll be really quick." She cast a worried glance towards the front of the house. "I just hope she doesn't come back while I'm in there—"

"Fear not!" said Viktor, pulling himself to his full height. "I shall go and divert her."

"Uh, no, no, Viktor, I don't think that's a good idea—"

"Oho! You doubt my abilities, do you? You do not realise how skilled I am in the art of subterfuge! The finesse of deception! The command of artifice! The flair of—"

"Er... yes, I get the idea..." said Caitlyn. "But I still think you shouldn't—I mean, it's not that I don't believe you'd be great at it—" She broke off as she realised that she was talking to empty air. "Viktor? Viktor?"

She whirled to see the old vampire tottering determinedly towards the front of the house.

"Viktor! Wait!"

He disappeared around the corner.

Great. Caitlyn sighed, wondering if she should run after him. Then she decided that if Viktor was going to provide a distraction anyway, she would be stupid not to take advantage of it. She slipped back to the kitchen window. A quick glance over the windowsill told her that there was no one inside, and she reached up to swing the casement out farther, grateful that the warm summer evenings meant that windows had been left open everywhere. She hitched herself up and over the window edge, rolling in and sitting on the counter for a moment, before jumping down into the middle of the room.

It was a modern kitchen, all cold marble and gleaming chrome, which was slightly at odds with the country look of the outside of the house. Still, it meant that the kitchen units followed the standard pattern and Caitlyn was able to easily find the baking equipment stored in the large bottom drawer next to the pantry. She crouched down and, as quietly as she could, lifted out various baking trays, cake tins, loaf pans, and cooling racks... And then her eyes lit up. Piled at the bottom of the drawer was an assortment of cupcake liners, spatulas, whisks, piping bags, and nozzles... and a silicone mould tray.

Caitlyn grabbed this eagerly. *Aha!* She held it up, turning it this way and that in the light to see it more clearly. Yes, each cavity showed the outline of a little toadstool mushroom, complete with spots etched on its domed top.

A noise outside the kitchen made her stiffen. Was someone approaching? She strained her ears to listen. No. It must have been a false alarm. Still, she was nervous now and she hastily began to return everything to the drawer. Then her ears caught another sound: a familiar cranky old voice raised in indignation. *Viktor!* She could hear a female voice too, arguing with him, getting shriller and shriller. She groaned inwardly. What was going on?

She rushed to the window and swung herself out, then ran alongside the hedge until she reached the front of the house. There she found Viktor splayed against the open front door, his arms and legs spread-eagled, barring the way for a plump, middle-aged woman in an apron, who was trying to get back in. She was diving left and then right, trying to push past him, her face purple with indignation.

"I don't know what you're playing at! Let me pass, you crazy old loon!" she shouted, tugging ineffectually at Viktor's bony shoulders. "If you don't move aside, I am going to call the police!"

"Ahh... unhand me, madam... you shall not pass!" cried Viktor, bracing his scrawny form against the doorframe. "Even the great troll armies could not overcome me when I was defending Glastonbury Abbey—did you think a loud-mouthed shrew like you could—"

"Shrew?" the woman shrieked. "Who are you calling a shrew, you miserable, demented—"

"Viktor!" Caitlyn hissed. "*What are you doing?*"

"Eh?" The old vampire looked up and saw her.

He stepped aside suddenly, out of the woman's way, causing her to plunge forwards into the open doorway. There was a crash and the sound of breaking china, followed by a stream of shrill, angry exclamations. Caitlyn winced as Viktor tottered over to join her. She grabbed him and retreated around the house, until they were a safe distance away, tucked up against the hedge.

"What were you doing?" Caitlyn demanded.

The old vampire sniffed and said importantly, "I was distracting Lady Pritchard, as we discussed."

"Yes, but that wasn't Lady Pritchard," Caitlyn said in exasperation. "That was probably her housekeeper..."

"Eh?" Viktor blinked owlishly. "Are you certain? She looked just like the woman in the sitting room."

Argh. Caitlyn clutched her face in her hand. She should have remembered that she couldn't rely on Viktor's eyesight. "Never mind... I suppose Lady Pritchard must have gone upstairs or something. The important thing is, nobody saw me in the kitchen and I—"

She broke off as she looked down and realised that she was still clutching the silicone mould. *Oh no!* In her panic to leave the kitchen, she had forgotten to shove it back into the drawer, along with everything else, and had inadvertently taken it with her when she rushed out. Did she dare climb back into the kitchen to return it? She looked at the house again. She could still hear the housekeeper ranting from somewhere inside. In fact, the shrill voice seemed to be moving towards the rear of the house—the woman was probably heading to the kitchen. It would be crazy to return now. But if she didn't put the mould back, how could the police find it in Lady Pritchard's kitchen?

She sighed in frustration. "Rats!"

"...hmm? Rats? No, I doubt it—they wouldn't be interested in teeth," said Viktor. "No, no, I'm sure they dropped out of my mouth."

Caitlyn looked at him blankly, then realised that he was talking about his lost fangs again.

"In fact, I think I must have dropped them the night I was feasting on those marvellous red currants—"

"You mean the night of the Fitzroy dinner party," Caitlyn said. "When Evie and I were lost and we met you."

"Yes, that's right... the bush was alongside the path and I suppose the fangs could have dropped out as I was walking along... although I have been up and down several times already and I still haven't seen them."

He sounded so forlorn that Caitlyn felt sorry for him. Putting her own impatience temporarily aside, she said:

"What about the red currant bush itself? Did you look under there? If you were eating berries from it, chances are the fangs might have fallen out there and might be under—"

"Yes, yes, I looked there first, of course, but there was nothing under the bush, other than those silly chocolates—"

"Chocolates?" Caitlyn gripped Viktor's arm. "What do you mean? How could there be chocolates under the bush?"

"Well, I suppose they might have rolled under there. I saw some similar ones on the path nearby. Maybe somebody dropped them..."

"Oh my God—yes!" cried Caitlyn, gripping Viktor's arm. "Professor Thrope told me that he saw the tramp eating chocolates and then suddenly stagger and collapse. If the tramp had flailed around, the rest of the bonbons would have scattered everywhere. And if your red currant bush was nearby, the chocolates could have easily rolled under..."

She trailed off as she thought of something else. She looked down at the mould she was holding. This was good evidence but it didn't prove to the police that the chocolates which poisoned the tramp could have come from Lady Pritchard's kitchen. The only reason she knew that was because of Professor Thrope, who had seen it when he was the Black Shuck. Somehow, she didn't think that Inspector

Walsh would take her seriously if she insisted that her information about the tramp's chocolates came from a ghostly dog's vision!

But if she could find one of the chocolates left by the tramp and match it to the mould in her hand...

She turned eagerly to the old vampire. "Are the chocolates still there, Viktor? When did you see them?" She shook her head impatiently. "Never mind, can you show me where this bush is?"

CHAPTER TWENTY-EIGHT

Looking slightly bewildered by her request, the old vampire led her back to Dead Man's Walk and shuffled along it until they came to a large, sprawling bush at the side of the path, covered in berries which gleamed like pearls in the moonlight. Caitlyn dropped the mould she had been carrying and knelt down to peer underneath the bush, pushing the weeds aside. There were dead leaves, curled and brown, fallen berries in the process of rotting, pebbles and rocks, and an empty snail shell... but she couldn't see anything that remotely resembled chocolates. Caitlyn felt a stab of disappointment. *Well, what did you expect?* she told herself. It had been over a week since the tramp had been found, and even if some chocolates had rolled under here, they would have long been since eaten by animals or insects... or simply decomposed.

Then she saw something. She squinted, trying to get down lower. *Is that...?* There was something lodged against the very base of the bush, next to the trunk. The moonlight didn't penetrate well through the branches and it was hard to see clearly... but whatever it was, it looked very round—too perfectly round to be a stone. Caitlyn hunched down and stretched her right arm under the bush. But she could only grope blindly.

"What *are* you doing?" came Viktor's querulous voice.

"There's something—something very round—at the base of the bush, just beside the main stem. I think it might be a chocolate bonbon... but I can't reach it—"

"Ah, why didn't you say so before? Stand back!"

Caitlyn sat up and turned to see that Viktor had shifted into his bat form. Instead of the stooped old man in the ancient black suit, there was now a fuzzy brown fruit bat with fox-like ears, a pointy nose, and big black eyes. It squeaked importantly as it hopped towards the bush and Caitlyn moved back to let it crawl under the spreading branches. There was a rustling, more squeaks—grumbling this time—and a few minutes later, the little fruit bat emerged, its fur slightly dishevelled but triumphantly holding a gleaming brown lump in its mouth.

Caitlyn reached for it eagerly. In the pale glow of the moon, she saw that she was holding a chocolate bonbon. It was shaped like a little round mushroom, complete with spots etched over its domed surface—a toadstool—exactly like the ones she had seen in the box at Dr Nichols's office... and also exactly like the shapes in the chocolate mould from Lady Pritchard's kitchen. She picked up the mould and slipped the bonbon into one of the cavities. It fitted perfectly, every groove and every line snug against the silicone surface.

"What's that?" said Viktor, back in his human form and peering over her shoulder.

"Oh, Viktor, it matches!" said Caitlyn. "It's proof—proof that Lady Pritchard made those chocolates which poisoned the tramp! And she probably made similar ones to poison her husband too. Lady Pritchard is the murderer!"

She sprang to her feet. "I've got to return this mould to Pritchard House, so that the police can find it there when they search."

"Aha, I can replace it for you. With my power of vampire invisibility, I can—"

"No, no, I need you to go to the Manor," said Caitlyn. "You can get there faster if you fly in your bat form. Find James—Lord Fitzroy—you remember him, right? Tell him that I have proof of who the murderer is and ask him to call the police. They'll take it more seriously coming from him. Then tell him to come to Pritchard House. I'll wait in the gardens... Please, Viktor," she added as she saw him hesitate. "Please just trust me and do as I ask. I'll be fine—I promise. I won't take any unnecessary chances. If I can't get in the kitchen, I'll just shove the mould in through an open window or something—anywhere that's convenient. Hopefully, the housekeeper will find it and think that it had been misplaced, and return it to the kitchen."

A few minutes later, Caitlyn watched the little brown fruit bat disappear into the night sky. Then she turned and started towards Pritchard House. But she had barely gone a few steps when a dark figure stepped out from behind a bush. Caitlyn gasped as she recognised the slim, attractive blonde woman.

"Bravo..." said Lady Pritchard, clapping her hands with exaggerated slowness. "We're quite the little detective, aren't we? I thought it was that journalist that I had to watch out for... but oh no, it was the nosy chocolate shop girl who worked everything out. Maybe the rumours are true and you *are* a witch after all." She laughed shortly. Then she came closer and narrowed her eyes. "Where's that old man you were with? He was here just a moment ago—I saw you talking to him. Where is he?"

Caitlyn took a step back, keeping the distance between Lady Pritchard and herself. She couldn't see the other woman holding a weapon, but Lady Pritchard sounded too confident to be unarmed.

Otherwise, why would she be confronting Caitlyn and admitting to the murders? Caitlyn fought the urge to turn and run; she didn't want a bullet in her back to be how she found out that Lady Pritchard was holding a concealed gun.

"I... I don't know who you're talking about," she stammered.

"That old man in the weird black suit who was with you! I saw him—don't try to pretend—when you were leaving my house. You didn't realise I followed you, did you? I was upstairs—at the window right above where you and your friend were hiding by the hedge, actually—and I heard everything you said. Besides, when I saw that you had the chocolate mould, I knew you would figure things out sooner or later—"

"But I still don't understand," Caitlyn interrupted. "Why did you kill the tramp? What did he have to do with anything?"

Lady Pritchard smiled. "Darling... as we say in the business, never do anything without a rehearsal first. I needed to make sure that my dosage was right, that the poison I injected into the chocolates would kill within the hour, and I needed a guinea pig. How convenient that I should find a tramp sleeping in the garden shed by the orchard! I'd been growing some foxgloves especially for my purposes, you see, behind that shed, and I knew nobody normally went out there except me. So I made up a trial batch of bonbons, took them out to the tramp that night, and sent him on his way with the chocolates as a consolation gift." She laughed. "You should have seen how grateful he was, the poor sod! Couldn't believe his luck: homemade luxury chocolates! And the next morning, I heard the news." She clapped her hands with glee. "Success! So I got ready for the real performance."

Caitlyn looked at the woman with disgust and horror. "This wasn't some silly part you were playing in a theatre—this was a real man you murdered!"

"Ah, but you're wrong. This was the greatest part, the most thrilling role, I have ever played in my whole life! I never thought all those years of acting in crummy second-rate plays and budget movies would pay off like this. But I was good, wasn't I?" Her eyes gleamed. "I fooled everyone— even you, for a while! Everybody swallowed the poor, grieving widow act. And it was as if the Fates themselves had stepped in to smooth my way. I mean, I had been planning and waiting for the right moment... and then the stories about the Black Shuck began circulating around the village. It was perfect! I know Tillyhenge—I knew those superstitious old busybodies would jump to blame any unusual death on evil monsters and black magic. And that would just muddle the murder investigation even more. So all I had to do was watch and listen and stir the pot every so often: drop a few hints about possible suspects here and there, mention the legendary ghost hound and how scared I was..." She laughed again. "Did you know that fear is the most infectious emotion of all?"

"But Sir Henry... why did you kill him?"

Lady Pritchard pulled a face. "Bloody hell, do you really need to ask? You saw him at that dinner. Can you imagine being married to that male-chauvinist boor? Oh, I know what you're going to say—that I only married him for the money anyway, so I should have known what I was getting into. Well, that might be true, but there's only so much a woman can stand! How would you like your husband to smack your bum in public and treat you like livestock? After ten years of it, I had to get out."

"But you could have just divorced him—you didn't need to murder him!"

"What, and break my prenup? No way! It was bad enough that the bulk of the estate was going to that smug git brother of his, but as Henry's wife, I was entitled to a quarter of the money. Well, that's more than enough to keep me comfortable... at least until the next gullible rich fool comes along!" She chuckled. Then she sobered and scowled. "But if I left Henry, I'd be entitled to nothing. Those were the terms of the prenup contract. So I had to find some other way. I wasn't going to sit around, getting older and losing my looks, waiting for that stupid old sod to die... even if there were—*ahem*—'other diversions' in the meantime." She gave a coy smile.

"Dr Nichols," said Caitlyn, thinking that Pomona

had been right. "You're having an affair with him, aren't you?"

"Oh, I wouldn't call it an affair..." Lady Pritchard purred. "That has such romantic connotations. It suggests tragic passion... obsession... star-crossed lovers! This was more of a... a spot of entertainment, shall we say? A woman in my position has certain needs... Ben is very young... and very handsome..." She laughed throatily. Then suddenly, she was by Caitlyn's side. "Now, it's been very nice chatting to you, but it's getting late..."

Caitlyn gasped and went rigid as hard fingers suddenly clamped around her neck. She realised with horror that while she had been distracted by Lady Pritchard's explanations, the woman herself had sidled up close and taken her by surprise. Now, her head was yanked back by a cruel grip while Lady Pritchard raised her other hand and thrust something towards her face.

Caitlyn gave a strangled cry as the moonlight caught the silvery glint of a syringe, the deadly needle aimed at her throat.

CHAPTER TWENTY-NINE

"I wouldn't move if I were you," said Lady Pritchard softly next to her ear. "See this syringe? It contains a concentrated solution of digitalis extract... yes, I can see you know what that means. A few drops would be enough to stop your heart, especially if it was injected straight into a vein." She laughed softly. "It's quite handy shagging a doctor, you know... you can learn all sorts of useful things—like where the jugular vein is and how to use a syringe effectively—and all he thinks is that you're a wide-eyed little woman admiring his manly medical knowledge."

"The police... they're going to be here any moment—"

Lady Pritchard laughed. "You don't think I'm going to fall for that old cliché, do you?"

"It's true! My friend—the old man—he's gone to the Manor to tell James about you and call the police—"

"Do you think I'm stupid? It's at least a twenty-minute walk to the Manor from here—and that's if you're young and fit. That doddery old fool looked like he could barely stand up. He would be lucky to get there in an hour. By the time they listen to his story—assuming they believe him—and call the police... and the police arrive... hah!"

She jabbed the needle closer and Caitlyn flinched. But at the same time, she felt a flicker of hope. It was obvious that Lady Pritchard didn't know Viktor's true identity. If the woman had been spying on them from behind a bush and Viktor had been in the shadows, she wouldn't have seen the old vampire shift into his bat form. So she had no idea that he would be flying, not walking to Huntingdon Manor. And however wobbly and decrepit Viktor might have looked as a human, he was swift and agile in his bat form. (Well, okay, maybe agile was going a bit far. But he was certainly fast enough once he was alight in the air.) Caitlyn swallowed. If she could just keep the woman talking and that deadly needle away from her throat, she might still get out of this unscathed.

"I don't believe you're really going to kill me," she said boldly. "Otherwise, why wouldn't you have done it by now?"

"Ah, that's because I want you to tell me who

else—apart from that old geezer—you've been telling your little theories to. I need to know who else I might have to deal with. James Fitzroy and the inspector are fixated on Swanes and Julian as suspects, so they should be no problem... But what about that journalist friend of his... Nathan? Have you told him your suspicions about me?" demanded Lady Pritchard.

"No... but he's not stupid. And neither is James. No matter how much you try to set up Swanes and Julian Pritchard as scapegoats, it won't stop them realising it's you once they join up the dots like I did. All the clues are there. Your biggest mistake was making some chocolates for your lover using the same mould as for the poisoned chocolates."

She scowled. "No one knows I was the one who gave Ben those chocolates."

"But they can work it out from your note. Just like I did," said Caitlyn. She knew she shouldn't antagonise the woman, but Lady Pritchard's conceited overconfidence pricked her temper and she couldn't stop herself adding, "Were you trying to be clever with that card? That's your problem, you know—you take stupid risks because you think you're so much smarter than everyone else and nobody will get your little jokes."

Lady Pritchard made a hissing sound and her fingers clenched on the syringe. Caitlyn jerked her head backwards as the needle jabbed towards her. Suddenly she regretted provoking the woman. She felt the fingers tighten around her neck and she froze, bracing herself for the sting of the needle...

A loud rustling next to them made Lady Pritchard stop and look up sharply.

There was silence, except for the murmur of the breeze through the trees and the distant call of an owl. But it was a heavy, loaded silence... as if something was there in the shadows, watching and waiting...

"Wh...who's there?" Lady Pritchard shouted, staring around with wide eyes, all her previous arrogance gone.

She was answered by a low growl.

Caitlyn felt the hairs stand up on her neck, and Lady Pritchard trembled next to her. A minute later, the bushes parted and a huge, shaggy black dog stepped soundlessly out. Caitlyn felt a sense of relief and delighted recognition, but also a thrill of fear because she had never seen the Black Shuck look so ferocious. This was not the playful phantom hound that she had met the last few times by herself—this was something out of horror stories and nightmares. A monstrous beast with teeth bared and fangs gleaming, and eyes that glowed a sinister red. It crouched, then launched itself at them.

Lady Pritchard screamed and thrust Caitlyn in front of her. But the demon hound ignored Caitlyn, darting around her and lunging at the other woman. It threw its massive paws on her chest and knocked her down. She thrashed and screamed, and Caitlyn cried out too... and she heard—almost like echoes—distant voices shouting as well.

Everything became a noisy confusion of wild movement, terrified cries, and blurred images... waving torchlight... figures running towards them... an eruption of snarling, barking, growling... the Black Shuck pinning his victim to the ground...

"No, don't hurt her!" Caitlyn cried instinctively.

Then she saw that the huge dog was not biting Lady Pritchard. It was just holding her in place and snarling in her face—although that seemed to be enough to terrify her, and she was screaming and carrying on as if she was being eaten alive.

Then a tall figure rushed up... Caitlyn heard her name, felt herself being thrust behind a hard, male body... then she saw the gleam of a rifle barrel in the moonlight...

"*NO!*" she shouted, throwing herself at James as he aimed at the Black Shuck and fired.

She smacked into his arm just as he pulled the trigger and the gun jerked wildly. There was a whine of pain and her heart lurched. She saw a shaggy black shape limp off into the shadows and disappear between the trees. James raised the rifle again.

"No, no—don't shoot!" she cried, grabbing his arm.

"Caitlyn, are you mad?" James stared at her, angry and confused. "That creature was mauling

Lady Pritchard—"

"No, it wasn't—it was just scaring her!"

"What do you mean—" He broke off and made an impatient sound. "I need to find it before it hurts someone else. Wild animals that have been wounded can become even more dangerous." He plunged into the woods after the phantom hound.

Caitlyn started to follow but her arm was caught by Nathan Lewis, who had arrived with James.

"Caitlyn—"

"Let me go!" She yanked her arm out of his grasp and plunged after James. Thankfully, he seemed to be on a trail of some kind, otherwise she would never have been able to find him in the forest. She put on a burst of speed to catch up with him.

"James!"

He swung around in surprise. "Caitlyn! What are you doing? Go back! I don't want you getting hurt—"

"James... listen to me... please!" she gasped, struggling to keep pace with his long legs. "The Black Shuck—you mustn't hurt it! It isn't what you think—it isn't what *anyone* thinks!"

They'd come out into a wide space in the centre of the forest, where the canopy thinned, letting light in, and a narrow stream cut across the path. An old stone bridge had been erected across the stream and, in the pale moonlight, Caitlyn saw the bloody tracks leave the path; they led down to the water's edge and out of sight beneath the bridge. She darted in front of James and blocked his way as he started to follow.

"James, listen... listen... the Black Shuck is *good*. It's a guardian... it protects night travellers; it doesn't harm them."

He sighed. "Caitlyn, I understand there are different versions of the legends and you'd like to believe the nice ones, but—"

"No, it's not just a legend! It's the truth! I know because I... I've met it."

"You've... '*met*' it?" James was looking at her like she had lost her mind, and she couldn't really blame him.

"Yes, have you heard of shape-shifters? Well, the Black Shuck... it's the canine form of a man." Caitlyn took a deep breath. "It's... it's Professor Thrope."

"*What?* That's... that's the most ridiculous thing I've ever heard!" James looked like he didn't know whether to laugh or be annoyed.

"It's true! I confronted him about it and he admitted it. But even if he hadn't, I knew already, because... because the signs were all there—"

"What signs? This is nonsense," said James irritably. Then a familiar look of disappointment crossed his face. "This is like that witch thing, isn't it? You're just making things up, pretending a magic identity where there is none! Why can't you just accept that you're living a fantasy—"

"I'm not making it up!" Caitlyn shouted, losing

her temper. "Why can't *you* just accept that maybe—just maybe—magic could exist? Why won't you even consider it?" She glared at him, her eyes blazing. She couldn't remember ever feeling such furious frustration and all her usual shyness around James evaporated. "Why can't you open your mind for once, and stop being so smug in your scientific superiority?"

James was looking at her like he'd never seen her before, but Caitlyn was beyond caring. She took a step closer to him and said fiercely: "If you shoot that dog tonight, you'll be murdering a man! Because however much you don't want to believe it and however much it doesn't fit into your neat little scientific world, that creature is Professor Thrope."

She turned and stalked towards the water's edge. There was a small hollow underneath the bridge and she crouched down, peering into the shadows. The moonlight, which lit up the clearing, didn't penetrate much under the bridge, but she could just see a dark form lying against the earth, the shaggy fur rising and falling rapidly as the creature panted. Then, as she watched transfixed, the huge beast seemed to shimmer and start to shrink: the snout shortening, the pointed ears disappearing, the black paws extending into human fingers, the shaggy black fur smoothing and flattening out...

There was an involuntary cry behind her and Caitlyn glanced over her shoulder to see James standing there. His grey eyes were wide, and his mouth was slightly open, as he watched the transformation.

Caitlyn turned back. The Black Shuck was gone. All that was left was an old man with enormous sideburns, lying on his side, his hair dishevelled and his clothes ragged, and one arm bleeding from a gunshot wound.

CHAPTER THIRTY

"Yes, he's awake now. You can go and see him if you like."

Caitlyn followed the nurse to the rear of the ward, where she was shown into a private room with the name *"Professor Kynan Thrope"* on the label next to the door. Lying in bed, his arm bandaged and held in a sling, was the cryptozoologist. His face lit up as he saw her and he attempted to sit up.

"No, don't get up," said Caitlyn. She settled herself in the chair by the bed and smiled at the professor. "How do you feel?"

"Like I've been shot," he said with a hoarse laugh. "No, but seriously, I don't feel too bad. Arm's very sore, of course, and I'm a bit groggy from the anaesthetic... but all things considered, I just feel lucky to be alive." He gave her a grateful look. "And I believe I have you to thank for that, my dear,"

Caitlyn looked down in embarrassment. "It was nothing, really. I mean, I'm sure James wouldn't have shot you if he had known who you really were..."

Professor Thrope raised his eyebrows. "So does Lord Fitzroy know...? He came to see me as soon as I got out of surgery, but he didn't say much, other than to apologise again. Of course, I assured him that accidents happen and I didn't blame him at all. In fact, he has been more than generous—" he waved a hand around the room, "—arranging for me to have a private room and insisting on covering all hospital expenses."

"Yes, James does know," said Caitlyn quietly. "He saw your transformation."

"And... his friend, Nathan?" asked Professor Thrope, his face alarmed.

"No, Nathan didn't see. He arrived a moment after you'd shifted back, and neither James nor I mentioned it. We just said that you must have been chasing the Black Shuck too and been shot by mistake in the dark. He seemed to accept that explanation."

The cryptozoologist relaxed a bit. "So Lord Fitzroy is the only one who knows, except you?"

"Yes, and you don't have to worry... I think he will keep your secret. I... we haven't spoken about it, but I know James..." Caitlyn blushed at the intimacy implied in those words, and added hastily, "Actually, my grandmother knows too. In fact, she knew about you before I even suspected."

Professor Thrope smiled. "She is a very wise woman, the Widow Mags. I hope to see her again before I leave."

"Will you be going soon?"

"As soon as the doctors say I can travel. Lord Fitzroy is very kind but..." He gave a wry smile. "I feel that I have outstayed my welcome. In any case, I think my work here is done. I heard one of the nurses talking earlier—apparently the police have arrested that gang of men who had been attacking women in the countryside?"

"Yes, I heard that too. Inspector Walsh arrested them yesterday afternoon. I'd tried to reach him at the station and they wouldn't let me speak to him. They said he was busy interviewing suspects. I guess that's what he was doing: questioning the members of the gang."

"So, it turned out to be quite a busy day for the local CID," said Professor Thrope with a chuckle. "First this gang and then Lady Pritchard last night. Has she confessed?"

"Yes... and in fact, I think *you* helped with that, Professor."

"Me?" he said in surprise.

Caitlyn laughed. "Yes, she was so terrified after her encounter with the Black Shuck, she was practically begging to tell the whole story to anyone who would listen. Perhaps she thought she was being haunted by the demon hound for what she had done and the only way to get rid of the ghost was to confess to everything."

"Well, I'm glad I was able to help in some way."

Caitlyn rose from her chair. "I'll leave you to rest now. Oh, I nearly forgot..." She lifted a small box and placed it on the professor's lap. "These are from my grandmother."

Professor Thrope opened the box to find it filled with ivory white bonbons, in various shapes and sizes.

"They're white chocolate," Caitlyn explained. "They're made from a blend of cocoa butter, milk, and sugar, with no theobromine—so they should be safe for you to eat."

"Thank you, my dear—and please thank the Widow Mags for me," said the cryptozoologist, beaming. "She's a very good woman. I think it is a great shame that so many in the village fear and shun her."

Caitlyn gave him a hopeful smile. "Well, things might be slowly changing. One of the farmers— Jeremy Bottom—is holding an Open Day at his dairy farm today, and he has invited the Widow Mags as the guest of honour."

She didn't add that what was even more surprising was that the old witch had accepted. She had thought that—after the horrible scene at the pub—the Widow Mags would refuse to venture out of her chocolate shop again. In fact, Caitlyn could hardly blame her grandmother for not wanting to face all that hostility. But strangely enough, the events of that day seemed to have had the opposite effect. It was almost as if, now that she had faced the worst, the Widow Mags didn't care anymore.

"Ooh, I'd better get going," said Caitlyn, glancing at her watch. "I'm supposed to pick up some things from the cottage and meet her there." She smiled warmly at the professor. "Do come to the chocolate shop and say goodbye before you leave, won't you?"

He returned her smile. "I certainly will."

***

Caitlyn found a note from Bertha waiting for her on the kitchen table, together with a basket of freshly baked chocolate fudge brownies and several jars of homemade toffees.

Have taken Mother and Evie, and the other things, to the Open Day first. Can you please bring the fudge and toffees when you come, as we couldn't carry them? Thank you.

Love, Bertha

P.S. Have left you a pair of wellies by the back door. Ground can be very muddy at the farm.

Caitlyn looked across the kitchen and saw a pair of rubber boots standing by the rear door of the cottage, then glanced down at herself. She had better change out of her pretty summer dress. Upstairs, she found that Nibs had made himself comfortable on her pillow and was curled up fast asleep. The kitten awoke as she came in and opened his mouth in a wide yawn, showing a little pink tongue and tiny white teeth.

"*Mew?*" he said sleepily.

"Hi, Nibs," Caitlyn said absently, as she stripped off her dress and rummaged in the chest of drawers for a clean T-shirt and her best pair of jeans.

She dressed quickly, then pulled her red hair back in a ponytail. But her fingers slipped and she dropped the elastic band in her haste. Making a sound of annoyance, Caitlyn crouched down next to the bed to retrieve it, then paused as she remembered the hag stone. She hadn't had a chance to look for it again since yesterday lunchtime, when she had dropped it with Pomona. Now she crawled once more under the bed and squinted in the dark, dusty space. *Where is it?* She spied a gap between two of the floorboards. The hag stone could have rolled in there. She wouldn't be able to look into the gap easily from this angle—the best thing was to shift the bed sideways so she could get access.

She crawled out again to find Nibs perched on the edge of the mattress, peering down curiously, trying to see what she was doing under the bed.

"*Mew?*" said the kitten.

"Brace yourself, Nibs," said Caitlyn as she grabbed the posts at the foot of the bed and gave a heave. The bedframe moved sideways with a shuddering creak. Nibs gave a *mew* of surprise at the sudden movement and leapt off the bed. Caitlyn gripped the bedposts again and gave the bed another sideways shove, then knelt down in the empty space revealed. Nibs scampered up next to her and watched as she felt in the gap between the floorboards... Yes! There was the hag stone. It was wedged snugly in the space between the two boards, but with a bit of wriggling, she managed to pull it out.

"*Mew!*" said Nibs, putting out an inquisitive paw as she held the hag stone up to the light.

"Ah-ah... not for you," Caitlyn admonished gently.

She rose and placed the hag stone temporarily on the windowsill, then returned the bed to its original position. It seemed to be much harder to shift back and it took her two or three attempts before she was satisfied. She was panting and sweating slightly by the time she was done. Turning back to the window, her eyes widened in horror as she saw that Nibs had jumped up on the windowsill and was batting the hag stone playfully with his paw.

"No! Nibs, no!" she exclaimed, diving across the room.

She grabbed the hag stone just in time, before

the kitten's paw sent it flying out of the window. Giving Nibs a stern look, she clutched the hag stone tightly in her hands and gave a sigh of relief. Then, as she opened her fingers and gazed down at the strange stone with the hole in the centre, she had an idea. Yesterday, she and Pomona had been using the hag stone to try and decipher the meaning of the symbols on the parchment. And something had happened: viewed through the hole in the hag stone, the symbols had seemed to transform, to take on the shape of letters...

She had been keen to try the hag stone on the parchment again, but now that she thought about it, she had a better idea. If the symbols on the parchment were similar to the symbols on her runestone, then that meant that the hag stone could also be used to decipher the meaning of the marks engraved on her runestone!

A thrill of excitement went through her. Hurriedly, she untied the ribbon holding the runestone around her neck, then held it up to the light. With her other hand, she raised the hag stone and held it in front of the runestone, lining it up so that she could look at the symbols through the hole in the centre.

"*Mew?*" said Nibs, coming closer and peering at the stones in her hands.

"Hush, Nibs..." Caitlyn muttered. "I'm trying to concentrate."

She tried to remember what she had done the

other day. *A deep breath*, she reminded herself. *And then focus your mind on the hole in the stone. Fade out everything else around you.* Slowly, her vision narrowed down to the circle through which she could see some of the symbols...

The engraved marks blurred... and then shimmered.

Caitlyn fought the urge to blink, scared that if she did, she might break the focus that enabled her to see the transformation. The shimmering intensified. And then, just like on the parchment the day before, the symbols began to uncurl and reform into different shapes... into letters...

Chameleon charm... Deflect, disarm... Fiends of evil, quartenate guised—

"*MEW!*"

Caitlyn jumped as a paw suddenly whacked the hag stone in her hands. She gasped and fumbled; the hag stone slipped from her fingers and fell on the windowsill, sliding to the outer edge.

"*Mew!*" cried Nibs again, rushing to pounce on the hag stone.

"No! Nibs, don't!" cried Caitlyn.

But the kitten ignored her and swatted the hag stone with glee. The circular stone shot over the edge of the windowsill and dropped from sight.

"Noooo!" groaned Caitlyn. She leaned over the windowsill and looked out. The cottage garden was right beneath her and there was no sign of the stone amongst the green foliage and flowers.

"Nibs!" she shouted. "Aaarrghh! Now, look what you've done!"

"Mew?" The little kitten looked up at her innocently.

She opened her mouth to berate him, then sighed and shut it again. It wasn't really the kitten's fault—he was only acting as kittens do. Like all cats, he was inquisitive, especially if he could see that you had all your attention on something. And she should have known, after his antics at the doctor's clinic, that he enjoyed batting things off ledges.

She leaned to look out of the window again. The cottage garden below was a mess of overgrown beds filled with herbs, wildflowers, and tangled shrubs. It would take her ages to search for the hag stone.

Caitlyn glanced at her watch. There wasn't time to search now—she had to get to the Open Day and, by the time she got back, it would probably be too dark. *Anyway, it isn't as if the hag stone is going anywhere,* she reminded herself. It was perfectly safe, buried somewhere out there between the herbs and flowers. She could look for it tomorrow.

And besides, I've learnt part of the message on my runestone, she thought with a tingle of excitement. *Chameleon charm / Deflect, disarm / Fiends of evil, quartenate guised—* It didn't make much sense to her, but that was okay. She smiled.

She would figure it out.

With a last look at the garden, she went downstairs to collect the chocolate treats and rubber boots, and be on her way.

CHAPTER THIRTY-ONE

It seemed like half the county had come to the Open Day at Jeremy Bottom's pretty little dairy farm. The air was filled with the sound of laughing and screaming children as couples and families walked around enjoying the activities laid on for them. There was a miniature bouncy castle, a "Pin the tail on the cow" on one wall of the barn, a display of milk products and confectionery (including the magnificent chocolate statue of Ferdinand the bull), a shed where you could try your hand at hand-milking a cow, a stall selling bottled fresh milk, and a pen where children could pet the calves and feed the rabbits and chickens. Several little boys were whooping with glee as they climbed all over the farm tractor, parked especially in the centre of the farmyard, whilst others played around bales of hay stacked in the corner.

The cows, of course, were the stars of the show, and they'd all come across the field to stand by the fence, basking in the attention from the visitors. The biggest attraction was Ferdinand himself and Caitlyn smiled as she watched the enormous bull nuzzle his head against a young woman, who laughed in delight. Although he had been accepted into the herd and didn't spend his days in a lonely field by himself anymore, it looked like the smoochy bull still loved getting cuddles and pats from humans.

"Caitlyn! Where have you been? I've been looking all over for you."

Caitlyn turned to see Pomona approaching, and marvelled at how her cousin managed to make a pair of faded jeans and green rubber boots look glamorous.

Pomona grinned as she came up and said: "You just missed the most awesome scene! Mrs Gibbs arrived, yeah, and freaked out when she saw the Widow Mags... but she didn't dare say anything directly to her 'cos James was there... so she started walking around the yard, pretending to talk to her friends and speaking really loudly... and making, like, all these mean comments about witches... and she was so busy talking, she didn't look where she was going, so she stepped right into a cowpat!" Pomona dissolved into giggles. "Man, you should have seen the look on her face! And it went all over her shoes and up her leg and everything... it was priceless!"

Caitlyn couldn't help smiling as well. She looked around, not seeing the woman. "Where's she now?"

"Oh, that Vera woman—you know, Jeremy's sourpuss sister—took her into the farmhouse to get cleaned up. But I can tell you, no matter how much she scrubs, she's gonna stink for days!" Pomona grinned wickedly and added, "Pretty fitting, really, when you think that so much of what comes out of her mouth is bulls—"

"Do you know where the milking shed is?" asked a frazzled-looking young woman with a baby on one hip and a screaming toddler in the other hand. She gave them an apologetic smile as the toddler let out another piercing wail. "He's having a bit of a tantrum. I thought I might be able to get him to calm down, if he has a go at milking a cow."

Pomona turned and pointed. "Yeah, it's just round the back of the barn..." She gave the woman a pitying look and said, "You know what? I'll show you." She turned to the little boy and held out her hand, while giving him her most dazzling smile. "Here... you wanna take my hand?"

He stared up at her, his sobs subsiding into hiccups, then slowly put his chubby little hand into hers. Pomona winked at Caitlyn, mouthed "Be right back", and walked off with the young mother. The little boy had stopped crying completely now and was gripping her hand and staring up at her in adoration. Caitlyn laughed to herself. It looked like Pomona's effect on the male population started at an early age!

She turned at the sound of a deep, male voice calling her name and her pulse fluttered as she saw James Fitzroy approaching. He was dressed, like Pomona, in faded jeans and wellington boots, with a crisp white shirt open at the neck and rolled up at the sleeves, to show tanned, muscular forearms. His dark hair was slightly tousled, and his grey eyes crinkled at the corners as he gave her a familiar lopsided smile. Caitlyn's heart skipped a beat. James hadn't smiled at her like that for ages, not since that day when...

"I was surprised when the Widow Mags and others arrived without you," he said, nodding across the yard to where Bertha was standing with the old witch.

"I was a bit late because I went to the hospital first—to see Professor Thrope."

"Ah." There was an awkward silence, then James cleared his throat. "I saw him earlier—he seemed to have come through surgery well."

"Yes, he has." Caitlyn squirmed at this inane, polite conversation. They both knew they were avoiding the proverbial elephant in the room: the subject of Professor Thrope's shape-shifting.

James cleared his throat again and fell back on every Englishman's standby. "Er... lovely weather we're having today, aren't we?"

Caitlyn didn't know whether to laugh or roll her eyes, and something of it must have shown in her expression because James laughed suddenly in a sheepish manner and the tension eased between them.

"I heard at the hospital that they've arrested the gang who was attacking women," said Caitlyn.

"Yes, it's terrific news, isn't it? What with Lady Pritchard and the other two in custody as well, the local CID have never had so many arrests within a day in their entire history," said James with a chuckle. "I think Inspector Walsh doesn't know if he's coming or going."

"What do you mean? Who else has been arrested?"

"Well, Derek Swanes was picked up this morning. He's been charged with embezzlement and fraud. And Julian Pritchard too. It seems that they'd been conspiring together—or rather, Pritchard had enlisted Swanes to do the dirty work."

"Oh, so that's what I'd overheard at the petrol station!" said Caitlyn. "They weren't discussing a plot to murder Sir Henry, they were talking about the embezzling racket."

"Yes, Pritchard approached Swanes last year and offered him a cut, if the estate manager helped him siphon off money from his brother's estate. Unfortunately, Swanes got caught, and to make matters worse, Sir Henry was then murdered, which meant that the police got involved... It's why

Pritchard was so against them investigating his brother's death. Not because he was trying to cover up a murder, but because he was worried that if they started digging around, they would find out about the embezzling."

"So he was willing to let his brother's murderer get away, just so he could keep his own back covered?" said Caitlyn in disgust. Then she remembered something else. "What about the deal with Blackmort?"

"I think, with Pritchard now awaiting trial, he'll have other things on his mind than negotiating a deal with Blackmort," said James dryly.

"So that piece of land is safe for now," said Cailyn, more to herself than to anyone else.

James gave her a quizzical look. "'For now'? I should imagine that the estate will remain unsettled for quite a while yet, what with both the heirs arrested for serious crimes. I don't think Blackmort will be getting his hands on that piece of land."

Caitlyn wasn't so certain. She felt that somehow, what Thane Blackmort wanted, he would get. She thought uneasily of Pomona and hoped that her cousin wouldn't be going back to London any time soon. Glancing across the yard, Caitlyn saw the subject of her thoughts coming back around the corner of the barn with the young mother next to her and the toddler still clinging to her hand. She smiled and wondered if her cousin would be able to get rid of her young admirer now.

The sight of the little boy reminded Caitlyn of James's story about his childhood friend who had created that piece of parchment with the mysterious symbols.

"By the way, James," she said, "you know you were telling me about that piece of parchment that we found the other day in the Portrait Gallery?"

He looked at her expectantly. "Yes?"

"Well, the young man who drew those symbols— the one who spent time playing with you—can you remember anything else about him? Like... his name?"

He shook his head regretfully. "I'm afraid not. It was so long ago and I was very young. I don't even remember what he looked like, really... just that he was tall..." He frowned in an effort to remember, then he brightened. "Oh, and he had green eyes."

"Green eyes?"

"Well, not green, exactly... more a sort of hazel... The exact same shade as yours, actually."

"As *me*?"

He looked at her so intently that Caitlyn began to blush.

"Yes... It's a very unusual colour, isn't it, your eyes? They seem to change with your moods: deep green sometimes, and yet other times a soft hazel... I remember thinking the day I met you that I'd only ever seen eyes that colour once before—it was this chap from my childhood."

Caitlyn stared at him as a crazy idea began

forming in her mind. But before she could say anything else, they were interrupted by Nathan Lewis.

"Smashing event, isn't it?" he said enthusiastically as he came up to join them. Then he gave a self-deprecating laugh. "Never thought I'd say that about a farm open day! It's funny... living in London, with all the trendy bars and posh restaurants and fancy shops... well, you forget how much fun you can have just doing simple things." He glanced across the yard again, taking in the crowds. "And there's something so nice just seeing the families out and about, and the children laughing—"

He broke off suddenly and frowned. "Hang on a minute... that old fellow..."

Caitlyn turned in the direction he was pointing and groaned inwardly as she saw a scrawny old man in an ancient black suit going up to people in the crowd and tapping them on the shoulder. His quavering voice drifted across to them.

"Have you seen my teeth?" he said to a startled couple. "Four inches, a bit yellow—not terribly stained, mind—and there's a chip on one of the fangs. Got it fighting off those wretched hobgoblins during the Napoleonic Wars, you see, and the stupid dentist never fixed it properly..."

The couple gave him a wary look and hastily edged away. Undeterred, Viktor turned to another couple nearby: "Have you seen my teeth?"

H.Y. HANNA

"That's him!" spluttered Nathan, jabbing his finger in Viktor's direction. "That's the chap I was telling you about, James! Last night... he showed up at the front door, babbling about Caitlyn being in danger, and by the time I went to get you and we came back, he'd disappeared... Remember?"

James looked startled. "I... yes, I suppose so... although I didn't see him myself. I only saw you rushing into the Library—"

"When you went to get the gun, I tried to find him again, but no one had seen where he got to, not even Mosley..." Nathan frowned. "Although I doubt Mosley was paying much attention—he seemed to be trying to catch a bat that had somehow got into the house..." He pointed a finger at Viktor again. "Anyway, that's him! There! And I saw him the other day too—he was skulking around the Manor by himself—seems to believe that he's a six-hundred-year-old vampire, can you believe it?" he laughed. "Absolutely barmy."

Then he sobered as he watched Viktor shuffling farther away. "Must speak to him and find out which nursing home he belongs to. Might be lost, poor chap... need to get him back safely..." He hurried off after Viktor as the old vampire disappeared into the crowds.

"Excuse me, Lord Fitzroy..."

James turned to find a good-looking teenage boy with sun-streaked blond hair standing behind him. "Ah, Chris... For goodness' sake, do call me James."

Chris Bottom grinned and inclined his head in acknowledgement, then said, "My dad was wondering if you could join him—he's with some of the village committee members..." He pointed to the other side of the farmyard, where Jeremy Bottom was arguing with several of the village residents. They were gesticulating and frowning at the chocolate statue of Ferdinand the bull, while the Widow Mags stood on the other side of Jeremy, her arms crossed and her bottom lip jutting out defiantly.

"Oh dear... here we go again," said James with a sigh. "Yes, I'll come right away."

Giving Caitlyn an apologetic glance, he excused himself and followed Chris across to the group. He was joined by Bertha, her face anxious, and Evie, who gave Chris a covert look. Caitlyn noticed that her young cousin's rubber boots seemed to be glowing a strange shade of green. *"Oh dear... here we go again" is right*, she thought.

She was about to cross over to join them (and ask Evie what was going on with those rubber boots) when Caitlyn felt her elbow being grabbed, and she turned in surprise to see Pomona tugging her arm excitedly.

"Omigod, Caitlyn, you gotta come and try it. It's so much fun!"

"What is?" she asked in bemusement as her cousin hustled her in the opposite direction across the farmyard.

"The milking! C'mon... you gotta give it a go..."

"But Pomie, I don't want..."

Her protests ignored, Caitlyn found herself being dragged behind the barn to a small shed lined with straw, where a dairy cow with an enormous udder was calmly chewing the cud as she stood tied to the inside wall. There was an empty metal pail under her udder and a three-legged wooden stool next to it. Pomona shoved Caitlyn onto this.

Caitlyn eyed the cow nervously. "Um... are you sure we should be doing this by ourselves?"

"Oh, there's a girl here showing people how it's done... I dunno where she's got to..." Pomona looked around, then said: "You stay here! Don't move! I'm gonna go find her." She paused, then pointed to a large tub of cream on the floor next to the stool. "You can put some of that udder cream on her while you're waiting. It's supposed to be really good for cracked teats."

"But Pomie—"

Caitlyn found herself talking to an empty doorway. Sighing, she turned back to the cow and gingerly reached out to touch the pink udder.

"*MOOO!*"

Caitlyn yelped and nearly fell off the stool. She shifted back slightly so that she was farther from the cow. It turned its head and regarded her with big, long-lashed eyes, and its jaws moved from side to side, chewing, chewing, chewing.

"Um... hello..." said Caitlyn. "I'm... er... I'm just

here to milk you..."

Oh, this is ridiculous, she thought, standing up. She wasn't going to sit here in a shed, waiting for someone to come and show her how to handle a cow she never wanted to milk in the first place! But even as she had the thought, she heard steps hurriedly approaching outside. A minute later, James Fitzroy burst into the shed.

"How is she?" he asked. "What have you done so far?"

"She's... she's fine," said Caitlyn in surprise. "Pomona said I should put some cream on her teats, but I wasn't sure if that was—"

"I beg your pardon?" James gaped at her. "On her *what?*"

"Her teats..." Caitlyn faltered. She gestured to the tub on the floor. "The udder cream."

"Oh, the *cow!*" James looked immensely relieved. "But what about Mrs Gibbs?"

"Huh?"

"Pomona said Mrs Gibbs was having another seizure and you were dealing with her in the shed and needed my help."

"Pomona said...?" Caitlyn suddenly had a horrible suspicion. But before she could do anything, the shed door slammed shut. Caitlyn heard the sound of a bolt being shot into place. She rushed to the door and shoved against it.

"Pomona!" she shouted. "What are you doing? Let us out!"

The only response she got was a giggle. Then footsteps fading away. She tried the door again but it was locked fast—it wouldn't budge. She turned around to find herself standing in a cramped, dark shed with James... and a cow.

Oooh, I'm going to kill Pomona when I see her! she thought.

"I take it we're victims of a practical joke," said James with an ironic smile.

"I'm sorry. It's... er... Pomona's sense of humour."

"*MOOO...*" said the cow.

Caitlyn eyed the big animal nervously. "Um... maybe you'd better stand at this end, near her head... I don't know anything about handling cows—do you? I don't know if they kick like horses..."

"She's probably fairly placid and used to being handled, so we should be fine," said James, moving slowly to join her. Then he added dryly, "Just as long as she remains a cow."

Caitlyn looked at him quickly. This was the first time James had made any reference to Professor Thrope's shape-shifting. There was a long silence, then he said:

"I almost couldn't believe my eyes... when I saw... last night..." He shook his head. "I've tried to come up with every scientific explanation that could make sense but... well, nothing explains how a dog could transform into a man! Nothing except...

magic."

Caitlyn held her breath. There was silence again except for the sound of the cow's placid munching. Finally, James spoke, his voice low:

"What you told me last time about you being... a... a witch... Is that true?"

"Yes, yes, it's true," said Caitlyn breathlessly. "I mean, I don't go flying around on brooms or anything like that—but I can work magic, especially magic related to chocolate. Look... look, I'll show you!" She glanced around, then grabbed a handful of straw from the ground near their feet. She held this up to show James. "I'll change this into chocolate... watch!"

She focused hard on the wisps of straw, trying with all her might to direct her will onto the dried strands. She imagined them changing, darkening, turning into strands of smooth, milk chocolate...

Nothing happened.

Caitlyn gritted her teeth and tried harder. She was concentrating so fiercely that her hands shook and beads of sweat formed on her forehead. But still, nothing happened. The bunch of straw clutched in her hands remained unchanged.

"Caitlyn—"

"No, no... I can do it!" she insisted. She couldn't bear it. Now that James finally seemed to be willing to open his mind, to accept the impossible, she had to convince him... she had to! She looked feverishly around. "Maybe something else... that rag over there... I'll just try that—"

But as she reached towards it, James caught her hand.

"Stop, Caitlyn... it's all right," he said gently.

"No, no... I must show you—"

"You don't have to show me anything," he said, taking her hands into both of his.

Caitlyn stared up at him. "But... but I want you to believe me—"

She felt his strong fingers interlace with hers.

"I do believe you."

She stared up at him. "You... you do? But how... I thought you said... you can't see—"

"No, I can't see it with my eyes," admitted James. His hands were warm around hers. Then he smiled at her—that heart-stopping, lopsided smile. "But I don't need to, Caitlyn. I can feel it with my heart."

THE END

The BEWITCHED BY CHOCOLATE Mysteries

Dark, Witch & Creamy (Book 1)

Witch Chocolate Fudge (Book 2)

Witch Summer Night's Cream (Book 3)

Blood, Sweets and Tears (Book 4)
~ *previously published as*
Witch Chocolate Bites

Bonbons and Broomsticks (Book 5)

Have you tried my other mystery series?

OXFORD TEAROOM MYSTERIES

"Scones, a tea shop in England, a kitty & a murder - yes, please!"

The Oxford Tearoom Mysteries

Books in the Oxford Tearoom Mysteries:
A Scone To Die For (Book 1)
Tea with Milk and Murder (Book 2)
Two Down, Bun To Go (Book 3)
Till Death Do Us Tart (Book 4)
Muffins and Mourning Tea (Book 5)
Four Puddings and a Funeral (Book 6)
Another One Bites the Crust (Book 7)
Apple Strudel Alibi (Book 8)
All-Butter ShortDead (Prequel)

ABOUT THE AUTHOR

H.Y. Hanna is an award-winning mystery and suspense writer and the author of the bestselling *Oxford Tearoom Mysteries*. She has also written romantic suspense and sweet romance, as well as a children's middle-grade mystery series. After graduating from Oxford University with a BA in Biological Sciences and a MSt in Social Anthropology, Hsin-Yi tried her hand at a variety of jobs, before returning to her first love: writing.

She worked as a freelance journalist for several years, with articles and short stories published in the UK, Australia and NZ, and has won awards for her novels, poetry, short stories and journalism.

A globe-trotter all her life, Hsin-Yi has lived in a variety of cultures, from Dubai to Auckland, London to New Jersey, but is now happily settled in Perth, Western Australia, with her husband and a rescue kitty named Muesli. You can learn more about her (and the real-life Muesli who inspired the cat character in the story) and her other books at: **www.hyhanna.com**.

Sign up to her newsletter to be notified of new releases, exclusive giveaways and other book news! Go to: **www.hyhanna.com/newsletter**

ACKNOWLEDGMENTS

As always, I am forever grateful to my beta readers: Connie Leap, Charles Winthrop and Basma Alwesh for making time in their busy lives to read the first draft and give me such helpful and insightful feedback. My thanks also to my editor and proofreader for being such a great team to work with.

And to my wonderful husband, for his constant support and encouragement – for always listening, always cheering me on and always believing in me.

Made in the USA
Middletown, DE
30 October 2018